W9-BZK-200

THE
COFFIN SHIP

Books by Peter Tonkin
Killer
The Journal of Edwin Underhill

THE
COFFIN SHIP

Peter Tonkin

Crown Publishers, Inc.
New York

Copyright © 1989, 1990 by Peter Tonkin

All rights reserved. No part of this book may be reproduced or transmitted in
any form or by any means, electronic or mechanical, including photocopying,
recording, or by any information storage and retrieval system, without
permission in writing from the publisher.
Published by Crown Publishers, Inc., 201 E. 50th Street, New York, New
York 10022. Member of the Crown Publishing Group.
Originally published in Great Britain in different form by Headline Book
Publishing in 1989.
CROWN is a trademark of Crown Publishers, Inc.
Manufactured in the United States of America
Library of Congress Cataloging-in-Publication Data
Tonkin, Peter.
    The coffin ship / Peter Tonkin.—1st ed.
      p. cm.
    I. Title.
PR6070.0498C6   1990
823'.914—dc20   90-31245
                                                                  CIP

ISBN 0-517-57523-X
10 9 8 7 6 5 4 3 2 1
First American Edition

For Cham

Coffin Ship: *A ship sent to sea in an unseaworthy condition, destined to sink before the end of its voyage as part of an insurance fraud.*

—First used 1833, *Oxford English Dictionary*

A ship has happenings according to her weird. She shows perversities and virtues her parents never dreamed into the plans they laid for her.

—H. M. Tomlinson, "The Sea and the Jungle"

Gulf

1

11 P.M., Gulf local time, July 15. The Very Large Crude Carrier (VLCC) *Prometheus* lay at anchor off Kharg Island and nothing at all seemed wrong.

She lay deep in the black water, fully laden with 250,000 tons of Gulf light crude, like a massive battery waiting to be connected; charged with enough dormant energy to light New York when released. To light New York or destroy Hiroshima. But all that massive energy lay caged in the three cathedral-size tanks, held still by baffles of steel stretching like unfinished walls from side to side, from top to bottom of the huge chambers. Its volatile elements, capable of igniting at the merest spark, lay smothered by the inert gases pumped into the ullage, the gap between the surface of the liquid and the roofs of the tanks.

She lay dark and quiet, lit only by the riding lights denoting Ship at Anchor and the brightness of the illuminated bridge; giving off only the gentle hum of the generators necessary to keep those lights alight. The bulk of her only visible because she blotted out the timeless stars and their reflections in the sea.

Manoj Kanwar, third mate, was standing watch. He should have been on the bridge, not running, terrified, through deserted corridors. But he had to get to Nicoli. That was the most important thing. Nicoli was first mate. He would know what to do. If he didn't, they were all as good as dead.

The thick soles of his desert boots screamed on the linoleum decking. The rasping of his breath filled the still air. He reached the door of the first mate's cabin and thundered on it with his fist. Then, scared by all the noise he was making, he knocked once more, quietly.

There was a distant groan as Nicoli came awake. A wash of light over Kanwar's boots from under the door. Unable to wait any longer, the young Indian turned the handle and all but fell in. Nicoli was on the point of opening the door and so they found themselves standing chest to chest: a short, dusky boy and a tall, bullish Greek with wise blue eyes and salt-and-pepper hair.

"It's Gallaher," wheezed Kanwar. "He says we're all dead men."

"No," said Nicoli calmly. "We'll get off all right in the lifeboats when the time comes. I've told you. Stick by me."

"It's not that," cried Kanwar in an agony of apprehension. "It's something else. Something no one else knows about. He said he'd only tell me if I slept with him. It's something bad, Nicoli. Something he was paid to do in secret."

Gallaher gazed at the pair of them with his disconcerting eyes. "Of course," he slurred. "Now would I be telling this lovely boy lies?" He fell back, sprawling, into the captain's chair on the bridge.

He was a small Irishman, red-headed and covered with freckles. His face and arms were terribly marked with scars. So fair were his brows and lashes that his pale eyes looked naked. His once lean body was running to fat. Only when he was totally drunk did his hands stop shaking. He never seemed to sleep in his berth and prowled the ship at night, often settling, as now, in the captain's chair up here. Nicoli knew nothing of Gallaher, the ship's electrician, and wanted to know nothing. But he knew the truth when he heard it. And he could just see this strange, sadistic man using whatever he knew to try to seduce the boy.

"Where?" he demanded.

Gallaher leered up at him. A shadow moved the depths of those naked eyes. What was it? Fear. The man was terrified. "They expected me to keep it down in me berth," said the Irishman.

4

"Sleep with it under me bunk till it was time. Not me! Never again! Not for any amount of money. I've been blown up, you know. Under me bunk! I should fuggin' think so!"

"Where did you put it, Gallaher?" Nicoli's voice was quiet now, appealing. He suspected all too clearly what "it" might be.

Gallaher grinned like a death's head. "I'd have gone mad with keeping it so close." He gripped Nicoli suddenly, with bruising force. "You do see that? I'd have come to pieces with it under my bunk!"

"'Course you would, Gallaher. I can see that. But where did you put it?"

Gallaher started giggling helplessly. "You'd never guess," he said. His eyes rolled up in his head.

Nicoli glanced over his shoulder then. "Wait outside," he ordered Kanwar. And, from the tone of the first mate's voice, Kanwar was glad to go.

It took ten minutes. Kanwar stood well clear of the door, so he never found out what kind of duress the mate used. But after ten long minutes they came out together, Nicoli's arm firmly round Gallaher, supporting him as though they were friends.

"Quick!" snapped the first mate, with uncharacteristic rudeness. "Take his other side." Kanwar obeyed at once. And so, three abreast, they proceeded.

They crushed into the tiny lift and hissed down into the bowels of the great tanker. Kanwar's fear of being discovered by the captain was at once replaced by the fear of discovery by the equally terrifying chief engineer, the tall, taciturn American, C. J. Martyr. Indeed, rounding a bend in the corridor suddenly, they bumped into two figures so unexpectedly that Kanwar cried out aloud. But it was only two of the Palestinian general purpose seamen coming off engine-room watch. Kanwar knew them: Ibrahim and Madjiid.

"You two!" ordered Nicoli at once. "Come with us." Obediently, unquestioningly, they fell in behind.

Kanwar paid them no more attention, all other thoughts wiped from his mind by the sudden realization of where Gallaher was taking them: the Pump Room.

The thought had no sooner entered his mind than the great steel bulkhead door was before them.

"Open it," ordered Nicoli. When Kanwar hesitated, Ibrahim stepped forward and lifted the great iron handle. Like the door to a bank vault, or a nuclear bunker, the huge steel portal swung wide. All of them hesitated on the threshold, as though they feared what awaited them within.

The Pump Room was the heart of the supertanker. When the computers in the Cargo Control Room four decks above worked out the optimum loading schedules, every drop of oil aboard, even the bunkerage that fueled the engine, could be moved through here.

The room itself was three decks high—nearly ninety feet—and was palisaded with silver-colored pipes around the walls. On the far side from the doorway they were now hesitating in, some forty feet inside, a single ladder led rung by rung up to a hatch on the main deck just in front of the bridge. On their right, built out from the pipe-covered wall, almost like a stage house in a play, was the Fire Control Room.

In the Fire Control Room great racks of carbon-dioxide canisters stood attached to the automatic firefighting equipment; for a fire here was the most dangerous thing that could possibly happen aboard. At the slightest hint of a spark, the automatic equipment would fill the whole Pump Room with carbon-dioxide. This process took the merest seconds. It was the only way of stopping the whole ship exploding.

And in this terrible place, Gallaher had been up to his mad mischief.

Nicoli moved first, then the drunken Irishman, then the reluctant Kanwar. The two GP seamen followed. Ibrahim, last in, closed the door behind them.

In the harsh white lighting, the room gleamed dead silver like a pathology lab in a hospital. The pipes dominated everything, like massive robot snakes frozen to silence in the midst of some sinister, serpentine orgy.

At once they were in the middle of the room. "Where?" snarled Nicoli.

The semiconscious Irishman looked around, as though surprised to find himself here. Then his face cleared. Even the habitual drunkenness in it vanished, to be replaced by horror at what his lust- and whiskey-loosened tongue had done.

"Mary, Mother..." he began, turning to escape from the place and his folly alike.

But Nicoli caught him by the arm and swung him back. "Where is it?"

"Sod you, Nicoli! You've got the pretty boy. You don't get no secrets."

All the rage in the Greek, held pent through the whole episode so far, exploded to the surface. Without a further word, he drove his fist into Gallaher's face and the Irishman hit the deck without ever knowing what had hit him.

For a second they stood looking down at him. There was no sympathy in their faces. They were a hard crew—except for Kanwar, perhaps—on a hard ship. And Gallaher had never been popular. "He's in the way there," observed Nicoli coldly. Ibrahim and Madjiid took an arm each and dragged him clear, but Nicoli was already looking into that harshly gleaming forest of pipes. "Now we'll have to do it the hard way," he observed. "You three. Look around for anything out of place. Anything unusual at all."

It took them nearly an hour, but at last Kanwar's keen eyes saw the tiniest twist of green wire in a junction of pipes twenty feet up. "There's something!" he called, his excitement boyish.

Nicoli was at his shoulder at once, the crows' feet at the corners of his eyes deepening as though he were gazing at some far horizon. "Yes!" His broad hand clapped the third mate on the back. "Well done, boy!"

"We'll have to get a ladder." Kanwar was all professionalism at once. He turned even before the first mate nodded and led Ibrahim and Madjiid to the Fire Control Room.

The low, stage-set door opened inward and Kanwar held it wide. The ladder stood, telescoped down, amid the canisters on the back wall of the small room. It was the work of a moment to release it.

The two seamen lifted the ladder up onto their shoulders, turned, and took two steps forward, back toward the door. The ladder was slightly unwieldy. As they moved, the front rose just enough to hit the lintel above the door. It momentarily snagged on some wires there, but pulled free easily enough when the two men stepped back again. Ibrahim lowered the front and they stepped safely past Kanwar and out into the Pump Room. Kanwar closed the door and followed them at once. He did not hear the faint sound of wires shorting in the room behind him, the wires that the ladder had caught and so easily—so fatally—twisted.

Within a minute, the ladder was extended and in place. With the other three at the bottom, Nicoli climbed up for a look.

It was surprisingly innocuous; a gray box about one foot square, hardly more threatening than a neatly wrapped present, with its gaily colored wires. Without thinking, Nicoli reached down and touched it. His fingertips no more than brushed it, but that was enough. It fell back into the junction of pipes and wall with a loud *clunk!* Nicoli jerked back, turning away. He would have fallen had the ladder not been so firmly held below. But nothing happened.

After a mental count of three, Nicoli turned back, pushed his arms through the rungs, and hugged the safe steel to his broad chest, waiting for the shock to die. Waiting for his heart to stop racing; waiting for the roaring in his ears to fade.

But then he realized that the roaring in his ears was nothing to do with shock. It was real.

Automatically, he looked down. At the foot of the ladder, Kanwar stood, gazing up. On his face was the most frightening expression Nicoli had ever seen. The boy's fists were locked onto the ladder and his whole body, like his fingers, seemed closed in some kind of seizure. His eyes were wide and his mouth stretched open, as though he were drowning. His lips and tongue were blue.

He was standing there screaming silently up at his friend and he was dead.

Nicoli saw all this in the time it took for the first agony to rip through his chest like a breaking heart. And in the instant it took him to die, he understood: something had switched on the automatic firefighting equipment. There must have been a short-out in the wires in the Fire Control Room. Every single atom of oxygen had been driven from the place.

From everywhere in the Pump Room: including their lungs.

He tried to move. He was too late. When the fatal spasm hit him, he locked onto the ladder and remained where he was, frozen in a purposeful attitude; looking just as much alive as Kanwar, Madjiid, and Ibrahim, the three other corpses at the ladder's foot.

The roaring of the automatic firefighting equipment continued for five more seconds. Then, as there was no more oxygen left anywhere in the Pump Room, right up to the ceiling ninety feet above, it switched itself off. There was only silence and stillness.

2

Captain Georg Levkas was an angry man. Even when nothing had happened to enrage him, he still went about life as though in the grip of an overpowering fury. In truth, most of Levkas's fury was directed against himself for failing to live up to the heady dreams of his youth, but he was far too proud a man to admit this to himself, and so the anger that filled him at all times was poured upon everything around him like molten metal boiling over in a crucible.

He had always been a buccaneer, a blockade runner. As a young man he had learned the sea, smuggling between Europe and Africa. He had carried something of that romantic apprenticeship with him when he had worked his way through his first real set of officers' papers and beyond; into the glittering world of commercial shipping. Onto his beloved tankers.

But the price. In the end the price had been too high. The price of getting his tanker captain's papers; the price, now, of keeping them.

At half past midnight local time, July 16, he was standing in the Radio Room yelling at the owner over the radio. The objects of his considerable ire were, at that precise moment, the ship's electrician, Gallaher, and the chief engineer, the American C. J. Martyr.

It had begun as a routine midnight report that the cargo had been loaded from the Iranian oil terminal that day. The oil was currently—on paper at least—the property of the Abu Oil Company, but it was likely to pass from owner to owner during the voyage according to the vicissitudes of the oil market. Their papers to transport the cargo from the Gulf to the huge refineries in Europoort near Rotterdam in Holland, sailing via the Cape of Good Hope on the standard route were all in order. The report had contained all this information but then it had somehow turned itself into a diatribe against the men the owner had sent aboard—the men Levkas refused to take into his confidence.

Hamstrung by the fact that he could not be absolutely sure who else was listening to the open radio link, and by the knowledge that he could never be explicit if there were the faintest chance he might be overheard, unaware of just how drunk he really was, Levkas was trying to explain that Martyr simply did not fit in with his crew, who otherwise seemed perfect for the business in hand: "...hand picked. All of them. Men I know. Men I can trust. I don't have to like them. I do not like any of them particularly, except the boy Kanwar and Nicoli, but I know them. I know what they have done and will do. I know nothing of these men Martyr and Gallaher except that I do not trust them."

"Captain..." The owner's voice was irritated. The man had a Greek name, thought Levkas. Why did he never speak in Greek? Had he no pride? "Captain Levkas, can you hear me?"

"I hear you."

"I understand your concern, Captain. You must understand me. I vouch for these men. I guarantee they will fulfill everything required of them. In any case, you know there is no time to get replacements out to you. You sail in the morning."

"I understand that. I understand how tight the schedule is. But you could get new men to Dubai in three days. I have names, numbers. There is the launch which comes out from Ras al Kaima..."

"I don't see how that would solve anything, Captain..."

"You do not understand the nature of the problem. My crew is a well-tuned instrument, involved in a dangerous undertaking. Each one knows his place. They do not trust this American, or..." An idea struck Levkas. He threw open the door of the Radio Room. Outside, the radio officer, Tsirtos, was talking to the Hong

Kong Chinese chief steward "Twelve Toes" Ho. "You two!" bellowed the captain. "Get the mate down here. He'll be on the bridge..."

But Tsirtos returned a minute or two later to report that Nicoli was not, in fact, on the bridge. Nor was he in his cabin. There had been no officer on watch since Kanwar had disappeared over an hour ago. This was too much for Levkas. With a bellow of rage, he broke off connection with the owner and stormed out of the Radio Room. "Sound for lifeboat drill!" he ordered. "I want everyone up and out!"

Ten minutes later, with the alarm still sounding, everyone was at his assigned post for lifeboat drill. Everyone except Nicoli, Gallaher, Kanwar, and two seamen.

"We'll search the ship!" announced Levkas, unconsciously slurring his words.

It took them half an hour to reach the Pump Room. Captain Levkas himself swung the great bulkhead door open with a sort of explosion of rage and there were the missing men, grouped around a ladder at the far side of the room. The scene was so natural it didn't occur to him that anything might be wrong. He looked up, saw Nicoli standing twenty feet up and, calling his name, stepped in.

With a ragged cheer, the others began to follow him in. After the long search, it was the natural thing to do.

Two steps over the threshold, Levkas knew there was something badly wrong. One more, hesitant, step and he knew just what it was. He turned, solid enough to stem the rush, but not to stop it. Tall enough to see over their heads to Martyr's face outside the door. A terrible roaring began, filling all the room. The first drunken officer tottered away, collapsing, surprised.

"Out!" yelled Levkas, but he knew it was already too late. The face outside the door asked an agonized question, although its lips did not move.

Strange, thought Levkas dreamily; now he was putting all his trust in one of the two men he had said he could not trust at all.

There were simply too many people coming in, away from the

door. All his officers now except the chief engineer and the boy Tsirtos. There was no time to repeat the order; to explain to them that they should all turn and get out. The carbon-dioxide, heavier than air, would spew out of the door until at first the corridor, and then the Engine Room and everywhere else level with or below here was also deadly. The only real chance they had for rescue came from the deck-hatch ninety feet above. And then only if the men immediately outside the door survived.

There were half a dozen of them in here and half a dozen oxygen masks in the Fire Control Room. Christ! if only his head was clearer! Another man sat down, faintly surprised at being unable to catch his breath. Only a millisecond had passed since his eyes had met Martyr's. There was no choice. Whatever the chances of the people inside, the door had to be closed. Almost wearily, Levkas nodded. The massive American's face twisted with the effort. The great slab of steel swung closed and the flat clang of its closing echoed in the bright room like the chime of a cracked bell. The captain was sealed inside the deadly Pump Room with ten other officers and crew—five dead and five dying fast.

Levkas was already moving, shouldering his way through those few still standing, looking away from their desperate eyes. Useless to all until he got to an oxygen mask and was able to breathe himself. It was years since he had bothered to train for anything like this. He had all but forgotten the rules. Of course he was holding his breath now but had he already breathed in a lungful of the deadly gas, like the others, dying with every new breath they took? Should he hurry and risk passing out from overuse of the little oxygen left in his system; or should he walk more slowly and risk simply running out of time? In the end he walked as fast as he could toward the Fire Control Room. Blackness swirled around the periphery of his vision. Lightning flashed before his eyes. The door, coming closer, suddenly became much taller and he never realized he had fallen to his knees.

All he could feel was the pain in his chest. It was like fire but he would not breathe. He fell forward and gashed his head on the jamb of the door. The blood came out blue. The shock of the fall surged through his system, giving him an iota more strength. As though in a dream, he pulled himself to all fours and crawled. Weaving from side to side, a terrible parody of the numberless drunken staggers of the last few years, he crossed the room until his head hit the wall opposite. By a supreme effort of will he found the strength to reach the masks a mere three feet above him, and he pulled one off the wall. Dizzy with relief, he placed the face mask over his nose and mouth and switched the equipment on.

And nothing happened. It was empty.

3

Martyr was a fit man, lean and hard; and yet he was completely out of breath by the time he reached the Pump Room hatchway on the deck. He stood, back straight, head up, gazing at the pearl-bright stars and filling his lungs with oil-tainted air, the backpack caught up from the Emergency Room on his way here held erect before him on the deck. The pause gave him time to think—not about the danger he was going into, but about the man he was going to save.

He had nothing but contempt for the other officers aboard. Oh, Nicoli looked a little better than the rest on the surface; Kanwar and Tsirtos, perhaps, just young and in the wrong company, but there was not one of them who could have called on an instant's loyalty from him until tonight. That one professional gesture. That one silent command from Captain Levkas. That one act worthy of a captain, unexpectedly putting the safety of ship and majority of crew before his own life. That deserved a little of Martyr's hard-won respect.

And, as senior officer left alive, even in this situation—even on this ship—he had a duty.

He checked the pressure reading on the backpack's oxygen canister, slipped it over his shoulders, and pressed the mask over his mouth. Then, suddenly full of energy, he knelt and tore the hatch clasps loose.

When he looked down the ladder, at first he felt a swirl of

15

vertigo. The steel uprights looked thread-thin as they plunged ninety feet straight down. The rungs blurred into one another, making the ladder look like a slide. But there was no time for hesitation now. Perhaps he had taken too long already.

He swung one leg over the raised rim of the hatch and placed his foot carefully on the first rung. Then deliberately, hand over hand, he began to climb down. He breathed slowly and evenly, watching the rungs go by. Watching the backs of his hands. Watching the display on his digital watch. It was 00.50 Gulf time when he started climbing down and he never remembered seeing the display change from that reading; but when he checked again, consciously if automatically as he stepped off the last rung, it read 01.00 exactly.

He hesitated an instant before turning. He had seen enough of death already, and had hoped to see no more. It was not fear; more a weariness. He was exhausted deep inside, as even the strongest will become after a while when tested near to destruction. As especially the strongest will become when they will not—cannot—share their burdens. But now he was here. He had no choice. He drew strength from that and turned.

Most of them were piled by the door, sitting or lying at ungainly angles; eyes and mouths wide, as though incredibly shocked at what had happened. A glance at them was enough to satisfy him that they were all beyond help. Another glance at Nicoli and his men clustered round their short ladder scant yards away. At Gallaher propped against the Fire Control Room, apparently peacefully asleep. Nine bodies. No captain.

Without further hesitation, he crossed to the Fire Control Room: his first priority still Levkas.

The captain was lying at the foot of the far wall, curled on his side, clutching an oxygen cylinder. The mask was loosely over his nose and mouth. Martyr crossed to his side at once, pushing the mask more firmly into place. He checked the cylinder pressure. It was empty. He replaced the whole thing. Only when the mask was firmly in place and pumping oxygen did he check for vital signs.

He could find none.

He straightened quickly, searching for the manual override to the firefighting equipment. It was on the wall nearby. He switched it off and the fans on. They would clear the inert gas in time, but in hours, not minutes. Only then would the atmosphere in here be safe. Only then could the bodies be moved. Until then, there was nothing to be done.

He looked down at the captain curled uselessly around the life-giving bottle like a dead child in the womb. He thought he might as well finish the job he had come down here to do. He took the hunched shoulders and tore them off the floor with a massive effort. He propped the inert body against the wall and stooped, letting it fall over his shoulder. Then he straightened, lifting the dangling feet into the air.

For some reason he glanced up as he passed through the Fire Control Room door, saw the blackened, shorted-out wires above the lintel, and began to understand.

He was breathing like a bellows when he reached the foot of the ladder up to the escape hatch. He glanced up at the distant hatchway and the one bright star that seemed to fill it. Should he go across and open the door? He could hammer on it to warn anyone who might be still outside. For all he knew the corridor was still full of the carbon-dioxide that had leaked out before he had closed off the Pump Room. And, ultimately, that was the trouble. There were decks and working areas below this. The engineering decks—his own domain. The thought of filling them with deadly pockets of heavier-than-air inert gas was something he could not accept. He turned again and started to climb. With each rung, the captain's inert body became heavier. With each added strain on his own body, Martyr's consciousness closed down, keeping pain and fatigue at a necessary distance until he had completed his task.

How long it took him to complete the ninety-foot climb was something else he would never be sure of. He didn't even notice when the ladder ended. He fell out of the open hatchway with his grim bundle onto the cool iron deck, to lie there like another dead man until Salah Malik, leader of the seamen, had the pair of them carried away.

* * *

17

But there was too much to do. He struggled back to wakefulness before they even reached the bridge, then stood watching as they lugged the captain's body on into the brightness.

"Our first job is to contact the owner," he said to Malik, who loomed competently at his side. "Then we'd better start clearing the Pump Room. I'll write the Accident Report and make up the logs, since there doesn't seem to have been a watch officer on the bridge for nearly two hours. Nor in the Engine Room since the lifeboat drill.

"I'll have to guess what happened to Nicoli and his team, I guess. Any idea what they were doing down there with that ladder?"

Ghostly in the shadows, Malik's shoulders shrugged.

"Well . . . Let's get to it then. Two of your seamen gone I know. The rest just officers, I think. And Gallaher. Tsirtos in the Radio Room?"

"I suppose."

He was. Sitting wide-eyed with shock, staring at the bright displays. "They're all dead, aren't they, Mr. Martyr? Everyone who went into the Pump Room," he said as the chief put his head through the door. "Thank God you stopped me from following them! I walked round the ship after you closed the door. The stewards were all in their berths. The seamen are around somewhere. I've seen Malik. But the ship's just empty. Corridors. Cabins. Everywhere. Empty. Like the *Marie Celeste*. Ghost ship . . ."

Martyr let him talk. There was time. Little enough, God knew, but time to let a shocked boy talk away his fear.

Gently he said, "Can you reach the owner?"

"Will we go down in history, like the *Marie Celeste?*"

"Maybe get a spot on the six o'clock news. Those reporters sure seem to love a good outbreak of death. Can you contact the owner?"

"And when I was wandering around the corridors, I could hear some kind of pipe playing. Ghostly. Like ghosts singing."

Into the eerie silence, Martyr agreed, "Sure. One of the stewards plays a flute. His name's Nihil. He's the only one not from Hong Kong I think. It's real pretty."

"I never dreamed there would be anything like this, Chief. This is really my first berth. Nicoli got it for me. We're from the same village. *Were* from the same village . . ."

"That's tough. Can you get the owner for me now, Sparks?"

"What? Oh, certainly. He's still at his hotel, I expect. The captain was just talking to him."

"Well, get him!"

It took a few moments, during which Tsirtos calmed a little, soothing his way past an angry night porter, getting the phone rung in the owner's suite in spite of the unusual hour.

As soon as the ringing tone filled the small room, Martyr said, "That's enough for now. I'll take it from here." And he gently ushered Tsirtos out.

Just at the moment the door closed behind the departing radio officer, connection was made.

"Yeah?" snarled the owner.

"Demetrios? It's Martyr. We got trouble."

$$4$$

Four thousand miles away, two hours later, Richard Mariner sprang awake in an icy sweat. He lay for a moment in the tangled wreck of his bed as the sound of metal grinding on metal died in his ears. He always heard the terrible sound of the impact, never the explosion. But then, the impact had, oddly, been the more terrifying of the two, and the explosion itself had seemed silent to him. The explosion that had destroyed his last command, his last crew. His wife. His life.

Mariner swung himself out of bed and strode through into the sitting room. Long windows facing the river made the place seem like a ship's bridge and he stood where the helm would have been, looking over the Thames toward Nine Elms with the bright span of the Vauxhall Bridge on his left, unconsciously reliving those last terrible seconds on that other, real bridge.

He was tall, thin of waist and hip; but the breadth of shoulder and depth of chest gave him the appearance of rocklike solidity. The strength of his jaw might have suggested an equally resolute character to an old-fashioned expert in physiognomy, who might also have seen natural aristocracy in the aquiline jut of his nose, broken a little out of line now; and fastidiousness—perhaps tenderness—in the delicate line of his lips. In the half-light, his face seemed almost blue: hair so black as to have a hint of it; square jaw, even when shaven, with a tint of it; and eyes like magnesium flares behind a pane of sapphire.

And rings, bruise deep, below them.

On the sill before him lay his current reading, Nigel Balchin's *The Small Back Room*. Richard remembered Sammy Rice's first words in it: "In 1928 my foot was hurting all the time, so they took it off..." God! If only memories could be like that.

Every once in a while Richard Mariner's memory would start to play up. It would never be for any particular reason, never on the anniversary of his first meeting with Rowena Heritage, of his marriage to her, or of her death. Out of the blue he would suddenly find himself prey to nightmares. In his dreams great ships would blow apart. Then sleep itself would become a dream. He would become moody, violent. Unable to concentrate. Unable to work. Surrounded by ghosts wherever he was.

The phone rang and he picked it up without moving more than his hand. "Mariner."

"Good God! Do you ever sleep?" It was Audrey, the night secretary from the agency.

"As little as possible. What is it?"

"Emergency. Call from a Mr. Kostas Demetrios. Accident aboard his VLCC *Prometheus*. Can we replace the master and all deck officers except the radio officer? Also all engineering officers except the chief?"

"How soon?"

"Now."

He glanced at his watch. The steel Rolex his wife, Rowena, had given him just before they set sail that last, fatal, time. Why wear it? Waste not, want not.

The same reason he maintained the membership to the Royal Automobile Club Sir William, her father, had bought him so long ago. Maintained it even when his back was to the wall and it had seemed an unnecessary expense. But the marble halls in the basement of the club's Pall Mall headquarters, with their exercise areas, pools, and saunas had stood him good guard against the fat pot belly of city life ashore.

Rowena's Rolex said the time was a minute or two past midnight, British Summer Time. "I'll be there in twenty minutes," he said.

* * *

Seventeen minutes later, he stepped out of his long black E-Type Jaguar and walked briskly to the door marked CREWFIN-DERS. They owned a suite of three rooms on the fourth floor of a Victorian building overlooking St. Mary Axe in the City of London. Cheek by jowl with Leadenhall and Lloyd's, it was in the best possible position to keep his finger on the pulse of world shipping—as was necessary if it was to become what Mariner dreamed: the largest independent crew-finding agency in the world.

Twenty minutes later, to the second, he stepped out of the lift into the reception area. "Any idea what went wrong?" he called to Audrey.

Audrey was at the night desk, with a small switchboard on her left and a slave monitor on her right connected to the computer's central file. "No," she answered at once. "Must have been something big, though; unless it was industrial action."

"An officers' strike, led by the captain?" His tone said it all.

"Have to be one hell of an accident. An explosion..." She tailed off in horror. She had uttered the forbidden word. Mariner seemed hardly to notice. "...would hardly have left enough of the ship to require a full complement of officers."

He swung past her, already in his shirtsleeves and ready to get down to business. When he sat in his deep leather chair at the main console it was exactly 00.30 British Summer Time. Exactly three hours since he had left, exhausted, for home.

He got up again, with the back of the assignment broken, at dawn. And, had he been one for keeping anniversaries, he would have known that it was exactly five years to the minute since the nightmare began.

After the disaster, Mariner had chosen to remain ashore, yet at first sight, this man, one of the great sailors of his generation, seemed ill qualified for life on the beach. He had been a sailor for twenty-four years, a captain for eight, and a senior captain with Heritage Shipping for six. In all the long years before he had settled down as senior captain, heir apparent, husband to Rowena, his boss's eldest daughter, he had moved about and worked for all and sundry. Before he became senior captain at Heritage Shipping and Mr. Rowena Heritage, he had not only earned the papers to command almost anything afloat, he had also set up an unrivaled network of contacts.

Contacts which, during the years of estrangement with the Heritage family after Rowena's death, had formed the backbone of Crewfinders. It was not a company that would ever rival Heritage Shipping, even though Heritage had been half crippled by the loss of Richard's last command, but it was Mariner's own company. And it was growing stronger every day. And would continue to do so as long as its reputation remained intact.

That reputation rested on one fact: Crewfinders could replace officers and crew faster than any other agency in the business. Between one and three days. Any officer. Anywhere in the world.

But never before had they been asked to replace almost all the officers on a supertanker all at once.

Dawn came slowly and late, edging into a low gray sky only the thinnest strip of which was visible to Richard Mariner in any case, looking up as he was from a small side window between high building frontages. He watched it, nevertheless, deep in thought, with a huge mug of coffee cooling in his fist. The junior officers were already on their way, summoned by Audrey from beds and other haunts all over the world. But the first mate was proving more difficult to find. And there were no captains at all.

It was the merest chance, nothing more. He had four captains on paper, but none in fact. One had gone cruising somewhere in the Greek Islands. One had fallen off a ladder. One had been involved in a motor accident on the Kingston bypass, and the last had run over his foot with a lawn mower late yesterday evening. The soonest he could supply a captain was in about a week. Which would not be good enough.

Still, first things first. Let him get the mate sorted out and he would worry about the master then. He put the cold coffee down and went back into the computer room. He had no sooner sat down in front of his console than his phone purred.

"Yes?"

"I've just had a call from Ben Strong. He's available."

"Are you sure? I thought he was still in Bangkok. So did the computer."

"He's just reported back. The computer will be updating his

23

file now. And it's an expensive city, from what I've heard..."
He knew that tone in Audrey's voice. Ben had spun her a hard-luck story and flirted with her a bit to get preferential treatment.

Well, he deserved it, God knew. He was an excellent officer. And his father had been Richard's own mate, once upon a time. He was Ben's godfather. The closest thing to a real father Ben had left.

"Get him back. Tell him he's now first mate on *Prometheus*. He needs to be there as soon as he can."

After that he hit a block. He could not replace the captain. With all favors called and all debts cleared, he was still that one vital crew member short. There was simply no one he knew who could take command.

When the idea popped into his head he would never know. Suddenly he saw his own master's papers as he had thrust them into his desk drawer at home after the inquiry five years ago. At first he dismissed it, but as his desperation grew the vision persisted.

He made excuses: he had always run a one-man show; there was no one to look after Crewfinders if he went. But he was in a cleft stick: if he didn't go, there would be no more Crewfinders in any case. And anyway; he knew perfectly well that his capable, dedicated secretarial team could run it flawlessly without him.

So, at last, in spite of his bone-deep feelings of foreboding, he drove back to his flat by Vauxhall Bridge, packed his bags, and settled his affairs as though he knew he weren't coming back.

Then Audrey drove him to Heathrow to catch the last flight out to the Gulf. Then, exhausted herself, she went straight home to bed. As soon as she arrived at the office next morning, she telexed *Prometheus*.

John Higgins heard about it first, because he happened to be outside the Radio Room when the telex came in and was able to take the flimsy off Tsirtos because the young radio officer was still disoriented by all the new arrivals and so easily browbeaten.

"Well, blow me down!" said the wiry Manxman, and, clutching the stem of his cold pipe firmly between his teeth—one of a range of pipes he sported constantly but never, ever, smoked—he strode off in search of his old friend the mate.

Ben Strong, here only a few hours but already very much in charge, was on the bridge. He straightened up as Higgins came in and caught his eye. "What is it, Number Two?" he asked at once. Higgins was one of those men who almost sparkle with ill-controlled energy—every muscle in his lithe frame always seemed at full stretch and he chewed through pipe stems at an alarming rate. Now he was almost luminous with glee.

"Message for the owner, Number One. Seen him?"

"In his cabin, I expect. Anything I should know?"

"New captain due aboard later this afternoon." Higgins tried to keep it nonchalant. He failed.

"Oh?" Ben was suddenly all attention. "Anyone we know?"

"I should say so. Mariner's coming himself."

Ben just managed to hold himself in check, refusing to rise to Higgins's bait. "Is that so?" he asked equably after a while. "Well, you'd better run along and let the owner know at once, if you'd be so kind. And we'd better get the last of the coffins ashore as soon as possible."

"Righty-ho." Higgins refused to be dashed by his cold reception and loped off in search of the owner, pipe jutting jauntily up toward his left ear.

As soon as he had gone, Ben mopped his brow. "Christ on a crutch," he muttered. "Dick himself. Now, who would have thought of that!"

He was by no means alone on the bridge. As well as the seamen on duty, the third mate Danny Slope was there. Like John Higgins, Slope was of medium height, just topping Ben's shoulder, but unlike the Manxman, he was plump and furtive. He habitually wore a veiled, secretive look. He was an unknown quantity among the Crewfinders men, not on the list long enough to be known to anyone other than the computer in St. Mary Axe. "What's that all about, Number One?" he asked now, his voice high.

Ben looked at him with something akin to distaste. He had nothing against the third mate, indeed he seemed quite a competent man, but he looked and sounded like the school sneak in the sort of books Ben had enjoyed reading as a boy.

"Don't you know anything, young Danny-me-lad?" he demanded; a schoolteacher with a criminally inattentive pupil. "Richard Mariner's the man you work for. The man who owns Crewfinders."

"Well, I know that..."

"You just don't know what that has to do with the price of eggs. Right? Well, I'm precisely the man to tell you.

"Five years ago, Richard Mariner was senior captain of the Heritage Shipping fleet. He was married to Sir William Heritage's eldest daughter and was captain of his most beautiful new tanker. Both the daughter and the ship were called Rowena. He took Rowena aboard *Rowena* for her maiden voyage—a sort of second honeymoon because their marriage had hit a bumpy patch—then lost them both in a collision and explosion in the Western Approaches.

"The inquiry exonerated him. Came out smelling of roses to everyone except Sir William Heritage, who was short one ship and one daughter—and was not happy about either.

"And the long and short of it is, Dick Mariner brushed the dust of supertankers off his shoes. Set up Crewfinders. Swore on the grave of his beloved, which was empty of course as her body lies blown to atoms at the bottom of the Channel, never to sail in these iron monsters again."

"God," said Slope, simply awed by the story. "How come you know so much about it?"

"You see before you a poor orphan boy, Number Three. Lost my mum on the day I was born. Lost my dad five years ago, almost to the day. He was Mariner's first mate on that Heritage tanker."

The news went round the ship like wildfire after that. Mariner was the sort of man legends clung to. Everybody in Crewfinders had their own favorite tale or memory of the great man. Tales that grew in the telling.

Chief Steward "Twelve Toes" Ho had no trouble in finding out all he wanted to know. As well as being perfectly trained stewards, his men were a finely tuned information-gathering machine.

Salah Malik, leader of the seamen, also heard what he wanted to hear, when he wanted to hear it. He was not displeased. The previous officers—late and unlamented, in his book—had not been the sort of men he relished dealing with.

The pair of them got together in the galley later that afternoon, prompted by almost telepathic communication, and decided what should be left and what concealed of the previous occupancy. They decided to conceal nothing and let matters take their course.

Only two men aboard remained relatively unaffected by the news. The owner, Kostas Demetrios, was a shipping man and not a sailor. He knew of Mariner's reputation distantly. He knew nothing of exploding tankers, lost loves, and lost fortunes. It seemed to him fitting that on a contract this size, the boss should get his hands dirty too. He thought no more of it than that, as far as anyone else could tell.

Martyr heard. He heard some of the story from young Andrew McTavish, third engineer supplied by Crewfinders. It moved him not at all. It spoke to him of a man who had married the boss's daughter for advancement in the firm; who only took her on the fatal voyage because he had been told to and was afraid of queering his pitch with the old man; and who had fouled up anyway and run away from the sea.

It was a story utterly without romance, as far as he was concerned; the tale of a man who by luck or circumstance had built himself a reputation, but when the testing time had come had simply cut and run. So now, probably down on his luck again, with his vaunted company at full stretch, he was being offered a fortune to come and get his hands dirty again. Dirty in more ways than one, Martyr thought.

As far as the taciturn American could see, this was just the man to replace the late, unlamented Levkas.

5

They had left the last three coffins close to the top of the accommodation ladder so that they were the first things Mariner saw as he pulled himself wearily onto the deck.

They were the worst things he could possibly have seen during his first moments back aboard a supertanker and he froze, horrified. For a moment even his massive reserves of emotional strength were taxed to their limit.

Ben Strong pushed forward at once, shocked to see his godfather's long, aristocratic face all bone and line; the massive chin steely with stubble; the incendiary blue eyes dull and dark-ringed, sunken with fatigue. His hand was raised, but more to support than to greet.

He was unceremoniously shoved aside by the owner. "So this is the great Richard Mariner," boomed Kostas Demetrios. "Welcome aboard, sir. Welcome aboard."

Mariner took Demetrios's hand and shook it formally. He dragged his tired eyes away from the boxes and glanced around the deck. He saw little enough—only the expanse of green overlain with huge pipes, fifteen feet above, running fore and aft; port and starboard. Odd-shaped columns of manifolds, winches, hatches, tank tops; all standing to shoulder height—all dancing and wavering in the furnace heat of a Gulf afternoon. And beyond them, the incandescent brightness of the bridge. Five stories high. Far, far away.

Ben succeeded Demetrios at last, shaking Mariner's hand. "Hello, Dick," he said quietly. "Welcome back. No ceremony, I'm afraid. I thought you'd rather not..." His eyes, gentle brown in a mahogany tan and deep-slitted against the murderous glare, searched Richard's pale face anxiously. Then, as his godfather's eyes came alive again, he gave a broad grin. They shook hands vigorously and might have embraced, had Demetrios not interrupted. "C'mon. Let's go. Time's money."

Richard looked at him properly, and didn't much like what he saw. Demetrios was a short man, lean in body but with something self-indulgent, almost decadent, about his huge dark eyes and full red mouth. His luxuriant black curls just topped Mariner's square shoulder. As he spoke, sunlight blazed on a gold tooth. And when he spoke, it was with an American accent. Among the most dangerous combinations in the world, mused Richard grimly. Greek pirate's soul and a Harvard Business School mind. And greed. Demetrios had greedy eyes. But then, which self-made millionaire did not? he wondered. And pushed the bluff, honest gaze of his father-in-law out of his memory.

These thoughts occupied his mind for the walk up to the blessed shade cast by the port bridge wing. He opened the bulkhead door and stepped ahead of the others into the cool of the A deck corridor. There was a distant hum of generators. The lights and the air-conditioning were on. He shivered. Then Ben was by his side. "Good trip out, Dick?" Richard was momentarily distracted. Ben's cheerful smile, dark tan, and sun-bleached hair seemed to give off energy. He gave a wry smile.

"Fine. How soon can we weigh?"

"As soon as the owner, and...and the others leave."

If Richard closed his eyes he could see the coffins. The three, full no doubt, at the head of the accommodation ladder. Others, older, at the memorial service five years ago: empty every one.

They got under way at 16.35 local time. The interim was taken up with a brief conference between the owner and his new captain, during which Demetrios seemed determined to answer as few questions as possible and to emphasize the overwhelming need for a swift passage. When he left, he took the last three coffins with him.

At 17.00, Richard began his inspection.

He started high in the navigation bridge with Ben Strong at his side. Then they went down to the bridge and chatted briefly to John Higgins on watch there; checked the equipment, chart table, course, logbooks. Looked down the long deck, changing color from green to ocher in the early sunset. Went down to C deck, then B deck, then A; then the crew's quarters and the rest.

Here Richard met his crew. Vague names, quickly forgotten at first—only Salah Malik and Twelve Toes Ho standing out from the crowd because they were so obviously in charge. Salah somewhere between a mullah and a chief petty officer; Ho named "Twelve Toes" because of his uncannily sure footing.

He took the Accident Report Book into the Pump Room and read through the concise notes above the chief engineer's signature. He tried to reconstruct the sequence of events those bland words described. He walked into the Fire Control Room and looked around, narrow-eyed. The wires above the lintel were all new and meticulously fitted. "Your work?" he asked Ben.

"Chief engineer's."

He walked across to the rear wall and looked up at the pipe junction where Kanwar had seen the twist of green wire. There was nothing. "Anything up there?"

"Not that I could see. They were maybe checking the pipe junctions. Some of them are ... Well, let's just say some of the pipework isn't all it looks."

Richard looked at his first officer, frowning, then up at the pipes again. "No, no," said Ben. "Nothing to worry about. It's fine. I've had a good look round. Next time she's in for maintenance she might need a little work, that's all."

They checked that the oxygen cylinders and the carbon-dioxide canisters all read full-pressure and left.

Then they went deeper into the bowels of the ship, down into the roaring inferno of the Engine Room. And here at last the captain met the chief engineer.

In the air-conditioned relative quiet of the Engine Control

Room, overhanging the three-deck-deep hole that contained the huge engine, C. J. Martyr stood with the statue stillness that characterized the man. He must have heard the surge of sound as Ben opened and closed the door, but he did not move until Ben took him by the shoulder. Then he swung round incredibly fast, as though he were going to fight them.

His face was absolutely closed. What lay behind that statuesque mask they might learn in time, little by little, but what struck Richard immediately was the cold hostility. Martyr had tremendously expressive green eyes astride a great beak of a nose that overhung an uncompromising mouth extended by deep lines down to his square, gray chin. Only his ears added a touch of levity, sticking out like jug handles to draw attention to the width of his cheekbones; their size emphasized by the sand-gray stubble of his crew-cut hair. He was six feet four inches tall and as thin as a rake.

He stuck out a massive hand. Richard looked down as he took it. It was as gaunt as the rest of the man—fingers thin between scarred knucklebones, tipped with great square nails.

"How do you do?" In the face of the baseless hostility, Richard spoke stiffly, and then felt very stage-English, as though he were putting on airs to belittle the American. Martyr scanned him from head to toe, able to look down on him—just; the blue-black waves perhaps half an inch below the sand-gray crew-cut. He nodded once, coldly, silently.

It was like a declaration of war.

Dinner was held back to 20.00 that evening, waiting until the captain's inspection was complete. Richard had told Ben to proceed with Pour Out while he showered and changed. Although exhausted, he hurried, knowing that the first social meeting with his officers was of the greatest importance.

At precisely the same moment as Richard stepped out of his cabin door, Martyr stepped out of his a few feet away.

"Evening, Chief," said Richard guardedly. "You've missed Pour Out."

"Yeah."

They crossed to the lift, shoulder to shoulder, in silence, while

Richard sorted out in his mind the sequence of questions he wanted to ask. Martyr pushed the button.

"What exactly happened in the Pump Room?" asked Richard at once.

Martyr, his face closed, turned. There was something Richard could not read, moving in his glass-green eyes. "Murder," he said.

"*Murder*?"

"As good as."

The lift came. The doors hissed open. They stepped in together.

"What do you mean?"

"Goddamned amateurs," yelled Martyr, suddenly overcome by the enormity of what had happened. "You've never seen anything like it in your life. Rotten wiring. Empty emergency equipment..."

"Did you look at the pipework that Nicoli was checking?"

"Yeah. Nothing wrong with it. The biggest disasters have the smallest causes. That's always the way."

They arrived. The doors hissed open. Martyr's face snapped closed again.

The silence between them still cool, they walked down to the Officer's Bar and entered together at 20.00 precisely.

Everyone was there, except the third mate and the third engineer, who had just begun their respective watches above and below. They were rowdy and cheerful. Even young Tsirtos looked blearily happy, holding a pint of beer—clearly not his first—very much more at home with this crew than he had been with the other.

John Higgins bustled across to them, beaming, an empty briar wedged jauntily in his mouth. "Evening, Captain. Chief. Would you like a drink, sirs?"

Richard at least was tempted—Martyr rarely drank—and he hesitated for a second. It seemed too long, all of a sudden, since anyone had called him "sir" like that. He grinned enormously, feeling all the weariness drop away and an old excitement stir inside him. Then he clapped the second mate on the shoulder. "No, thanks, John. I've kept you all from your meal long enough. Ben, Chief. Let's go through."

The meal started quietly because both senior officers were silent; but as course succeeded course, each more excellent than the last, conversation became a hum and then a contented buzz.

An hour or so later they trooped back to the bar, picked up a few more drinks, then proceeded to the lounge. The food had sharpened Richard's mind—the food and a simple joy in existence he had almost forgotten how to feel. He had spent the meal studying his men. He felt able to invest another half hour in this crucial exercise before retiring at last. He took his beer and followed.

In the lounge there was a TV, but it could only pick up Arabic stations. There was also a video. "Where are the tapes for this?" demanded Martyr unexpectedly. He, too, had been watching the captain and officers during the meal and he now looked less hostile—perhaps even a little confused. Certainly this was the first time he had ever come into the lounge with the others. Truth to tell, it was also the first time Tsirtos had dared come in here as well. The young radio officer was as willing to oblige as an excited child.

"There are some tapes in the library, I think," he offered at once.

"Try and get a good movie, son," demanded Martyr. Tsirtos vanished to obey.

Martyr seemed to have reached a decision. He crossed to Richard's table and sat, uninvited. Richard swung round until his back was to the screen, facing Martyr. The chief put his great scarred hands on the table and leaned forward above them. "Richard Mariner," he drawled. "Do I know that name?"

Richard knew when he was being tested. He had no idea of the stories that had circulated, anticipating his arrival, and would have been surprised to hear half of them. He thought instead of the collision; the explosion . . . He sat quiet, watching his adversary. The cheerful hum of conversation continued unabated. That was good, he thought; he didn't want this clash of wills too public, or the authority of one of the combatants must inevitably suffer, no matter what the outcome.

"Captain Richard Mariner . . ." The American drew it out, apparently using the sound as a goad on his recalcitrant memory.

Suddenly, with breathtaking vividness, Richard saw three hundred feet of pipe-forested deck rolling back toward him as he stood, unbelieving, in his bridge. Three hundred feet of steel plate, rolling like a carpet. Like the top of a sardine can with an invisible key turning.

His whole body jumped and flinched. Martyr's eyes focused on him sharply at once, but Tsirtos unwittingly saved the situation by bustling back importantly, holding a handful of black video cassettes. Martyr swung toward him, a glimmer of interest lighting his bronze hatchet face. "Anything good? Any westerns?" he asked almost wistfully.

"I don't know what they are, sir. No labels."

All the officers turned back into their little groups. Martyr turned back toward Mariner, the temporary distraction over. The test began again. "Mariner. Now I'm sure I know that name ..."

Richard ran out of patience. He opened his mouth to tell the chief to play up or get out of the game, but caught his breath in shock. At the very moment he looked up, Martyr's face changed.

The eyes blazed. The thin lips drew back from marble-white teeth. Nostrils flared. Ugly veins wormed their way across his broad forehead.

At the same time, all conversation stopped, stunned into silence. Discordant music blared. Richard swung round, knowing a crisis when he found one.

Tsirtos was kneeling down, checking the video machine as it ran. Above him, on the screen, a young girl was hanging from the branch of a tree. Her legs were lashed to pegs, wide spaced in the ground. She was utterly naked. As they watched, in stunned silence, a hooded man appeared and began to beat her with a stick. She looked sixteen years old, if that.

"Tsirtos!" snapped Mariner, but his voice was lost in Martyr's roar. The table rose in the captain's face as the chief launched himself forward. Richard toppled to one side, rolled over, and came up just as Martyr hauled Tsirtos to his feet. Holding the boy's shirt left-handed at his throat, Martyr launched a murderous right hook low to his belly. Another.

Captain and first officer leapt forward as one, each catching an arm. Martyr dropped Tsirtos and pulled free, swinging round. He drew back his fist, eyes completely mad. "Ben!" called Richard, at whom the blow was aimed. Ben caught Martyr's wrist and turned the blow. Richard stepped back, kicking away the table and chair.

"Right! That's all. Look after Tsirtos."

His whole stance changed. The English stiffness went out of his back and shoulders. His heels left the floor and his knees bent slightly. His chin tucked down toward his chest. "Come on, then," he said quietly. His voice and face had changed too. When he raised his fists, they were surprisingly big.

Martyr, far beyond control, threw another huge haymaker at the icy Englishman. Mariner rocked back slightly and let the blow pass within an inch of his nose. Then he leaned in over the chief's guard, hooking a vicious right to the angle of his jaw. Martyr staggered forward and Mariner danced behind him delivering a crisp combination of right-left-right jabs to his kidneys. Martyr answered with a right hook to Mariner's ribs concealed by his turning body and delivered like a landslide. The Englishman hissed and staggered back a step or two before starting to dance again, using the movement to swing a left of his own back over Martyr's guard to the side of his head.

Any of these blows would have destroyed lesser men, but the captain and the chief were hardly slowed. Martyr, his turn stopped by the simple physics of Mariner's counterblow, put his head down and charged. After two steps, he gathered the Englishman to his shoulder, but Mariner twisted before the American's grip could tighten and, taking that great cannonball head under his arm, he ran forward, using the chief's own weight and the force of his charge, guiding the blind man into the door.

He had closed the heavy teak door behind him as he had entered, last of the officers, a few minutes ago. Now he opened it again with the top of Martyr's head and his own shoulder. Not so much "opened" as "demolished." And the massive force of the movement, centered on the top of Martyr's skull, knocked him unconscious at once.

Richard let go as they exploded through the door and spun away, catching at the handrail along the wall, saving himself from falling, turning back at once to see Martyr landing face down like a dead man. And in motion once more, stepping back over his adversary through the splintered door. There was a cheer quelled instantly by the look in his eyes.

Tsirtos was on his knees, puking weakly and swearing viciously in Greek. Suddenly the radio officer looked less boyish. His brown eyes were hard. His face vicious. Making Richard remember inconsequentially, that it was the Greeks, not the Sicilians, who invented the vendetta.

The video picture had changed. Its subject matter had not. "Switch that off!" snapped Richard Mariner.

There was a click. The screen went mercifully dark.

"Sweet Jesus!" said somebody.

Mariner glared around the room, suddenly overcome with absolute fury. *"Quite so!"* he snapped. Even Ben Strong quailed before his gaze.

And Richard really began to remember what it was like to be the captain of a ship.

6

A short while later, Richard was standing on the bridge by the helmsman looking past his reflection and the twinkling lights on the console before him into the black velvet of a Gulf night. There was no moon. The dancing stars were like the huge, misshapen pearls they collected from the shallow seabeds here. He was thinking of a dawn five years ago. Of a beautiful, spoiled woman lying alone in her berth rigid with loathing for him. Making her plans for a messy, painful divorce; looking forward to hurting her husband and her father as much as she possibly could, out of pure childish spite.

She was in his thoughts almost constantly, this woman wasting the last seconds of her life on hatred.

Slope was behind him to his left, looking down into the green bowl of the Collision Alarm Radar. In those days the Gulf was too busy to let the *Prometheus* do everything for herself. There were always dhows up to no good, smuggling guns, pearls, slaves; small tankers and cargo ships; VLCCs; the odd ULCC, twice as big; SMBs; sandbars; rigs; tiny, uncharted islands; heaven knew what else. It was almost as bad as the Channel and no place to be sloppy or off guard. There were lookouts with night glasses on the bridge wings and in the forecastle head.

As first officer, Ben Strong was also acting medic. After they had cleared the mess in the Officers' Lounge, Richard had sent the others to their cabins and closed the bar; detailed John Higgins to go through the rest of the videotapes, and ordered Ben to report to the bridge when he had seen to Tsirtos and Martyr.

Now he shook himself mentally and cleared his mind of its ghosts. He had more immediate problems. He started pacing the bridge, head forward, hands clasped behind his back, trying to focus clearly on the jumble of events at whose center he stood. It seemed obvious that the previous officers had, to put it mildly, been a strange lot. And they had met a pretty strange end. Martyr probably knew more than he was saying—but he was strange himself, and there was no guarantee he would confide anything more to his new captain—especially now—beyond what he had said, and the accounts that bore his decided signature in the logs and the Accident Report Book.

Why did he seem to regard the others, and Richard in particular, with such suspicion?

Why, if he held the dead crew in such contempt, had he been persuaded to join them?

Was there something going on, or was it just that sort of mild lunacy that sometimes breaks out at sea?

But they had only been at sea for six hours.

Ben and John came up together. "Did he, by God?" Ben was saying. "I'd like to see that."

"Anytime you like, Ben. That and all the rest. But watch out for the chief."

"All the rest, John?" snapped the captain as they came round the great bank of instruments standing like a low wall across two-thirds of the bridge. John nodded, his open countenance twisted with disgust. His gaze flickered across to the young third officer's back, then up to the captain again.

"All right, Mr. Slope," said Richard. "You can slip down to the Officers' Pantry and make yourself a coffee. Take ten minutes."

Slope hurried off, not too happy about missing the gossip.

Richard turned to Ben first and received a brief report on Tsirtos's bruises and Martyr's abrasions. Tsirtos had accepted aspirin. Martyr had not. As far as Ben could tell, they were none the worse for their experiences.

"I see," said Richard, turning away. "John. What about the rest of that stuff?"

"It's all the same. Most of it worse." His voice was hoarse; emotion pulling his Manx accent into prominence. For once he was not chewing on a pipe; he looked pale, genuinely sickened.

"Oh, come on," erupted Ben. "Blue movies on a supertanker— and all this fuss?"

John swung on him. "This isn't just blue, for God's sake. This stuff's sick. Some of it looks like snuff."

"Snuff?" asked Richard, startled into thinking of Regency gentlemen sniffing tobacco powder from silver boxes. "What's that?"

"That's where they actually kill people, right in front of the camera," said Ben, soberly. "Jesus! That's no joke. Are you sure?"

"How can I be? But that's what it looked like to me."

"Jesus. That's horrific. Sorry."

"I looked in the library too." John held out a pile of books and magazines. One glance told Richard they were companion pieces to the videotapes.

Tankers' libraries are usually stocked with old books brought aboard by previous crews. *Prometheus* had had three crews recently. A skeleton crew who had brought her out of mothballs in Valparaiso and sailed her to Lisbon for refitting. Another, who had brought her from Portugal to the Gulf. The only full crew she had had in recent years had died soon after coming aboard, leaving only Tsirtos and Martyr. And, judging from tonight, neither of then had known what was in the library.

Wearily, Richard mentally filed away a few more questions to be asked in the morning.

Slope sidled back at that moment. "Okay, John," said Richard. "That's enough for tonight. Destroy all that filth—I'd chuck it overboard in weighted sacks if I were you—and then turn in. It's late and you have the next watch." He automatically glanced at the two brass chronometers above the helm. One read 20.30, the other 23.30. GMT and Gulf Time respectively.

Richard had reached the end of his strength.

As he turned to go, however, Ben said, "Dick!" in an urgent undertone.

"Yes?" Richard turned back.

"I wasn't going to bring this up, but that porn has put my teeth on edge."

"What is it?"

Ben motioned Richard round to the chart table where he opened a deep drawer to its fullest extent. He lifted something out of the back and handed it over. It was a bottle of ouzo, half empty. "Makes you wonder; doesn't it, Dick?"

It did indeed. All the way to the blessed oblivion of his bunk, Richard's mind was filled with the nightmare vision of *Prometheus* under Levkas's command sailing up the Channel on a black night with the off-watch officers below enraptured by the torture and murder of pretty young girls, and the on-watch officers getting blind drunk on ouzo.

He could hardly have been expected to know it, but his fears were almost identical to those of Captain Levkas. Except that Levkas had known *Prometheus* would never reach the Channel.

Richard sprang awake out of a deep, dreamless sleep. He was absolutely sure there was someone in his room. He groped for his bedside light, wondering in a panic about the rhythmic surge of sound. Nothing was where it should be.

This was not his bed!

Totally disoriented, he swung his feet to the floor. The vibration told him he was at sea, but that only confirmed his suspicion that this was part of a nightmare.

"Rowena?" He called his dead wife's name as he always did in his nightmares and waited: sometimes she would answer; sometimes not. He took a hesitant step toward where the shadows were thickest, knowing that was where she would be. He took another. And barked his shins against a chair. The pain brought clarity.

He turned and reached for the light switch unerringly, knowing exactly where it was now that he knew where he was.

The cabin flooded with light. It was empty apart from himself, and yet the impression lingered that someone had been close at hand.

He crossed to the door and opened it. The tiny, dark vestibule was empty. So was his shower on the right. So was his dayroom straight ahead. He had been sleeping fully clothed. He opened the door and looked out into the corridor. It was empty, but it contained a hint of a footstep, a subliminal memory of movement. The silent echo of a softly closed door. Thoughtfully, he closed his own door and returned to bed. This time he undressed and got properly beneath the sheets. The last thing he did was to check the time. It was 03.00 on the dot.

Far below, in the Pump Room, a green illuminated display on the gray box Nicoli had disturbed just before his death switched silently to 00.00; a clock-timer set not to Gulf Time, but to GMT.

7

The next morning, Richard held lifeboat drill before breakfast. It had been one of Slope's first duties aboard to draw up and publish the lists, and it was one of the captain's duties before the end of his first twenty-four hours in command to hold a drill.

It went perfectly satisfactorily, although Richard had hoped to catch one or two slackers and identify potential weaknesses in the running of his ship with the unexpected timing of the exercise. But the only man apparently caught with his trousers down was the chief. Richard was faintly disappointed in the man. They had taken an instant dislike to each other; but Richard had thought him at least efficient.

He stood by his lifeboat. The crew was lined up nearby. The cover was off, the davits swung out. He looked at his stopwatch. *Martyr* was two minutes later than everyone else . . . Three . . .

The sun beat down out of a hard blue sky. There seemed to have been no dawn, no cool morning—simply an abrupt transition from stuffy darkness to blazing heat sometime when no one was looking. There was that faint headwind that bespeaks flat calm—it was *Prometheus*'s movement, not the movement of the air, that made the wind.

The sea, forty or so feet below the lifeboat's keel, was like oil; the waves flat and sluggish, disturbed only by the great ship's passage. The horizons were far and golden, concealing Shiraz behind leagues of Iranian desert to the north and Doha to the south. *Prometheus* was heading east.

... Four minutes.

Martyr appeared at last, walking briskly, looking as if he would rather have been running. His face, as usual, was absolutely closed but there hung about him a thunderous atmosphere of rage.

"Good morning, Chief," said Richard, putting his stopwatch away. "Now that everyone is at his station we can clear away and go down to breakfast."

Martyr could have made any excuse: it would have been accepted as a matter of course. But he seemed content to oversee the repositioning of the boat he was responsible for, then follow the others down and to eat his food in silence.

Richard watched him doing all these things, thinking of the long-gone days when a captain could treat a chief as though he were a junior. No longer. Nowadays captain and chief had to work hand in hand—equals, except in the most extreme circumstances. Nowadays, a captain would never dream of belittling his chief.

But then, at breakfast, things began to make more sense. Richard suddenly found himself leaning forward and squinting. The sun bludgeoning through the window of the Officers' Dining Room fell upon the white cloth of Martyr's sleeve like a magnesium flare. Bright enough to reveal, just above the immaculate cuff, a series of tiny, dimpled pinpricks and a couple of short-cut threads.

Richard's hard blue gaze switched to the far end of the table to where Third Officer Slope and Radio Officer Tsirtos together were rapidly ridding the world of half a dozen eggs and much of a pig. There was about them an air of barely suppressed hilarity that explained almost as much as the marks on Martyr's cuff.

The captain sat back in his chair, thin-mouthed. This was not a happy ship, and, for all his attempts to pour oil on troubled waters, the situation was not helped when junior officers sewed up the arms and legs of the chief engineer's uniform while he slept. An act of insubordination which, he strongly suspected, would only make the situation more explosive.

* * *

But the rest of that day left little room for mischief. They moved farther east in that tight arc south of the Jezirehs, which guard the Gulf approaches to the Strait of Hormuz. Here, the great 250-mile width of the busy sea lanes is compressed into a mere forty miles before opening out again, into the Gulf of Oman, the Arabian Sea, and the magic fastnesses of the Indian Ocean.

But all that lay far beyond them at the moment.

As in the English Channel, the Strait of Hormuz is divided into lanes like a motorway. First Danny Slope, then John Higgins, then Ben Strong guided them through the day into the first stages of this invisible motorway; plotting their position with careful precision, checking to within scant yards on the Sat Nav equipment up above the chart table, giving orders to the seaman at the helm.

The engineering officers took their corresponding watches below.

Richard, by no means relieved of the burden of fatigue he had carried aboard, filled his morning with paperwork. Not a difficult task. He had forgotten how much everything that happened on board his ship depended on his whim. He had to agree—amend, if he wished—all the menus for the day. The power made him grimly self-mocking: they would all eat baked beans from here to Europoort if he so desired.

He began to detail a list of the conferences it would be necessary to hold. The ship would have to be carefully maintained as they proceeded south toward the wintery Cape. Only a fool would take a summer-laden tanker around those dangerous, stormy, sharp-rocked shores if she were in anything other than tiptop condition. Then, as they proceeded back up the west coast of Africa, they would have to repair the ravages of the southern winter. When *Prometheus* reached Europoort, Richard wanted her to be in even better shape than she had been in when he assumed command. So he drew up schedules of maintenance and penciled in times and dates. He suspected Ben would have drawn up similar lists. They would compare notes later. Now, who should he get to check the paint lockers? He made a note to ask the chief to draw up a corresponding list for engine maintenance, though he suspected it would have been done long ago.

In the absence of much in the way of videos and books—he had already dispatched his own travel reading, C. S. Forester's *The Happy Return*, to the Officers' Lounge in the hope of starting a new library there—he drew up a short list for an entertainments committee.

He made notes of what he wished to say during his noon broadcast and checked with Tsirtos for any interesting pieces of international news. There wasn't even a test match.

He gave his noon broadcast.

And at last he had run out of papers to sign and lists to make and dates to pencil and committees to draw and things to do and so he went up onto the bridge.

John Higgins was busy at the chart table. The Collision Alarm Radar, which observed the position of every ship and obstacle nearby, was set on its closest range and would warn them automatically if anything came too near. A GP seaman stood by the helm—a wheel no larger than the steering wheel of a rally car.

Jezireh Ye Queys lay off the port beam, its low golden shoulder shrugging aside the ripples of mercuric water. A VLCC inbound slid a few miles south to starboard—perhaps three miles—riding high and looking huge. Richard watched her for an instant before John appeared at his shoulder. "Captain?"

Richard turned at once, alerted by something in the Manxman's tone. "Yes?"

"Take a look at this, would you?"

On the chart table lay a litter of pipe, papers, rulers, dividers, chinagraph pencils, calculators, and a sextant.

John Higgins, the second officer, was an old-fashioned sailor at heart. He had a yacht that he kept in the marina at Peel on the Isle of Man, in an anchorage under that tall, frowning castle—an ocean racer, as if he didn't get enough of the ocean in his line of work. But then, thought Richard indulgently, as he crossed to the chart table, he himself had kept a yacht when he was John's age. The yacht that had started it all: *Rebecca*.

On board, John was as modern as anyone. Calm, quiet, executive; perfectly at home with the modern machinery and the high-tech aids. But once in a while, Richard knew, some old seadog of an ancestor (a Viking, perhaps, come ravishing after the fair Manx maidens a millennium ago) would peep out of those calm dark eyes; and you would find those small, callused hands of his at some task that sailors had been about for centuries past.

Today he had taken a noon sight of the sun.

"I read it at meridian passage on the dot. Not quite when you started broadcasting. Had Tsirtos check with the World Service pips in case the chronometers were off. Perfect conditions. Perfect sights. Perfect instrument. Never been wrong. Never." He picked up the instrument lovingly and Richard didn't like the repetition of "never," suspecting at once where the conversation was leading.

"So?" he prompted.

"I've checked my calculations three times now. Even used the calculator." An admission of deep desperation.

"But they still disagree with the Satellite Navigation System," Richard said, giving the Sat Nav its full name, for once.

John nodded. "Look," he said, sweeping aside the litter on the plastic sheet over the chart. There were two black crosses marked, some inches apart. "According to my sights we're here." He pointed to the northernmost.

He reached up and pressed the buttons on the Sat Nav. Figures clicked onto the LCD. "This thing says we're here." He pointed to the southernmost cross. He looked starboard suddenly. Richard swung round to follow his gaze. The unladen tanker had moved exactly abeam of them, three miles south.

"If the Sat Nav is to be believed," said John grimly, "we've just collided with her." Then he caught his breath at the enormity of what he had just said—especially to Richard Mariner—and he stuck his pipe in his mouth at once to cover his confusion.

Richard felt the flesh on his forearms quiver. He took a deep breath. "Keep checking our position against positions obtained from the islands using radar," he ordered tightly. "And warn the others. I'll send Sparks up to see what he can do with it."

On the face of it this worked well enough. Tsirtos, the radio officer—"Sparks"—spent the next couple of hours pulling the Sat Nav to pieces, checking, then reassembling it. He missed lunch. Without him, Slope was quieter.

Lunch was all too short. Officers bustled through the meal and departed busily. Only Martyr showed any disposition to linger, and Richard got the impression the chief wanted to talk to him but didn't know where to start.

Richard sat, also silent, wondering how to help. But he had been away from the sea too long and had fallen out of the way of ruling a pride of officers.

In the end, both men remained silent and rose when lunch was over with that unspoken conversation rankling between them and making matters worse.

Richard went up to his office and began to make more lists and draw up the agenda for the first captain's conference, which he wanted to hold in the morning.

After an hour, Tsirtos came to report that the Sat Nav was fixed. Like Martyr, he gave the impression that he would have liked to have said more than he did say, and the captain began to get the measure of him, seeing beneath that curious Mediterranean mixture of shy immaturity and boyish bravado another, more calculating, man.

Driven by abrupt restlessness, he rose and gazed along the deck. He had been aboard twenty-four hours now. The Gulf had used that time to get under his skin, in spite of all the tightly enclosed world of *Prometheus* could do to keep it at bay.

There was an easy chair convenient to the window. He made himself sit down in it to watch the sea and think.

At first, as he woke, he thought something incredibly horrible had happened. Every surface around him seemed to have been rinsed in blood.

Prometheus seemed to be sailing a sea of blood through a downpour of blood.

That was what he saw before he understood what he was seeing.

It was the Shamaal.

The desert wind had crept up behind them, carrying sand like a plague of locusts deep within it. They were traveling at fifteen knots and the wind a little faster. The sand grains and the supertanker were all but still in relationship with each other. The tiny specks of red sandstone and crystal mica percolated through the air with the balletic grace of snowflakes. The sun, halfway to the horizon, looked like a huge blood orange.

Abruptly, the deck beneath Mariner's feet vibrated to a different beat. He glanced at his watch. 16.30.00. Ben Strong, on the bridge, had cut the speed.

16.30.30. A knock at the door.

"Come!"

It was Slope, sent down to inform the captain of the new situation.

"I'll come up," he decided, inevitably.

Even from the bridge, it was difficult to see the forecastle head at the far end of the deck. The usually clear lines of the deck itself were already slightly out of focus, the geometric angles cloaked by curves of drifting sand.

Ben was on watch as Richard entered, standing behind the helmsman's left shoulder, glaring into the murk. John Higgins, although off duty only half an hour, hovered over the Collision Alarm Radar. As Richard crossed the threshold, he glanced anxiously across at the mate's back. "Sand's giving false echoes on this now, Ben," he said tensely.

"What are we, Ben?" asked Richard, crossing to the captain's chair. With his arrival, some of the tension seemed to leave the situation.

"Half ahead, making eight knots," answered Ben, a measure of relief audible in his voice. He drew both hands back through the sun-bleached shock of his hair.

"Come to slow and make five." Richard stood for a moment by the big black leatherbound chair on the port side of the bridge; then he sat with every appearance of ease.

"Slow ahead," acknowledged Ben, his hand moving on the Engine Room telegraph. The pounding of the engines slowed further, pulsing to a funereal beat. "Five it is."

The light thickened. Shadows crouched like monsters in corners, under tables. The Sampson posts, two vertical, white-painted loading posts twenty feet high halfway down the deck became almost invisible. "Jesus!" said Ben. "This is impossible. How's the radar?"

"Murky," answered John.

"Start the siren, please," ordered Richard quietly. Immediately, the lost-soul howl boomed out over the Gulf.

The situation was rapidly becoming dangerous. They couldn't see the length of the deck. They couldn't rely on the radar. Only the Channel was busier.

"Sparks in the Radio Room?" asked Richard nonchalantly, already certain of the answer.

"Yes," said Ben.

"Good." He could warn local shipping if things got any worse. "But I think I still want a particularly sharp pair of eyes up for'ard. Mr. Slope?"

"Sir?"

"Take some glasses and a walkie-talkie. Stroll up to the forecastle head, if you'd be so kind. I'll arrange for a member of the crew to relieve you shortly."

"Right, sir." He turned to go.

For some reason he would never understand, Richard added, "And keep in touch."

"Right-ho, sir," said Slope cheerfully, and he was gone.

Richard leaned back against the headrest which, with the swivel foot, made his chair look like a dentist's chair. On the shelf beneath the port windows was his radio transceiver handset: his R/T. He picked it up and switched it on, ready to receive.

"Third Mate here. Sir?"

"Captain here. Receiving you loud and clear."

"Just going out onto the port . . ." Slope probably said more, but he cut himself off by switching to Receive too soon.

"Report when you reach the Sampson posts. Over. Can you see him, Ben? The port bridge wing's in my way . . ."

"No, sir."

"No? Strange. Must be thicker than I . . ."

"It's not that, sir. I can see the deck. He's not there."

"Third Mate. This is the captain. Do you receive me?"

The R/T hissed. Nothing more. Like sand grains brushing over silk. A sinister sound. Something's wrong, thought Richard.

"*Slope?*"

No reply. Nothing.

He was on his feet without further thought. His voice remained calm, but he let a little urgency into it. "She's yours, Ben. I'm going to look for the third mate." There was another R/T on the chart table. He gestured to it. "John. You monitor me."

"Aye, sir. But take care. She's a tricky ship."

Richard gave a bark of laughter, then realized the Manxman was quite serious.

Crossing to the lift, he left the R/T on, but only a hiss came in, ghostly enough to make him think about John Higgins's instinctive superstition.

The lift whispered down until the doors opened on A deck. Richard hurried across and stepped out onto the port side without pausing to think. Immediately, his face filled with sand. He had forgotten about this. Now that the *Prometheus* was at slow ahead, the wind was effectively gusting ten to fifteen knots; and freshening, by the feel of it. He slitted his streaming eyes and bundled his handkerchief over his nose and mouth, sneezing convulsively. The sand moved down his collar with a disturbing sense of personal invasion. Into his ears and up his nose. He sneezed again.

When his eyes cleared, he saw the monstrous tracks leading straight to the broken rail and understood at once the story they told of the third mate. Badly disoriented by the sand, he had stumbled forward into the rail which, like the Sat Nav, had not been all it seemed. Silently cursing the lackadaisical workmanship that had simply added another coat of varnish without checking the wood beneath, he shambled forward. There could be no mistake. "Man overboard! Stop engines! Man overboard!"

A second later, the whooping of the foghorn became the howl of the emergency siren. The throb of the engines stopped.

Richard was still by the broken rail, peering down into the red murk. Because of the sand he saw little. Because of the siren he heard nothing. Not the opening of the door behind him. Not the sand-muffled footsteps. Why he turned he would never know.

He saw Martyr's face locked in a strange rictus: rage—horror—surprise. He could not tell. The man might simply have been going to sneeze, his face, like Richard's face a minute before, unexpectedly full of sand.

Then their shoulders collided and Richard stepped back. Automatically, he caught the broken end of the rail. A substantial section of it filled his grasp, but then it simply crumbled as his full weight came upon it. Broke away and went to dust in his fist. One more step was enough and he was falling.

His mind spun as wildly as his body for a second. Images whirled like his arms and legs while the R/T sailed uselessly away. It occurred to him that Martyr might well have pushed Slope overboard in retaliation for this morning's prank. Or he might be trying to revenge on Richard himself the humiliation of last night's defeat in the Officers' Lounge. He did not yet know the man well enough to make any sensible guess. Or of course John might be right. Maybe *Prometheus* was trying to get rid of her second crew that week.

He jerked in a desperate lungful of air.

Then the water exploded around him and he was, abruptly, thinking with absolute clarity.

He landed upright, facing in, ten feet from the tanker's side. He plunged deep beneath the swirling surface, and was immediately sucked toward the huge metal wall. The black hull plunged down and down before him, curving away toward the keel. And that keel seemed to call to him, pulling him deeper and deeper still.

At the final end of his endurance, just as his lungs began to empty of their own accord, he felt the downward motion slow. He crossed his arms before his face and smashed into the unforgiving steel as he started up.

He exploded back into the air a bare few feet from the hull, still facing in. Immediately, even as he fought for the first, life-giving breath, he was half-thrown, half-sucked toward *Prometheus* as a wave worked with the ship's movement.

He brought his feet up just in time, pushing his sodden desert boots against the slippery metal and kicking. His feet were snatched to the left. He wrenched shoulders and upper arms, paddling wildly to keep his feet between himself and his ship, choking in great ragged breaths as he did so. Much less than a quarter of the hull to go, he thought. And as the engine stopped, so the great propeller stilled. If he kept agile and lucky, he might get past the end of the ship alive.

Then there would only be the Gulf to contend with.

He could imagine Ben on the bridge, bringing *Prometheus* round in a Williamson turn. Probably swearing like a trooper. The thought made him smile.

He slid down another hugely buoyant, incredibly salty wave and kicked back, legs and belly smarting with the strain, water rushing in over his head and shoulders, exploding against the steel, foaming back to bury him.

Damn! The stuff even tasted of oil!

Abruptly, the most unexpected thing happened. The white bow of a lifeboat grazed down his left side and collided with *Prometheus*. There was a sound like the biggest gong in the world. Richard watched, overcome by it all.

Then arms reached down from the point and unceremoniously dragged him aboard, past a wildly whipping vertical length of rope. Miraculously, Martyr had managed to put the small port-side lifeboat down less than an arm's length from him. Within seconds he had recovered himself and was kneeling beside the chief in the pitching little cockleshell. They leaned against each other gasping until another wave drove in, threatening to turn the boat to matchwood. Then their fingers were feverishly at work, trying to release the rope falls bow and stern before the sea ground the boat to splinters against the ship like a kernel of corn in a mill.

The next wave tumbled into them catching them still in the trough. Swamping them. Smashing them against *Prometheus* again. Something in the filthy foam wrapped itself lazily around Richard's thigh. He kicked it free at once, thinking of the Gulf's deadly sea snakes. It was only seaweed.

As soon as the fall whipped free of his hand, Richard pushed back past Martyr and swung the handle to start the engine. It caught at once. He opened the boat's throttle and turned her head into the teeth of the next wave. It hurled them back to slam against the tanker once more, then rose beneath them, launching them down its back as though down a slipway. Water exploded up in great arcs on either side of the bow, and they were whirled away into the storm.

Even though the wind had strengthened, its action with the waves cleared the air down here. Richard could see farther now than he had been able to from the bridge. But it was Martyr, crouching in the bow like some misshapen figurehead, who saw Slope first, on the crest of a wave some fifty yards ahead. He turned, yelled, gestured. When he turned back, the third mate was gone.

Inevitably, however, the random march of the waves threw up another winning combination so that the boat rose on the crest of the wave at the same time that Slope did, twenty yards away. He was either waving feebly, or the sea was playing tricks with them. But he wasn't wearing a life jacket, Richard reckoned grimly; so if he wasn't alive, he wouldn't still be afloat.

Waves rose up between them, their crests streaming forward in a continuous spray of filthy spindrift plucked off by the wind. The lifeboat began to seesaw sickeningly. Martyr yelled something unintelligible and raised his right arm. Richard brought the boat's head starboard. The arm dropped. They straightened. The waves came in on the port quarter, slamming the boat round like pile-drivers.

They tilted to starboard, crawled crabwise up the concave face of a ten-footer about to break, and there was Slope, three feet from the stern, swirled past them in a flash and into their lee.

Richard had the helm hard over at once. Martyr threw himself sideways, nearly capsizing them. He caught at Slope. Missed. Caught again. Slope seemed to be floating in a ghastly, foul syrup. His arms were waving madly. The dead white oval of his face projected terror. As Martyr reached the third time, Richard quickly scanned the golden maelstrom for sharks. There were none that he could see. Martyr was on his knees, legs spread, straining forward over the starboard bow. This time their hands met. Closed.

Held.

As the wave broke.

The boat's head slammed right round. Martyr went sideways so hard he nearly fell overboard. The whole length of Slope's body crashed against the gunwale. Richard let go of the tiller, diving forward. One hand went to Martyr's right ankle, steadying him. The other plunged over the side, deep into the sea, trying to grab Slope's legs.

Something brushed his wrist.

Automatically, he jerked it back out of the water. Then he had let go of Martyr and was reaching for Slope with desperate urgency, understanding the young man's fear. He was too late. He only saw it for a moment as it neared the surface, struck, and fell away again into the sand-clotted depths. That one glimpse was enough. It was perhaps four feet long, broad as a man's forearm, and bright unbroken yellow like a buttercup. It moved with the sinuous grace of an eel, but it had the scaly skin and flat, diamond head that could mean only one thing.

Precisely what sort of snake it was, Richard did not know. It had a tiny mouth—all Gulf snakes do—and a long black double tongue. And the fangs that it sank into the tip of Slope's bare toe, they were surprisingly long, too.

The boy's body went rigid. The snake fell away, writhing lazily. Richard, his arms in the foaming water to the elbow, grabbed an ankle. "Now!" he yelled, at the top of his voice, and heaved. Slope came in easily, like a length of wood.

Martyr had seen the snake as clearly as Richard had. No sooner was Slope's body inboard than he ripped the linen belt off his overalls and made a tourniquet, as best he could, halfway up the foot. The flesh grew taut as he pulled it tight, two tiny blue pinpricks leaking blood at the tip of the smallest toe.

"Wild West stuff," cried Martyr flourishing a knife. He cut once, hard. Something small and white fell overboard: the top joint of the bitten toe. It was a desperate act—but Slope was in mortal danger from the venom.

The next wave nearly swamped them. Only the weight of the water already in the bilges stopped them tipping over; but far too much more came in over the gunwales. Richard leapt back for the tiller, opened the throttle, and swung her round until wind and weather were at his back.

Just in time. The greatest wave so far lifted them. Crested. Broke. Tarnished silver foam boiled over the side and vomited into their laps. They surfed forward as though hitched to Leviathan through water like the surface of an erupting volcano.

It was like boating at the birth of the world.

Abruptly, the dancing clouds in front of them exploded as though a flare a hundred yards wide had been ignited there. It was *Prometheus*, with all her lights ablaze.

Five minutes after that, they were aboard. Slope's inert body was being rushed up to the sick bay. Martyr and Mariner were following side by side in silence, bone weary, slow, old with fatigue.

The whole rescue, which seemed to have taken a lifetime, had actually filled only twenty minutes.

In the sick bay, Slope was lying face-up on the bed. Ben was sticking a plaster over the stump of his toe. The third mate was unconscious, breathing with rasping gasps through a slack mouth. "How is he?" asked Richard.

Ben looked up, a troubled expression sitting ill on his usually open, cheerful face. "Not good. We'll have to get him to hospital in short order. Nice piece of surgery, Chief. Crude, but nice."

They were hove-to fifty miles north of Dubai. That was their best bet. There was a fast launch service out from Ras al Kaimah that was regularly used to ferry crews to and from supertankers. But even the fastest launch service was likely to be too slow for Slope.

"Radio for a helicopter," suggested Martyr, who was destroying a perfectly good towel simply by rubbing his hair with it.

"Couldn't get out here in this," countered Richard.

"Neither could the launch," concluded the chief, looking disgustedly at the oil-smeared wreck of the towel.

In the end, Richard radioed Dubai, who said they would have a helicopter and a launch standing by, each with a medical team. Whichever could go first would go first. Then he set Tsirtos to trying to locate Demetrios.

They went back to slow ahead, making five knots, and altered course slightly, moving slowly southeast, south of Jesireh Ye Sirri, down toward Dubai. At last Richard went to his own cabin, pulling off his soiled shirt as he went and bunching it up in his left fist. Halfway down the C deck corridor, he paused. One more thing, he thought. He crossed to Martyr's door and knocked.

Abruptly, Martyr was standing in front of him, also naked to the waist; one white towel wrapped around his loins, another draped over his shoulders. His face, neck, and a V on his chest where the collar of his shirt opened, were all deep mahogany. The rest of his torso was pale. The hair on his chest bunched sand-gray and curled down his corrugated belly.

"I wanted to thank you for pulling me out." Richard stuck out his hand.

Martyr gripped it briefly, then, "Forget it," he said. "I pushed you in first." And he began to close the door.

But Richard, now, was no longer willing to be put off. The flat of his hand pressed against the door to stop Martyr's action and they remained face to face. "I need to know what is going on here," said Richard, his tone held at reasonable calm by an effort of will. "I have taken command of a ship registered as A-1 at Lloyd's of London and yet there is some question about the strength of the pipework, the Satellite Navigation equipment is suspect, the radar is faulty, the railing round the deck is danger- ously rotten..."

"You know as much about that as I do, Captain," countered Martyr warily. "All I know is that the engine's fine."

"You know more than that! You know what happened in the Pump Room!"

"No more than I wrote in the Accident Report Book. Like I said in the lift yesterday."

"But you must know more than that, Chief. You knew Captain Levkas and his men..."

"Damned if I did, Captain. I tell you I didn't know these men. What they were up to, what they were like. I..."

"Like?" exploded Richard. "You know very well what they were like. They got drunk on bridge watch. They enjoyed watch- ing sick pornography. They were the scum of the earth and they were up to no good."

"That may have been the situation then, Captain. But now

56

they're dead and you're here..." Martyr's voice was calm but tinged with irony.

"Right, Chief! Now I'm here. And I give you fair warning, you and anyone else who thinks whatever Levkas and his men were up to might still be going on..." Richard paused for breath, and let his voice sink a decibel or two. "No matter what was going on then, what's going on now is that I'm bringing *Prometheus* to Europoort, and nothing—and nobody—will stop me."

By 17.35, Richard was back in the Radio Room, leaning against the doorjamb, his bright blue eyes wandering vaguely over the clutter of untidy wiring, green metal, plastic fascia, and flashing lights that made up Tsirtos's den. He had already been to the sick bay, again, and the bridge.

"No word from the owner?"

"No, sir. I've checked all the numbers he gave me, but no one can reach him."

"And the other number? His agent in Dubai?"

"No reply. I think they must have gone home for the day. Shut up shop."

Richard's mouth thinned. This was unsatisfactory, to put it mildly. They were an officer short on an almost skeletal crew. It was usual enough for an independent to sail with only three deck officers for bridge watch, but Richard was used to the Heritage way—four deck officers apart from the captain, plus at least two more partially qualified trainees: *Prometheus*, though perfectly legal, felt undermanned to him. Both the owner and his nearest recommended agent were unobtainable. He ought to wait until he could contact one or the other. But Demetrios had specifically, if unusually, ordered a fast voyage, and Richard simply wasn't prepared to go charging round the Cape with only two deck officers.

"Okay," he said, unconsciously sealing his fate. "Get me Angus El Kebir. Here's the number of his Dubai office."

Demetrios's agents might knock off early. Crewfinders did not.

8

Angus El Kebir was not used to being intimidated. There flowed in his veins the blood of desert princes and of Highland chieftains. At the court of his father's third cousin he wore—as was his right—the tartans of his mother's ancestors.

Offspring of an Arab prince and a Scottish governess, both now deceased, he had been educated at Fettes College in Edinburgh, where he had learned to admire industriousness and look down his long hooked nose at sloth; so, when the time had come for him to fulfill some kind of function in the world, he had scorned the thought of sponging off his princely relatives and hitched instead his rising star to that of Crewfinders, and that of his old school friend, Richard Mariner.

Yet now he found himself sitting, trapped, in his tiny Dubai office, trying his best to hold the cold gray gaze opposite, stroking the fullness of his bright red beard, and thinking like a fox at bay.

"There is the Shamaal," he temporized at last. "You cannot even reach her in the Shamaal."

"Oh, come on!" The accent was even more clipped than his own; impatient where his was conciliatory. "You're stalling. You know I have every right to be aboard. I have come to you simply because I cannot contact the owner or his agent. If you won't get me out, I'll charter a helicopter and fly on out myself."

Could this most unwelcome visitor also fly helicopters? Angus would not be at all surprised. There seemed little the offspring of Sir William Heritage would not do, if driven.

"I did not say 'Would not,'" he placated; "I said 'Could not.' *Prometheus* will in all probability be through the Strait before the Shamaal clears. To take a helicopter down into the Arabian Sea would be expensive, even for you. Besides, you must know this is none of my business. Richard is there simply as this man Kostas Demetrios's employee. It has nothing to do with Crewfinders or with me."

Robin Heritage jumped up out of the chair, too full of frustration to remain seated. A long hand swept a boyish lick of golden hair back out of those cold gray eyes. Angus shifted uncomfortably under the searching stare that seemed to see into his soul like the gaze of a jinni in a fairy tale—that saw how completely he was prevaricating.

It was just this glare, so he had heard, that had made the young Heritage something of a power in the City. The old man, so they said, had yet to recover from the shock of the collision; but this youngster was pulling it all back together for him.

Trained at sea, through the Heritage fleet, with a surprising range of papers to show for it; trained also, if briefly, at the London School of Economics and at the Wharton School, here was a mind of unusual quality. Here was a power in the shipping world not lightly to be crossed.

But Angus could not sacrifice his friend. "Now look..." he began, trying charm as a last, desperate, tactic.

"Don't bullshit me! I came to you as much out of courtesy as anything else. I can drop onto *Prometheus* by parachute if I want and Richard Mariner will be hard put to do much about it. Demetrios might own the ship, but by God I own the cargo; all two hundred fifty thousand tons of it. I own it as of 09.00 GMT yesterday morning and I have the right to ride with it if I choose."

"Hardly marine lore..." He faltered. The icy glance said it all: Robin Heritage had forgotten as much marine lore as Angus would ever know. Thank Allah and the Shamaal, he thought. Thank Him also for the fact that Richard had not got in touch.

Angus knew better than most what Richard had suffered during these last few years. He suspected very precisely what it must be costing his old friend to be back at sea again after all this time. He saw all too clearly the resemblance to the dead Rowena in the determined young face opposite. He saw the bitter twist to the lips every time they mentioned Richard's name.

There was no way Robin Heritage would get onto *Prometheus* if Angus El Kebir could help it.

Robin saw this clearly enough in Angus's strange, light eyes and drove a fist down onto his desk in a gesture of frustration.

The impasse was complete.

The telephone rang.

Doctor, nurse, and pilot had been sitting patiently in the little Sikorsky for over half an hour when Heritage showed up.

"You flying out to *Prometheus*?"

The doctor nodded toward the pilot as though he didn't speak English. The pilot turned and looked back. "If the sand clears," he said.

"They need a replacement for the man you're bringing back."

"You?" The pilot looked at the perfectly pressed whites, innocent of badges of rank or seniority.

"Yup. Me." The cool, confident voice allowed no room for argument.

"On your own head," said the pilot equably. "But that's a bad ship. Unlucky."

Robin climbed fully aboard. "You have a Florida accent."

"Fort Lauderdale. Born and bred."

"Ever fly the Bermuda Triangle?" The question seemed innocently asked, but the point was made. Some people pay more attention to superstition than others.

Robin dumped the bulky suitcase beside the doctor's medical supplies and came far enough up the Sikorsky's short body to see that the right-hand seat was empty. "Mind if I sit up front?"

"Can't say's I do."

Something about the way Robin's capable hands and feet rested on the controls prompted the pilot to ask, "Ever flown one of these?"

"No."

For some reason, the American felt mildly surprised by the simple negative. But there was more.

"I learned to fly helicopters in England. Westlands, mostly. I've never flown a Sikorsky, though this looks almost identical to some I have been up in."

"Well now, if that's the case..." The pilot grew expansive, warming to his passenger's quiet English modesty and charm. "I'll see about giving you a lesson as soon as this wind drops."

In the event, the wind veered almost immediately and the sand cleared rapidly from the south.

Within half an hour the Sikorsky was following the fading petticoats of the sandstorm north as fast as the pilot dared—given the odd unexpected buffet and jump that caused both doctor and nurse to make some very strange noises indeed; and the danger of sucking too much flying sand into the engine and taking them all for an unscheduled swim.

The pilot flew almost the whole way out, but it was Robin, given a flat calm, clear air and a floodlit landing pad—almost perfect conditions—who brought them down in the end, drifting the Sikorsky sideways gently and expertly to match the tanker's speed.

As soon as they touched down there was bedlam. Four men rushed down the bright-lit deck bearing a fifth on a stretcher, paying scant attention to the clouds of sand still whirling under the idling rotors. The side door of the Sikorsky slammed open and the doctor and nurse rushed out to meet their patient, equally oblivious of the sand. The pilot gave Robin an impressed thumbs up and was gone to see what he could do to help.

Robin was left alone for a moment, like a yacht with the wind taken out of its sails. Movement seemed too much to demand of muscles still thrilling with the excitement of landing. Was this such a good idea after all? What would Richard say? Nothing pleasant; that was for sure. Did that matter a damn? Nope. One thing was certain: there was no point in coming all this way, then vanishing again.

The hesitation lasted perhaps a second.

Everything was gone out of the body of the helicopter to make room for the stretcher. This included Robin's luggage. There was nothing to do but to leap down onto the sand-cloaked metal and get out of the way as the doctor pushed past, already attending to his patient.

The sand was settling now, revealing an effulgent white bridge, big as a block of flats; revealing the distant, more shadowy lines of the ship. She hadn't seemed all that big from the air.

Suddenly the pilot was there. "Doc says we got to go or the boy'll be dead before we land. Pleasure to've flown with you. You have a delicate touch..."

He paused in the doorway, looking back. He might have been going to repeat his warning; going to suggest a change of mind. Their eyes met and he shrugged. "Your cases are up with the second mate. Captain's on the bridge. Take care."

Robin raised a hand in reply.

Ten steps toward the bridge and the pilot had completed his preflight checklist. The engine coughed warningly. Robin hunched forward and broke into a run. The Sikorsky fired up. The rotors caused another storm, clouding everything with red sand from the deck.

The side door to A deck was open an inch or two and some-one—John Higgins—was waiting just inside it. Robin tumbled through in a rush and a choking cloud and they faced each other—much the same height, uniforms pink and faces like childrens' made up to be Red Indians because of the sand sticking to them.

John launched into his speech of welcome: "Welcome aboard. I'm John Higgins, second mate. I've had your cases taken up to the third mate's cabin, and..." He paused. His short briar pipe drooped comically as his jaw slackened with surprise. "Good God! You're..."

"I know I am," said Robin pushing past him; nervous suddenly, and uncharacteristically rude. "I know where the third mate's cabin is. And I know where the captain is. Thank you."

Ten minutes later, washed and brushed, the new third mate arrived on the bridge. The deck officers were all there. John Higgins, frowning with concern; Ben Strong, his face devilish with laughter—one glance showed that John had reported to Ben and the information had stopped there.

Richard turned. He looked older; tired; so distinguished.

In the grip of feelings far too complex even to begin to examine, Robin strode toward him, watching the color drain from his face.

Richard stood, ashen, and watched the exact image of his dead wife approach him across the shadowy bridge and stop.

Only when she smiled did he realize that this was Robin, not Rowena.

"Hello, Richard," she said.

Richard closed the door with his back then leaned upon it looking at her as she turned to face him. The owner's suite was large—as large as the captain's—but it seemed tiny now, far too small to contain the pair of them. He remained, apparently at ease, tense as a coiled spring.

She turned and there was no pretense of ease about her. "You want rid of me," she accused. "But you can't send me away."

He let his breath out, hissing, between his teeth. He hardly trusted his jaw muscles to loosen or his numb lips to frame the words. He certainly did not dare to deal with things on her tumultuous level. "It's been a long time," he said.

She stopped. Her eyes narrowed calculatingly. She had not expected this. Outrage, anger, hatred even; coldness no. Calmness certainly not.

But only Richard knew how fragile that calmness was.

They faced each other in silence across the narrow room. "A long time," he repeated quietly.

"Are you going to let me stay?"

"I'm working it out," he answered.

"You want rid of me, the same as always," she challenged again.

"Not the same as always, but this time, at first glance, yes! I'm thinking. This is no place for you."

"An unlucky ship?"

One corner of his mouth curled up. Almost a smile. "Perhaps."

"You need a third officer."

"That I do."

"And I am qualified."

"Eminently."

"But... What I am... My sex..."

He hesitated. There was no denying it. Pictures from the video and the magazines flashed through his mind. What if anyone who found such things exciting were still aboard?

But even as she threw down the challenge, so she raised her chin and he recognized that look—something that existed in natural leaders. Some quality he had seen in her father but never in her sister. A power he had never seen in her before, nor ever even suspected she possessed.

"Not only that, no..." He was suddenly fighting for time and they both knew it. Like a duelist more interested in testing competition than easy victory, she turned away and let him compose himself.

Let him face the inevitable question: Why not?

Why should he not let her do as she planned? She was capable. She was available. She was here. In many ways she was a better officer than he was expecting. She would strengthen his command considerably.

But would she weaken him?

And was she actually strong enough herself?

Had this Robin Heritage been the son that old Sir William Heritage had always wanted—a young man equally qualified, even with all the hatred that lay between them—would he have been hesitating now?

No, he would not.

He stopped hesitating, therefore.

When she turned back, she saw it in his eyes and her face became almost incandescent as she smiled.

Next morning, 11.00 local time, they were all on the bridge again, but Robin was on watch.

Salah Malik stood still by the wheel, eyes scanning instruments and then horizons in easy rhythm, hooded against the dazzle of the sun. Robin stood at his shoulder, hands clasped behind her back, rocking gently on the balls of her feet, calm, collected, confident.

Ben and John were at the chart table. Every now and then one of them would look at the Collision Alarm Radar, though there wasn't much to see. Both of them, of course, were really watching the new third mate. They would have been here watching any newcomer on first watch—especially one as important as this— but the facts of who Robin was, and what, added extra interest.

Only Richard was not watching her. He had arrived half an hour ago—precisely when expected—checked the lookouts on the bridge wings, checked logs, speed, course, and heading, all the things he would normally check, and sat himself down as usual. He paid his third mate the same courtesy as he would have given any other: he was on the bridge and responsible; she was on watch and in charge.

It had taken hours more of heated—impassioned—discussion, far into the small hours of the morning, to make him accept the situation, even though—as she had pointed out to Angus El Ke-bir—she held all the high cards.

And, she suspected, he had seen beneath what she was saying to some of her hidden, secret, desperate reasons.

But it was done: save that her bags were in the owner's suite, as befitted her relationship with the cargo, she was the third mate.

Richard's mind was full to bursting, for all the languid mien of his long body. Leaving aside the memories that Robin had brought with her, there were all the normal worries of running a ship; all the peculiar problems of running this one. The strange chief. The sorry state of a ship listed as A-1 for Lloyd's. The unreliability of apparently first-rate equipment. The last crew. The drink on the bridge. The pornography. As he had said to Martyr, he suspected all too vividly what might have been going on in the past. But now things were different. Regular. And he would do his utmost to ensure they remained that way.

"Captain!" Robin broke into his reverie, pointing to starboard.

There, a couple of miles away, lay the maze of low islands— lost in the glare for the most part—stretching out from the Mu-sandam Peninsula, climaxing in that pair of islands, used as a guide for uncounted generations, called the Quoins.

They were going out through the doorway of the Gulf at last. Overcome by an unaccountable rush of elation, Richard decided not to wait until they had "turned the corner" at Rass Al Hadd: "Good. Tell Sparks to make a telex," he ordered. "To the owner, Kostas Demetrios [wherever he is]: 'Left the Gulf at 11.10 local time, July twenty-first' . . ." He paused, then added. " 'All well so far, *Prometheus.*' "

Indian Ocean

9

They came for Robin six nights later when she was coming off watch at midnight as they crossed the Line.

Two burly sea nymphs sprang from the shadows of the corridor and caught her tired arms. Surprised, she looked over her shoulder but Ben was oblivious—crouching over the chart table already, rechecking her calculations of their course and exact position.

She opened her mouth but was immediately gagged. One of them giggled girlishly, reeking of alcohol, and she knew it would be useless to struggle against them. Although she hated the feeling of powerlessness even more than she had thought she would, she knew there was no alternative, so she gave a mental shrug and went along for the time being, wondering queasily what to expect.

On bare feet, silent except for the swish of their seaweed skirts, they ran her to the lift, then crowded in beside her. The light had been put out of commission so they plunged downward in absolute darkness.

Robin stood still and straight, her mind a whirl of possibilities, her long upper lip prickling with sweat. It was a stultifyingly hot night. The grip of the sea nymphs, one on each arm, threatened to bruise her tense flesh. She calmed herself by trying to work out who they were. She had been aboard a week now, after all, and she felt she was getting to know the officer complement well.

Ben Strong was on the bridge. That ruled him out for the moment, though Robin was firmly of the opinion that he would be involved in this somewhere along the line. The two of them had not really hit it off. Strong was Richard's godson, almost his adopted son, but no two men could be less alike. The first officer was brown-eyed, deeply tanned, sandy-haired, powerful but slightly plump. She felt he affected the languid, sarcastic airs of an aristocrat in a cheap romance: manners that only charm would have made acceptable. Ben did not charm her at all, for the strong-minded, energetic, enthusiastic young woman had found her superior officer either oversolicitous, patronizing, or bullying; constantly surprised that she knew what she was doing. And, if Ben was on the bridge, then Paul Rice, the Welsh first engineering officer, a dark, slight hard man from Tiger Bay who boasted a knife scar on his right cheek, would be in the Engine Room.

Unless the mysterious, unreadable chief was relieving him. That was possible. Not probable—schoolboy pranks did not seem to have any place in Martyr's character—but Robin had simply been unable to sum the man up; so anything was possible.

John Higgins would be involved. On the one hand, the quiet Manxman—possibly under Richard's unofficial direction—would be there to see things did not go too far. On the other hand, this was an important part of traditional sea lore and he would want to see it done right: she would have to keep an eye out for a strange sea creature sucking on an unlit pipe.

David Napier would be there too. The second engineering officer. A hard-faced Mancunian bully, a great square ex-boxer with thin stubble-hair and a flattened nose, Napier would delight in making things as unpleasant as possible. She would be well advised to keep out of the clutches of his massive, apelike hands.

That left McTavish and Tsirtos. They were the most likely candidates for sea nymphs. And while McTavish, good Glaswegian Presbyterian that he was, did not drink, Tsirtos most certainly did.

She began to explore the black air around her for the exact source of the fumes.

At no time did it occur to her that Richard might be directly involved in any of this.

The lift jarred to a halt. The door opened to a blaze of light at whose heart stood a gargoyle figure half fish, half man, bewigged and hideously masked like the sea nymphs. Two green arms reached out toward her and even before her vision had cleared from the glare, a bag went over her head.

During the last six days they had begun the voyage proper. As soon as the restrictions of the Gulf were left behind, Richard had ordered full ahead and *Prometheus* had answered with an easy fifteen knots.

At this speed, never varying, day in day out, they had proceeded on a course a little south of east out of the Gulf of Oman and across Cancer; a degree or two east of south across the Arabian Sea, east of the Red Sea approaches and past Socotra.

Now they were moving west of south, swinging toward southwest proper, preparing to pass down the inner arc of the Seychelles, the Amirantes, and Providence Island, to the Comoros and the Mozambique Channel approaches. They should reach the Comoros in eighty-four hours' time—midday on the 29th.

Now they were at the equator: 0 of latitude, 56 east longitude, at the heart of the Indian Ocean.

Richard lay on his bunk fully clothed and wide awake. His shoulders were propped against the wall, feeling the easy movement of his great ship through the long ocean swells. Such was the size of her hull that *Prometheus* did not ride the water as a smaller ship might have done, pitching as the waves passed beneath her; but she had her own special movement and it was familiar to him now.

The last six days had laid the ghosts of the Gulf to rest. The mysteries that had seemed so important then were in their proper place at last. Occasionally they nagged at the edge of his mind, like an unsolved crossword clue, but they remained secondary, a long way behind the efficient running of his ship.

And *Prometheus* herself seemed different. He supposed he should have expected teething troubles, and thought now he had overreacted to them. For the deep blue waters of the Indian Ocean seemed to have brought out the best in her. Her mysterious, unsettling little ways had departed and she showed her true colors at last. She was a strong, pleasant, reliable ship.

Worked by a strong, reliable, for the most part pleasant crew. Oh, Martyr might have been more approachable, but their discussion after Slope's rescue seemed to have made him less suspicious and antagonistic; Ben could have been less of a bully at times; "Slugger" Napier less of a hard man at all times; and Paul Rice less of a pirate, he was talking of wearing an earring to emphasize his scar: here was a man born a couple of centuries too late—he should have served with that other great Welsh sailor, Henry Morgan. But by and large they were fine. And Robin seemed to have pulled them together. At times she seemed their mascot, almost their pet. They took endless delight in teasing her, being gruff, avuncular, patronizing; indulging her, teaching her, testing her.

It was not a situation she enjoyed. She was her own woman, a fully trained, flawlessly competent officer. She deserved a great deal more respect than most of them tended to give her. But they had both known that this would be the case at first before he had agreed to take her on. And she was behaving perfectly under the added strain, slowly earning the respect of the most deeply entrenched male chauvinists among them. As he had never doubted that she would.

At first she had put on an act, becoming a wide-eyed innocent with an inexhaustible fund of energy and an open, enquiring, apparently guileless nature. Trained in the dour rigors of the North Sea, on tankers a fraction of *Prometheus*'s size, she made a game of the simple joy it was giving her to be on her first Cape run. She treated the whole thing as an enormous lark; a huge adventure. And this ebullient enthusiasm, showered on one and all, had proved a perfect buffer. And a necessary one, keeping her at a distance from them during the long days sailing these vast blue waters, sun-filled and monsoon-cooled; and during the black velvet nights with their mother-of-pearl moons and extravagant, gemstone stars.

Only occasionally, when they were together not as captain and third mate, but as master and owner of the oil, did she put the mask away with him and show how much it was costing to perform the role.

He worried about her, and wondered if that were patronizing.

He was tempted to protect her a little, too aware that the others were watching them like a teacher with a favorite pupil. On the surface, the tip of the iceberg, his relationship with her was the same as everyone else's, and turned around her efficiency as an officer and member of the crew. For the others, her sex made her an unknown quantity in a situation where unknown quantities were dangerous. It was the old story: their lives might depend upon her. They had to know how reliable she was under pressure. With a man, rightly or wrongly, they would take so much for granted. With a woman they would not. He found it distasteful, as did some of the others. But they could not protect her and nor should he.

They would have been foolish to try. She wanted no protection; required no special treatment. She was perfectly capable of handling them, individually or all at once. However they chose to test her, she would pass. On their terms, perhaps: on her own terms, certainly.

And below and abaft the bridge where he lay, she was undergoing her first real test—the ageless maritime ritual of the Crossing of the Line.

A great roar of "GUILTY!" greeted the completion of the charges.

"Guilty as charged!" thundered a single voice. "Remove the first prisoner for execution. Uncover the second prisoner."

At once, Robin stood blinking in the brightness.

Unbelievingly, she looked around *Prometheus*'s afterdeck. The security lighting revealed half a dozen weirdly dressed figures etched against the absolute blackness of the vast night, grouped around the ship's swimming pool. Beside them stood a raised platform with a table on it.

A GP seaman called Kerem Khalil was the only other person aboard who had never crossed the equator before. He was undergoing the ritual first. Having been charged, he was now being led, in chains, up toward the table. As he neared it, a huge figure, bizarrely dressed to resemble a cook, rose up to meet him, flourishing a massive meat ax.

Struggling silently, Khalil was laid on the table. The ax rose and fell, apparently splitting him open. The cook reached down and pulled free string after string of raw sausages, seemingly disemboweling the struggling man. The spectators howled their approval. The victim was swept off the table and hurled into the pool.

The two nymphs holding Robin's arms were in motion at once, hurrying her round the end of the pool into the presence of Neptune himself. He sat on a throne of shells, cascading water from his great gold crown whenever he moved. Everything about him gleamed green—his trident, his curling beard, his flowing seaweed robes. The nymphs forced her to her knees. At least she wasn't in chains like poor Khalil, whom she could hear trying to get out of the pool behind her.

"Who dares enter my watery kingdom?" boomed the same mannered voice that had just sentenced Khalil.

"Robin Heritage, third officer, *Prometheus*," cried her escorts.

"With what is she charged?"

Another, more sinister, figure appeared beside the vivid god. Someone dressed as a lawyer. Wigged and masked like the rest. "With being a woman!"

Raucous chorus of approval.

"With being aboard a man's ship . . . With doing aboard a man's ship a man's job . . . With doing it almost as well as the average man might do it . . . With robbing, therefore, the average man of his job . . . and so being guilty of the current levels of unemployment in the British Empire and of the collapse of the Western World!"

"GUILTY!" they chorused.

"Guilty as charged," yelled Neptune. "Remove the prisoner for execution!"

Robin was unceremoniously dumped in an empty chair that was immediately lifted onto the platform where the cook's table had been. Before she could react in any way, a shaving brush the size of a mop was thrust into her face, spreading stiff, green, stinking foam everywhere from shoulders to ears. In a moment she was ready. Gasping for breath, she opened her eyes only to be confronted with a fish-man wielding a cutthroat razor as long as her arm. The blade was metal, and sharp enough to scrape away a little skin as she was shaved to the gleeful shouts of Neptune and his cohorts.

After a few moments this, too, was over and she was lifted bodily from the chair. She saw Neptune rise to tower above her.

"One!" he shouted. She was swung like a hammock between two of them.

"Two!" The whole chorus as she went back, and . . .

"THREE!"

As she sailed through the air she twisted and landed badly. As soon as the water closed over her, she curled her body so her shoulders hit the bottom with a considerable bump. At once, she wedged her left hand into a filter on the pool's floor and waited, her right fist closed around the scissors hidden in her pocket.

The trick worked even better than she had dared hope.

After no more than a minute, Neptune himself came floundering to her rescue.

As soon as he plunged into the pool she was in motion, and before he knew what was going on, the sea king's heroic gesture was undone. She swam around him, snipping away carefully but ruthlessly. After a few moments, she rose out of the water in the far corner to throw his robes onto the deck, the scissors skittering away across the metal. Then, lithe as a seal, she was out herself, turning to sit on the corner of the pool looking in; her uniform transparent, but beneath it, instead of her practical but flimsy underclothes, her best black swimsuit. And in her left hand the final revenge: the remains of a pair of swimming trunks.

Neptune, on the other hand, was wearing only his mask and wig: the trunks, of course, had been his.

There was a moment of stunned silence; then two of the nymphs had torn off their masks and were cheering: John Higgins and Andrew McTavish. And all the rest joined in. Gentle hands grabbed her from behind and carried her shoulder high all the way down to the Officers' Bar, singing, "For *she's* a jolly good fellow."

When they were gone, Richard stepped out of the shadows with the towel Robin wasn't going to need after all. Knowing the instant they crossed the line, he had come down to see fair play. He climbed up onto the scaffold and looked down. Ben Strong had taken off the Neptune headdress and was standing, calculating what his shaken dignity and total nudity would allow him to do.

"Warned you, Number One," said Richard.

Ben looked up and grinned ruefully. "She fooled me all along the line," he admitted. "She's quite a girl. An officer but *no* gentleman!"

Richard gave a bark of laughter and threw him down the towel.

General Purpose Seaman Hajji Hassan laughed quietly to himself, uncertain whether he was more pleased with the humiliation of his friend Kerem Khalil, with the attempted humiliation of the unbeliever woman, or with her unexpected revenge upon the unbeliever mate whom he did not like. Whatever. It had been a memorable evening. One worthy of a little celebration.

Hajji was the last to have any hashish hidden aboard. The austere Salah Malik disapproved, and, while his attitude was not shared by all the seamen, his word was law. With all but Hajji. He would allow himself one swift indulgence, then he would retire happily to the uncomfortable berth with the others.

He had decided to hide his tiny cache in the Pump Room while helping the chief remove the corpses of the last lot of officers. None of the others was likely to come here unaccompanied after such an occurrence. Even Hajji, who was not in the slightest superstitious, found the atmosphere of the place oppressive. Especially this evening, for some reason. He hurried in, crossed to the Fire Control Room, and brought out the little silver packet from behind the sinister black canisters as fast as possible. The air around him seemed peopled with unnatural shadows. It seemed full of scarcely heard whisperings. Every now and then his heart would flutter as though something were just behind him, trying to steal his breath.

None of this was quite as imaginary as it appeared. In spite of the checks after the accident, in spite of daily maintenance, several of the cylinders had slow leaks. The air up to Hajji's knees was heavy with carbon-dioxide. When he left the door open, as now, it cascaded into the corridor and wound along the floor, sinking into guttering and runnels, seeping down and collecting in pockets where the air-conditioning could not reach, just as both Levkas and Martyr had feared it would; silent, invisible, odorless, deadly.

Still laughing quietly to himself, Hajji closed the Pump Room door and began to creep down the corridor. He had gone less than ten feet when Malik called his name.

Salah Malik stood, watching the man with distaste. At first he had seemed an excellent seaman, worthy of the pilgrim's title his parents had given him as a name: Hajji—one who has made the pilgrimage to Mecca; but it had soon become clear that this was an illusion created by the fact that he always worked in a team with Kerem Khalil, who was seaman enough for both of them. "Go to the Engine Room, Hajji," he ordered now. "You are late for your watch."

This was not true, but Hajji went anyway, muttering viciously, unaware that Malik had just saved his life.

10

The last evening in July found Robin hanging over the port bow of the supertanker, twenty feet below deck level, suspended from the forecastle in a boatswain's chair. In spite of the curve of the tanker's stem, she was close enough to inspect the rust-blistered area a foot or two in front of her. The stem of a super-tanker, never riding over the seas but always punching through them like a mobile pier, took unimaginable punishment. The slightest flaw down here had to be checked—even a rash of rust blisters. Kerem Khalil had reported it when he was repainting the ship's name earlier in the afternoon. Robin had come down to inspect them: as was her duty and her pleasure. Behind her, on the darkening horizon, lay the purple mountaintops of Mad-agascar, dark as thunderheads. Around her lay the massive beauty of the nightfall, making even this routine inspection almost un-bearably pleasurable.

Kicking against the side, she pushed herself out like a kid on a swing, feeling the bustle of life around her—something *Pro-metheus* normally managed to keep at a distance. A cormorant passed low overhead, having just launched itself from a Sampson post. The big black birds used *Prometheus* as an island, to the cheerful resignation of the seamen they kept swabbing day in and day out. Above the lonely cormorant, varying from specks to individual crosses, the gulls wheeled all the way up into the crystal sky. And if she twisted to look down into the equally clear, smooth sea, she knew she would see a school of dolphins playing in the great bow wave whose roaring filled her ears to the exclusion of all other sounds except the occasional keening of a low gull and the song of the wind in the ropes by her head. A warm, gentle south wind that had blown into their faces now unvaryingly for days; ever since they had pulled in toward the coast of Africa. This time of year there was a wind that seemed to blow from the Cape to the Gulf with hardly a break, following along the line of the coast; and even in midwinter at the Cape, the wind was rarely anything but warm. In Durban it might be as cool as sixty degrees Fahrenheit now. Here it was seventy-five.

Her reverie was broken by a muffled thump that made her jump as something hit the metal by her head and fell flapping into her lap. She had caught it with automatic revulsion and was just about to hurl it away when she stopped, realizing what it was. It was a flying fish. Holding tightly on to it now, she looked down over her shoulder just in time to see the whole shoal break surface and skim along the side of the ship, glittering like a golden rainbow, pursued by dolphins or a passing shark. As abruptly as they had appeared a foot or two above the swells, they were gone, sides glinting deeper and deeper until they vanished.

She swung back, looking up toward the tumblehome above, calculating whether or not she could lob the fish up and over the side. Probably not. It twisted in her hands again and she nearly dropped it so she thumped its head against the plank she was sitting on and it lay still, stunned. Impulsively she unbuttoned the top buttons of her shirt and stuffed it down to lie cold against her belly, held up by the waistband of her shorts.

They were a good team, the men on the forecastle deserving her loyalty as unstintingly as they gave theirs. She reached up and pulled the warning line. At once Salah Malik's head was thrust into silhouette against the darkening sky. She waved. He nodded. Vanished. A moment later she began to rise. After a few feet, she began to walk up the metal.

By the time she reached the top, the fish was no longer waving its bright tail from her cleavage—that would have been no fun— it was thrust into the waistband of her shorts at the back. As she stepped aboard it gave a wriggle and caused her to gasp as though she had been pinched, but no one seemed to notice. In an instant, the fish was out of her clothing and sailing through the air to land at their feet. There was a moment of stunned disbelief, then they all pounced except for Salah, who turned to look at her. With a howl of glee, Hajji Hassan straightened, holding the thing aloft. Robin sighed mentally. It was always the way. The one who hadn't earned it, always got it.

The Chinese stewards had started the pot, of course, inveterate gamblers to a man; but the seamen had joined in cheerfully, half expecting their money back in Rotterdam, for who had ever heard of a flying fish jumping nearly forty feet onto a supertanker's deck?

But here it was, a flying fish, right on the deck in front of them, and consequently worth over two hundred dollars.

Hajji was not popular, but such good fortune could not fail to lead to celebration. He and the fish were swept into the air and the team bore them off raucously, looking for "Twelve Toes" Ho, who was holding the purse.

Salah looked at Robin. Did she want the boatswain's chair dismantled and stowed? Should he call them back?

She shook her head. The mate would want to check her findings. They might as well leave it up for him.

He nodded, understanding more even than she suspected, and turned to follow his men.

After a moment, Robin followed too, feeling, in the aftermath of her elation, slightly depressed. No; it was not just after the elation. It was the thought of talking to Strong. Of handling his thinly veiled hostility, his nit-picking, double-checking, sexist, petty desire for revenge. She had come across men who found themselves incapable of seeing women as their equals—plenty of them—but, she realized, there had always been some sort of a buffer before. Now there was not. At the moment it was her and the first mate, head to head.

But, to be fair, it wasn't all simple sexism on his part: she couldn't think of many women who would be too charmed at having every stitch of their clothing stolen in front of thirty people, either.

* * *

But only John was on the bridge. "What happened down there?" he asked cheerfully, nodding forward, his trusty briar bobbing above the purposeful jut of his chin. "They going to chuck that lazy beggar Hajji overboard at last?"

"Found a flying fish."

"On the forecastle head? That's not a fish, that's Superman." He looked at her suspiciously. "You spoil that lot."

"They're worth it." She grinned, warmed by the comradely twinkle in his eye.

"Up to you. Anything wrong?"

"Everything's fine as far as I can see. Just rust blisters. Needs a paint job at the most."

"If you say it's fine, then it's fine."

"Better check with the mate."

"Look, Robin," John turned to her, "don't let him get you down. He's a picky sod, but nice enough. He'd be giving any junior a bit of a rough ride now, and you..." He hesitated, took his pipe out of his mouth, and scratched his chin with it.

"Bring out the worst in him?"

"You said it!"

"Bring out the worst in whom?" demanded Strong, coming onto the bridge at that moment. "Number Three, why is your team running riot below when there's still work to be done for'ard?"

"Looking for you, Number One. Thought you might like to double-check. Some nasty rust, but nothing dangerous: looks all right to me."

"Then I'm sure it is all right. Get your lot up and get that lot stowed." He turned to go. John glanced at her behind his back: told you so, he grinned.

Ben Strong turned back. "No, leave it," he ordered inevitably. "I'd better check it all for myself."

"Have you seen the Little Mistress?" asked Hajji of Salah Malik some time later. "I would like to share my good fortune with her." He had made up the nickname for Robin himself when one of his more intelligent colleagues explained to him that a pun existed in English upon the word *mate*.

Salah eyed him with even more disfavor than usual. "The third mate is a better officer than you have a right to expect," he said severely. "She is a better seaman than you will ever be and is superior to you in every conceivable way. I do not like to hear the wise insulted by the foolish, although I know it is the way of the world."

Hajji stalked off in high outrage at that. But he did not stay in a bad mood for long. He would attend to the Little Mistress soon. For the present, he was a fortunate man. And what do such men do? They celebrate. Now he knew for certain where the old woman Malik was, he would smoke the last of his hashish.

It was the work of only a few moments to liberate the little packet from behind the black cylinders and to slip out of the haunted Pump Room; then he was scurrying down and down to the secret hiding place where he could indulge his vice leisurely.

As he descended, the pounding of the engine grew louder. The air grew warmer, out of reach of the air-conditioning, and more redolent of oil from the engine room. Hajji liked it down here. The deeper he went, the more things shrank to an acceptable scale until, in the farthest depths of the great ship's bowels, he arrived at a tiny alcove. It was too small to be a room. It was deep and dark, though not pitch dark, and warm. The walls were covered in pipes. The engine throbbed like a heart.

Hajji sat contentedly on the floor and slowly rolled himself a joint. He regretted the loss of his pipe—Malik had found that and confiscated it as though the seaman were a child—but this way was better than no way. His fingers were clumsy but he persisted dreamily, his mind drifting from Malik back to the Little Mistress...

The cigarette was rolled by now, but he was having trouble with the matches. Were they damp? He could not get them to light. At last he tried three together and was rewarded with a small blue flame. He held it close and puffed hard. A trace of the drugged smoke filtered into his lungs. He took the matches away, holding them high as he drew on the joint again. His mind still on Robin, he glanced up, surprised to see that the matches were burning more brightly now. Slowly, he brought them down toward his eyes again, watching with wonder as the flame grew

82

smaller as it came nearer. No matter, the flame was still burning. He brought it back toward the end of his cigarette but for some reason he could not understand, at that very moment the deck came up and hit him in the face. He thought about getting up, especially as he seemed to have broken his nose and it was becoming difficult to breathe—but in the end, it was simply too much trouble.

11

"Think they'll ever find the little twit?"
    "Nope. I think he went overboard. Probably got drunk celebrating his win and fell into the ocean."
    "Didn't think Malik let them drink. Anyway, they're Moslems."
    "Think that'd stop Hassan?"
    "Probably not."
    It wasn't much of an epitaph, but it was almost all Hajji got.
    Ben and John were standing on the bridge at 07.30 next morning, chatting idly about last night's excitement as they watched Robin lead her depleted team down to the forecastle head. The boatswain's chair was still rigged there because Ben Strong hadn't had time to stow it between his cursory examination of the suspect area and the sudden first search for the missing man.
    The second, more exhaustive, search was going on at the moment, under the leadership of Salah Malik; with young McTavish notionally in charge, because they were in the engineering sections, and going on down.

    It was a glorious morning. The sky was high and brilliant, the sea translucently clear. The wind had shifted east of south and carried in each gentle gust a tantalizing complex of spicy scents born of Madagascar.
    Robin walked down the deck with a youthful spring in her

step, tired after last night's taxing searches but uplifted by the beauty of the day; utterly unaware of how close to death she was.

The chair itself was like a child's swing: a short plank of wood served as a seat; another plank, a few feet above it, held the ropes far enough apart to allow one occupant, lashed safely, to sit on the lower. Above the top plank, the two ropes supporting the seat became one, rising through a pulley. The pulley was raised six feet above the deck and angled out over the side by a carefully anchored tripod made of metal bars.

The equipment and its arrangement were to be found on any ship. Its use was entirely routine. Robin was not even supposed to be using it this morning. She was simply supposed to be stowing it away. But what she saw as she came onto the forecastle head changed all that instantly.

It was a ship. A felucca, with tall castles fore and aft; with what once must have been a proud mast bearing a gull-winged sail now snapped off short and gone over the side. She was not small. From stem to stern she must have measured all of forty feet. Nor was she a weak or ill-found vessel. That was obvious from the fact that her hull was still in one piece, wedged across the tanker's bow like that.

Robin stood on *Prometheus*'s prow and looked down upon her, scarcely able to believe what she was seeing. The others clustered round her, silently, also struck with awe. The two ships must have collided sometime during the night. After midnight, the forecastle head watch had been searching for Hajji Hassan with the rest. Such was the size of the supertanker that the shock of impact had gone unnoticed. The felucca's lights, had she been carrying any, had gone unseen. The cries of her crew, had she been manned, had gone unheard. She had simply ridden up onto the bow-wave above the great torpedo-shaped protrusion at the base of the bow, and hit at its thinnest part.

And there, in spite of the width of the forecastle, of the bluntness of the upper bow; in spite of the weight of the felucca herself sitting well clear of the water, there she remained: wedged across *Prometheus*'s bows like a tiny cross on a huge capital T.

Looking straight down from her current position, Robin could see where the tanker had chopped into the little ship, crushing her planking out to either side exactly amidships on the starboard side, cutting in almost as far as the broken mast. Cracks, some of them ragged and wide, stretched left and right, nearly from stem to stern, showing here and there a glimpse of what lay below. Everything on the felucca was still and silent, except for the hollow thud of the swells against her bottom.

Robin looked across at Kerem Khalil. "You ever seen anything like this?"

The Palestinian shook his head.

"The rest of you?"

"I heard of something like this," said one. Some of the others nodded. Robin found herself doing the same. They had all heard that it was possible. That it had happened before. None of them had ever seen it. Until now.

They stood, looking down at it for a few more seconds. Stories like this were once in a lifetime. They didn't want to share this one yet.

And then the screaming started.

Again they did nothing, looking askance at each other, knowing that what they could hear was some kind of illusion. Had to be some kind of illusion. There could be no crew left aboard. There could be no one left aboard. Unless some youngster was there, too badly hurt to join the rest. Unless it was not a crew member, but someone else. A slave, perhaps; for the felucca must have been up to no good, running dark and silent in the night.

Robin thumped the rail once, hard, as she had thumped Angus El Kebir's desk not so long ago, and was in action. "Swing the chair round here. I'm going down."

Kerem was about to argue, but he asked himself—as Salah Malik would have done—Would I argue with the mate? The answer was no. He saw no reason to argue with the woman, therefore. She was perfectly competent.

And the screaming was that of a child.

"What's that woman up to now?" asked Ben testily, looking down the length of the deck from the bridge.

"Checking *your* work, perhaps," John needled cheerfully.

"Damn cheek. She'd better hurry, though. She's due to relieve you in twenty minutes."

"I don't mind."

"I do. I'll have this run like a proper ship. Women or no women," snapped the first officer, and stalked off the bridge.

Kerem looked down at the woman walking across the felucca's deck, every bone in his body shrieking danger. He wished Salah was here. He glanced back at the bridge with an overwhelming feeling of frustrated impotence. There were four of the team now, instead of six. Himself and three others. He must keep an eye on the third mate. The other three must hold the rope. When the felucca went, they would have to pull her up at once, or she was dead.

He had no walkie-talkie and there was no one he could send for help.

Down here the noise was almost overwhelming. The drum roll of the bow wave sounded continuously against the felucca's keel. Each separate BOOM! of a larger wave was followed by a cacophony of screeches and groans as planks and pegs strained to tear apart. It was a wonder the child's screams could be heard above it all.

Yet there it was again: a plaintive, terrified howl. But where was it coming from?

Robin went down as though she were kneeling on broken glass. "Hello?" she called. Abruptly, the screaming ceased. "HELLO?" Louder. She knew the child wouldn't understand English, of course. But at least it would know there was someone near. She paused. Silence. "Where are you?"

Silence

She remained where she was, half kneeling, and looked very carefully around the deck. Both the fore and after castles were big enough to hold a child, and yet it seemed to her that the cries had come from straight ahead. And immediately in front of the stump of the mast there was an open hatchway. She crouched onto all fours, like a cat. Inch by inch, she began to crawl forward. Every now and then a wave slightly larger than the rest would explode against the bottom of the wreck, causing it to lift, causing great pieces of wood to spring free against *Prometheus*'s stem and fall rattling like dry bones into the sea, causing the hulk to scream even more loudly than the child. When this happened, Robin would freeze, watching her shadow on the deck, watching her sweat mark the dry planks beneath her as the drops cascaded off her face. And as they landed, increasingly frequently they would roll forward and down, away from her as the slope of the deck increased.

I'm going to die here, she thought. I'm going to bloody well die . . . I'm going to sodding well die . . . I'm going to . . . As she moved, so her language became fouler.

And the hatchway came closer.

At the lip of the hatchway, she was faced with a dilemma. Should she keep the chair on as she went down? The obvious answer seemed to be yes, and yet, if the felucca went while she was below and she was still tied in, she could all too easily be torn to pieces. On the other hand, if she untied herself, then went with the felucca, she would be just another man overboard.

And, of course, the rope would make it more difficult to reach the child if anything did go wrong.

It was that more than anything which decided her.

"What is she doing?" cried one of the others to Khalil as soon as he felt the rope slackening in his hands.

"She's taking the chair off. I think she's going below . . ." Kerem turned and deliberately started signaling to the bridge.

"Sir!" The helmsman noticed Kerem's signal first. He couldn't make out quite what the tiny figure was doing, however, because the forepeak was nearly three hundred yards away.

John had some trouble making out what was going on too, until he went out onto the bridge wing and used his binoculars. Then, at full magnification, it became obvious that something was wrong.

He walked briskly back onto the bridge proper, mentally cursing Ben for having left the bridge at just the wrong moment. He picked up the internal phone and dialed the captain's number.

* * *

With the wooden seat firmly wedged under her left arm, Robin crept gingerly down the ladder from the hatchway. The noise down here was incredible, the stench damn near unbearable, the sense of danger absolutely overpowering. The felucca was quite simply—but, thankfully, quite slowly—coming to pieces under her feet. On her right, sloping away at an increasing angle, was the single below-deck area, with the foot of the mast rising immediately ahead at a crazy tilt.

On her left, incredibly close at hand, was the huge, blunt metal blade of *Prometheus*'s bow. It rose through the crushed and splintered wood almost as though it had always been there. And yet, at the same time, it was an obscene intrusion, horribly out of place. Robin felt as though she were inside Mr. Borden's skull, just after Lizzie had delivered the first whack, looking out at the axhead.

"HELLO!"

Gripping the seat with bruising force, she stepped off the bottom rung, onto the deck itself.

There was an explosion of sound and movement immediately behind her, from under the ladder itself. This was so unexpected that she jumped forward, swinging on the rope and gasping with shock. The rope slackened at once, dumping her unceremoniously on her bottom. She sat still, looking up.

Beyond the ladder was a cavern of darkness stretching toward the bow. Still dazzled by the early morning brightness she had encountered on the deck, she could not see into the shadows. Even as she looked, however, her vision was aided by shaft after shaft of light. Like searchlight beams, like the light under storm-clouds, flat blades stabbed down in increasing numbers from the edge of that jagged wound as the felucca began to slide off *Prometheus*'s bow.

And this light revealed, just a step or two behind the ladder but chained helplessly to its perch, a scarlet, yellow, and blue Macaw parrot. And, as Robin watched it, the terrified creature opened its bill and screamed like a frightened child.

"Damn you!" Robin was on her feet at once, her rage beyond expressing—in direct proportion to her own fear. All this. And for a bloody bird! From the bottom of the ladder, looking through the rungs, she yelled at the top of her voice, "We're going to die! You know that, bird?" The parrot leaped toward her, but was brought up short in a flapping, squawking bundle by the chain.

"We're both going to sodding die!" At least it had the wit to sit still while she wrestled the chain loose from the perch. Then it jumped easily onto her right shoulder. "I wouldn't stay there, you dumb SOB," she warned it, "unless you can swim as well."

It screamed in her ear.

She stepped back onto the ladder.

The felucca fell into the sea.

12

It hadn't been as simple as Ben led Slope to believe that morning a fortnight ago, when he told him of Mariner's past. It hadn't been clean, cut and dried, full of simple rights and wrongs. It had been like any human relationship: messy.

Richard, Robin, Rowena, and Bill had met the second the sixties became the seventies at midnight, December 31, 1969. Their yachts were tied side by side at the unfashionable end of that long marina that makes up the seaward side of the main street of St. Tropez.

None of them had any particular reason for being in such a place in such a town when most of their friends were somewhere else anyway. Richard himself, who had bought the yacht *Rebecca* a few years previously to celebrate his first tanker captaincy, had sailed aimlessly out of Poole, alone, at Christmas and ended up here because there had been severe storms in Biscay preventing him returning. The champagne had been a pointless indulgence. Its cork hit Sir William on the head as he stood in the cockpit of the neighboring yacht. Apologies had led to introductions; introductions to mutual recognition.

Sir William was there with his two girls. It was exactly a year since the death of Lady Heritage and they had all wanted to get away. Why they had come here, none of them seemed to know, but Richard suspected it was Robin's idea: one of the vivid enthusiasms that seemed constantly to be impelling the gawky, sensitive, brilliant sixteen-year-old.

Certainly, it had nothing to do with the dazzling, slightly bored Rowena, who seemed to be following the debutante fashion of the time—he discovered later, she led it—in approaching everything with a chic ennui. The precociously mature twenty-two-year-old would rather have been almost anywhere else—and she made no secret of it.

Richard would never forget that first sight of her, sitting in the after cockpit of the Heritage yacht, sipping Bollinger, wearing Balmain, like Princess Grace come slumming it down the coast. Nor would he ever forget the fierce, feral passion that simmered just beneath that glacial surface.

How well he had fitted into the family; worshiped by one daughter, beloved of the other. Respected by a man whom he respected. Social calls in London soon became professional ones to Heritage House in Leadenhall Street. Richard's standing as an independent tanker captain eventually expanded by his appointment as senior captain to Heritage Shipping. Rowena and he married within the year, a red-eyed Robin as bridesmaid.

Neither of Richard's commitments to the Heritage family was a sinecure. Keeping Rowena in the style demanded by her position in society soon used up even his salary and he soon came to count himself almost fortunate when commitments to her father kept him away at sea where he at least lived free. But they were five heady, happy years nevertheless. He was building something lasting—or so it seemed. With his father-in-law, one of those hard-headed, down-to-earth northern businessmen who are the backbone of City institutions, he was creating a shipping empire of almost Greek proportions. During his increasingly rare visits home, he was feted as the dashing husband of a leader of the jet set, his name in the society as well as the financial pages; his picture at the front of *Tatler* as well as in the middle of *The Economist*. A coming man on every front.

It ended at Robin's twenty-first birthday party.

She was at the London School of Economics at the time, although her father would much have preferred her to be following in Rowena's footsteps at finishing school in Lausanne, or with her family friends at Oxford. The party itself was held at Cold Fell, the great house overlooking Hadrian's Wall in Cumbria, which had come to Heritage with his late wife, Lady Fiona Graham.

Richard and Rowena drove up; Richard, at least, unaware that anything was wrong. The house was full of undergraduates, echoing to youthful laughter for the first time since the thirties when Lady Fiona's parents had entertained the bankrupt Gertrude Lawrence and the young Noël Coward here, with the others of their set.

Sir William was in his element, dispensing punch and fatherly advice, insisting to one and all, "Nay, call me Bill," in his rich northern brogue, though none ever dared. Richard had joined him, of course, keeping an eye on all the excited young faces, discreetly checking all the more obvious places where virtue could be lost; feeling almost ancient in the process.

But it was Robin's night. Richard had never seen her look so lovely. She would never rival the cool perfection of her big sister. She remained slightly gawky, even when trying to be chic; even when dressed by Laura Ashley. Time and again their eyes met over the throng of her friends. Time and again they danced. He ought to have queued for the honor—he would have had to have joined a considerable queue to get a dance with his own wife—but she crossed out whole sections of her dance card and came to him time and again.

At midnight she demanded the vintage champagne. A bottle had been left in the library specially, and the two of them went through together. The great, book-lined room was empty, as was obviously part of Robin's simple plan. Richard suddenly found her in his arms. With all the overpowering enthusiasm she applied to everything in her life, she loved him; had always loved him: would always love him. As gently as possible, he pushed her away. He loved her too, but as a sister. Anything else would be unthinkable. And what about Rowena?

Stung by the simple unfairness of it, she told him about Rowena. How, during his absence at sea, she was busily sleeping her way through *Burke's Peerage*.

At first he had refused to believe her, but she was well stocked with proof. In the end, half convinced, he had gone to Sir William. Sir William had known for some time, but had hidden the truth; only Richard, it soon transpired, had not known.

Rowena herself was slightly surprised by all the fuss. She had always been given exactly what she wanted. The most expensive jewelry, clothes, and perfumes had been hers for the asking. She saw no reason why lovers should be any different. She really could not understand that this was where Richard drew the line. Like any spoiled child, she started throwing tantrums. There and then, at Robin's party, she threw the first. Richard had never seen her like this; nor had Sir William for many years: but then, Rowena had had everything she had wanted from the time she was seventeen.

The marriage turned to dross almost at once, and all Sir William's plans for Richard were automatically put at risk. The simple fact was that blood was thicker than water and so Rowena found it easy enough to drive a wedge between the men. This was not grand opera. It had not even reached the stature of tragedy yet. Richard and Sir William talked things through carefully. It seemed to them that the matter had not yet gone beyond the point where reconciliation was possible. And he still loved his wife. If she could remain faithful, he would welcome her back with open arms.

In succeeding years, going over the mess time and again in his mind, he looked back at himself with increasing wonder. He could not believe he had agreed to such a thing, for he was a fiercely proud man. Nor, indeed, could he see how Bill Heritage could have asked it of him. Only when Robin had smiled at him on the night she had first come aboard did he remember Rowena's smile, and the power it had once held over him.

Rowena had grudgingly agreed to try, as though it were she who had been wronged. A second honeymoon was mooted and agreed to: the perfect solution; a working holiday for Richard, a cruise for Rowena, who had never sailed the Cape Route before.

Sir William's new flagship was hurried into commission for the purpose and named *Rowena*. Time was short. Rowena was impatient, and Sir William so worried that he made one of the few serious business errors of his life. He insured his own bottom rather than waiting for the underwriters—desperate of course, but so confident in the massive tanker and in her captain that he bore the whole weight of the insurance himself, risking far more than he could afford to lose, instead of waiting for the consortium of businessmen who would normally share the risk with him on advice from Lloyd's of London.

The cruise passed off well enough until they reached the Channel. Then, quite simply and deliberately, Rowena kicked over the traces. She had never been a one-man woman. She could never be one. The strain of remaining faithful was going to prove too much for her. She backed out of the deal. She took the young third engineer to bed. Richard found out that morning, and had just backed out of the deal—and out of the family, and the company—himself, when the whole thing went up in his face.

That was the stuff of his nightmares—the massive power of the moment grinding closed on him like a great steel door that no power at his command could hold ajar.

Stage by stage he relived it in his dreams from the first sight of the pale, twisting bodies in his cabin, which had driven him back onto the bridge, to Daniel Strong's first urgent, "Sir!"

The vision of their bodies stayed before his eyes throughout the rest of it, though he knew the third engineer would have been back at his post before the end of it and Rowena, calculatedly, alone. The sight and sound of their coupling had remained more real to him than the death of his ship until that first grinding roar of collision. That was part of the horror of it—had the knowledge affected his judgment? Was there a moment when what she had been doing got in the way of what he had been doing? Had she caused him an instant of hesitation that had made him lose it all?

Not according to the Coastguards who had watched it all on their radar, nor according to the helicopter pilot who had seen the final impact through an eddy in the fog—and was lucky to live through the explosion. Not according to the survivors of the other ship who had watched their captain leave the bridge, putting an inexperienced boy in charge: a so-called third officer who, it transpired, had not been qualified at all. An overconfident, inept young man who had panicked and done everything wrong.

And yet Richard still wondered, remembering how remote he had felt during that sequence from the first warning on the Collision Alarm Radar, to formal warning by siren, radio, Coastguard; from standard avoiding action to sickening realization that the oncoming signal—they did not see the ship itself until the very end, of course—which was steaming the wrong way down the Channel's one-way street in any case, had turned onto a collision course and sealed all their fates.

The bodies had been before his eyes more vividly than anything until those massive bows came chopping toward him out of the fog bank. Their sighing had filled his ears with more reality than anything until the colossal roar of the impact.

And everything else had been darkness and silence anyway.

After the inquiry, the two men found themselves strangers. Rowena's ghost stood between them. Robin could see only the terrible cost of her infatuation with her dashing brother-in-law, and turned from Richard to try to make it all up to Sir William. She became the business partner, adviser, and son that Richard had almost been, working so much harder; gaining so much less of the credit. But almost single-handedly holding Heritage shipping together until her father recovered; and that recovery was years in coming. Even now, once in a while, he would do something ill-advised, almost suicidal in business terms.

Like buying the oil in *Prometheus*.

Richard lay on his bunk, chin on his chest, lost in these thoughts; wondering why Robin was really here. His memory of her twenty-first birthday was so vivid, he could still feel her hot in his arms, still smell the champagne on her breath as she swore undying love. How different things would have been had he loved the little sister. But ten years ago she had been a child: the idea was pointless. Or had been, then...

His phone rang and he reached for it, still lost in thought.

The moment Robin felt it go she hurled herself forward. She had just reached the bottom of the ladder when the whole felucca lurched left and so she was able to dive forward and upward in one, grabbing the rungs above while her legs pumped smoothly below.

The parrot, of course, deserted as soon as it saw the sky.

She had taken perhaps ten steps upward when the ladder toppled sideways with the rest of the hull. She twisted, reaching up for the lip of the hatchway with her right hand while keeping firm hold of her lifeline with her left. In this position she hung while the felucca pivoted round her. The hatch that had been a hole above her became almost a doorway framing her as she faced inward. She pushed off hard and stepped back into the dazzling, roaring day.

At once, the seat on the boatswain's chair under her left armpit took all her weight; but as it slid up past her ribs, it gathered her shirt into a pad which, during the next few minutes, protected her shoulder from serious damage.

As soon as she swung out of the hatchway, the deck fell forward into her face. She brought up her arms and legs, bouncing off it as best she could, with elbows and knees. Everything was happening far too quickly now to allow her to plan ahead or even to think clearly. So it was that the broken railing round the edge of the deck was able to slide down unexpectedly and bash her over the crown of her head. She felt giddy; almost slipped into unconsciousness. But her lithe body just would not quit. Everything went extremely bright. Reality wavered. She seemed to lose contact with what was going on around her.

The high aftercastle gathered her almost gently to itself, swinging in from her right as the wreck fell left. She flew out, spun around, came back in like a pendulum, in the grip of forces far beyond her control. When her mind cleared, she was just sliding off *Prometheus*'s huge torpedo-head protrusion on which the felucca had rested, and slipping down into the sea.

Horrified, she looked up. In a mess, hanging out over the side, destroyed by the same physical forces that had been sporting with her over the last few minutes, the tripod of the boatswain's chair protruded like a bizarre bowsprit. Then this, too, seemed to swing into dizzying motion as the water took her and swept her into the boiling bedlam of the bow wave.

Her head only went under for a second; then she was gripping madly with her left arm, the strain beginning to tell in her shoulder joint, and she rose above the surface a little. The weed-

and barnacle-encrusted side of the ship pressed against her. The movement of the monster through the sea tried to suck her under once more, but the trusty rope, and the trusty men on the far end of it, would not let her down. Instead, she ground back toward the stern, losing a little skin from exposed parts of her body, as though she were being keel-hauled. By this stage, she would have been glad enough to go free, even if it meant being sucked to oblivion under that long, long hull; but something in her made her throw her right arm up instead to grasp the rope above her head, relieve the pressure on her shoulder a little, and hang on like grim death.

The rope angled back from the forepeak now, tight as a fishing line, with her body riding the inner curve of the bow wave some twenty feet back. The pendulum effect had pulled her almost half out of the water and, because only her legs were still submerged, she was slowly spinning round and round, so that some of the time she was facing the black hull and some of the time she faced Madagascar nearly two hundred miles away.

It was on one of the occasions when she was facing out that the flying fish returned. Something really panicked them this time and Robin's mind was suddenly filled with visions of sinister shadows cruising the depths. Instead of running parallel to the ship, as they usually did, they hurled themselves straight at the side, and at Robin. One moment the sea rolled away smoothly, the next its bright blue surface exploded with bodies. Wings spread wide, they hurled themselves into the air just above her head. She quailed automatically, giving her shoulder a nasty twinge, and almost let go of the rope with her right hand, so overpowering was the desire to shield her face. Then they were on her. Luckily, only the youngest and smallest hit her. The rest smashed into the metal above her and fell back, stunned, down into the sea.

Those few that did hit her were quite enough, however, for there was no way for her to protect herself and no time to try to turn. They connected with bruising force. She tried to disregard them, grinding her heels against the metal in an effort to stay still as she looked for what had spooked them. But there was nothing there.

How long had passed since the felucca fell free she had no way of knowing, but the shock had cleared her mind and this was her first opportunity for anything approaching coherent thought. So, as she held herself facing out, as much by an effort of will as anything else, looking for a shark's fin near at hand, she began to wonder how she was going to get out of this.

The constant pummeling motion of the water over her skin had already killed off most of the sensation below her waist—if only it could do as much for her shoulder, which was really starting to hurt! Even if she could pull free, she could not trust three of her limbs to get her up the rope, then. But she wasn't looking forward to being hoisted up fifty odd feet by her shoulder either.

It was only at this point, really, that she began to regret the adventure.

"For a parrot?" Richard could hardly believe it. "She went down after a parrot?"

"It sounded like a child." Kerem was insistent: the third mate had not been foolhardy.

Neither of them was standing still to have this discussion. While the rest of the team were holding the rope safely, the captain and the young Palestinian were trying to put together enough of a line to lower some help. They rapidly tied several shorter pieces of rope together, testing the knots with vicious wrenches to ensure they were secure. In their skilled hands, it was the work of a few moments.

As soon as the second line was ready, Richard began tying it round his waist. There was no alternative to going himself. Ben was below somewhere, in his office, probably. John was on the bridge. There was no time to get either down here. Robin seemed safe enough for the moment, but there was no time to hang around practicing theoretical leadership. And in any case, it never even occurred to Richard that he should send someone younger, less senior, more expendable. He had never been the sort of captain—or person—who put his dignity first. If it was dirty, if it was dangerous, Richard had always led from the front; he saw no reason to change now.

And the fact that it was Robin suddenly made an unexpectedly powerful difference.

As soon as the rope was tied, Richard looped it around the rail twice so that it effectively went through a pulley, making it easier for Kerem to lower him unaided. Even so, Kerem looped the far end around his own waist, glancing up as he did so: if you go, I go. Richard had time to nod once, in curt recognition of the gesture; then he stepped over the rail and, leaning back against the tension of the rope, he began to walk backward down the side.

Things went wrong at once. The tumblehome was angled more acutely than it seemed, effectively giving an overhang. The metal was too wet and slippery for the grip even of his desert boots. What ought to have been a careful, controlled descent became an undignified scramble. But at least—by the skin of his teeth—he did not fall. And that was really all that counted.

Fifteen feet down, the side was perfectly vertical again, though even more spray-covered and slippery. He took the opportunity to slow his descent and to check below. Robin didn't even seem to have noticed that he was coming. She was flat against the side of the ship facing out, looking steadfastly toward distant, invisible Madagascar. He need not pause to look down again: he could judge how close he was getting to her by the angle of the rope stretching, almost straight, between her shoulder and the forepeak. He looked back up. High in the hard blue sky, vivid even at this distance, the parrot that had caused all this was heading for the massive, distant island.

He eased the rope around his waist and called up as loudly as he could. The rope lurched into motion once more. After a few more minutes, he could feel the spray from the bow wave on his bare legs and Robin's rope, straight as an iron bar, was angling down close by. He yelled again and his progress stopped. He turned carefully, and there she was, a matter of feet below him, at that instant looking up to see where the noise had come from. Their eyes met and she smiled. The smile of a perfectly happy woman.

"KEREM!" He was in motion.

Five seconds later, at the top of his lungs, "KEREM!" again.

He stood astride her and leaned inward to take her gently under the arms. Her face twisted at once and he saw the danger posed by the boatswain's chair. But there was little time to consider alternatives. He slid his hands round between her back and the cold side of the tanker, gathering her to him in a gentle bear hug. At once the rope round his own waist cut more deeply. No help for that either.

As soon as her feet were clear of the water, the weight of her rope pulled them left, nearly upsetting Richard's precarious balance. But the men on the deck understood the change in tension. A head was thrust briefly into silhouette over the edge of the deck and the boatswain's chair fell free. Richard and Robin swung back, his feet skipping and dancing over the metal, trying to keep their purchase. The strain on his arms intensified. The rope bit deeper at his waist. He took the first step on the long walk home.

There were willing hands enough to lift them in over the rail. John had remained on watch on the bridge, but he had got hold of Ben who had arrived on the forecastle head too late to do anything other than to heave with the rest. In that psychic way he seemed to have, Chief Steward Ho had heard too, and, having high regard both for his round-eyed captain and the barbarian woman, he, too, had hastened here, collecting on the way Salah Malik, who had just completed the second, fruitless, search for Hajji Hassan.

In the final analysis, their presence was the most germaine. As Richard and Robin sank to the deck, side by side, water spewed out of Robin's sea-filled shirt, and in it, the smallest of the flying fish that had bombarded her earlier. They all stood looking at it. Hajji's winnings had gone back into the pot. The fish was worth two hundred dollars.

Robin pulled herself up. Her shoulder hurt, but she would survive. And she was determined to get back on duty as soon as possible. She looked at them all standing watching the flying fish dance.

"Salah," she said firmly, "you'd better share the winnings from this one round the team, 'cause I'll be damned if I'm going to get you another one."

13

After the adventure of the felucca, *Prometheus* proceeded west of south and early August passed in a deceptive, haunted calm while they sailed under Capricorn and out of the Mozambique Channel. The calm was both haunted and deceptive almost all because of Hajji Hassan. The cause of his disappearance remained a mystery. Richard interviewed anyone who had anything to say, formed his own conclusions, and filled in the logs and the Accident Reports accordingly. After that, it seemed, he was gone for good. And yet he left something of himself behind. Something more even than Levkas's doomed crew. Perhaps because they had all known him; perhaps because none of them had liked him much; whatever the reason, it was he, the crew said, who was always there, just beyond the edge of your vision. Just behind you. It was his breath that stirred the hair on your neck when you paused in the flat bright corridors in the night to listen to the haunting music one of Ho's men played on a mysterious Eastern flute.

But, beyond this, the haunted calm was deceptive because on board there were plots and currents under the busy surface that boded no good at all. And because, far to the east and south, a weather system was building that would come close to destroying them all.

* * *

Robin had had every intention of returning to duty before the end of her first watch, but Ben had gone soft on her and filled her so full of painkillers before he dared try sew up the small wound on her scalp caused by the felucca's rail, that he knocked her out for nearly a day and kept her in bed for several more.

Richard took her watches, and this was no bad thing. While on the one hand it tied him down—he had to be on the bridge at certain times—it also brought him out of his captain's solitude and dumped him right back in the swing of things. With the action forced upon him, he was happier at once. Nor was this a quiet time for anyone else. There was painting to be done; all sorts of maintenance to be completed before they reached the Cape in less than a week's time. And, while South Africa is as near the equator as Florida, nevertheless it was winter in the Southern Hemisphere and rough weather could be expected.

The working day stretched from dawn to dusk and then beyond. Suddenly it became the rule rather than the exception for small groups of men to appear and disappear at odd times, and to demand food when everyone else had just eaten or were still fasting. The entertainments committee disbanded itself, without having entertained anyone other than themselves. The true brains of the ship moved from the bridge—and the Engine Room—to the galley. This was the time "Twelve Toes" Ho and his men came into their own. No demand was too great; no requirement too unreasonable. As the machine of the crew—above deck and below—ran more and more rapidly, they poured the oil of their service on all the working parts. No matter who left what berth in how much of a mess when called away on some errand, it was all neat and tidy on his return. No matter what nameless accident with what filthy part of the engine, there were always clean, freshly pressed overalls available. Ho even set up an elementary watch system so that there would be someone in the galley at all times.

At midnight, local time, August 4, however, there was no steward there at all. Which made it all too easy for the tall figure in white overalls to put the poison in the food.

He came into the galley with the plan already formed in his

mind, hesitant only about the final touches. Aware that he was unlikely to remain undisturbed for long, he paused, enjoying the pressure. He did not want what he was doing to take immediate effect but he needed it to be active at a certain time, in a particular place. Under predetermined conditions.

Yes! That was it! What did you consume under one set of circumstances that you tended to avoid under others?

He smiled grimly and went to work.

The storm came whirling out of the east two days later.

They had been trimming the edge of a seasonal high ever since they had left the Mozambique Channel and the barometer had been standing at 1025 for days, with wide skies and quiet seas to show for it. On the afternoon of the 5th it began to rise rapidly. By sunset it stood at 1037 and John was shaking his head while everybody else was perspiring in the sort of heat they should have left in the Gulf.

"I don't like the look of this at all," observed Ben when he relieved Robin at midnight.

"What can we do?" The third mate shrugged—she could shrug now with no discomfort to her shoulder, and was back on her first late watch. "I'd keep my eyes open, though."

"That's sensible," Ben agreed. "Only wise thing to do." But his tone was distant.

Robin didn't need to ask why. He was checking her records. She waited. "Back down to 1025 millibars," he observed.

"Yup." She shrugged again, wearily.

She went to bed.

By four, the barometric pressure stood at 1020. John noted the fact in the log when he relieved Ben.

By dawn later that morning, the 6th, John was on the port bridge wing looking narrow-eyed into the heart of the pressure system that was all that lay between them and Australasia. The glass was falling fast. The sky was still blue, but its cerulean face was marked with high streaks of cloud and the distant horizon was dark.

When Richard came onto the bridge at 07.15, John was still

out there. Richard went out and stood at his side, following his gaze.

After a while, John said: "'Mackerel skies and mares tails/ Make tall ships wear short sails . . . .' There's a nasty one coming."

"The glass is at 990," observed the captain coolly. "Of course there's a nasty one coming."

During the next twelve hours, they altered course a point or two south, letting the coast of Africa fall away west on their starboard, giving themselves more sea room. When the monster hit, they were at 30 south, 40 east, five hundred miles off Durban.

They had more warning than the falling glass and the darkening sky. They had more substantial danger signs than the increasingly agitated surface of the ocean and the hot, vicious gusting of the wind. Tsirtos started picking up distress signals as soon as the thing reached its full force to the east of them. Small ships and then large ones began reporting wind strengths off the Beaufort scale, mountainous seas, and unbelievably destructive electrics. They started asking for help, but nobody, it seemed, was too keen on going in to get them out. And as the day wore on, some of them started falling silent. Tsirtos's mood went dark, then foul, like the weather. After the briefest communication with the desperate men, he felt as though he were losing personal friends to the storm.

But soon enough he had worries of his own.

The first he knew about their own position was an unexpected lurch that he felt even in the shack, as though *Prometheus* had hit an impediment solid enough to stop her for an instant. Everything loose in the little room seemed to spring forward. Some of it hit the wall in front. Most of it went onto the floor. Tsirtos looked blearily around. He had been concentrating so hard on his messages he had lost all track of time. It was 19.14: an apt enough hour for war with the elements to be declared.

The great lurch was repeated, as though this were the smallest of trawlers and not a sizable tanker. Tsirtos switched off and went up to the bridge.

As soon as he stepped out of the shack, he heard the wind,

although it took him a moment to realize that it was the wind. It sounded like a rolling explosion in the near distance accompanied by the music of a mad orchestra. Over the artillery-barrage bass, a thousand different notes and tones rose and fell as the air tore at every individual strut, line, nut, and bolt with that microscopic fury that only the greatest disturbances are capable of showing. Quite simply, the wind was trying to tear the superstructure off. Even in the long corridors behind battened bulkhead doors, the air was mobile, whispering into drafts and breezes. Moving curtains, setting pictures aswing, making carpets and even linoleum seem to ripple and lift. Setting everything attapping restlessly. Slamming doors suddenly, as though moved by sympathy for its wild cousin outside.

Tsirtos had thought it was impossible for a supertanker to pitch. The hulls of such ships, he knew, were too long for even the broadest wave formation to place the stem on a crest and the stern in a trough. Supertankers, he had been told, were supposed to ride smoothly on the backs of several waves at once. But no one seemed to have explained this to the storm. *Prometheus* seemed to be pitching like a cockleshell. Tossing. Rolling. Performing complexes of motion totally at the mercy of wind and water, as though there were no one at the helm or in the Engine Room at all. For a wild moment in that wind-haunted corridor, Tsirtos was convinced they had abandoned without telling him.

He reached the bridge at an unsteady run. It was bedlam. While the storm had seemed distant enough in the passages below, here it was pressed up against the windows fighting madly to get in at them.

The twilight's last gleaming smeared the bellies of the low, scudding clouds with blood. From the near horizon, dark gray curtains of torrential rain hung in devastating series, torn from top to bottom continuously by great jagged forks of lightning. The sea in sympathy was a crystal gray—like a leaden gemstone—but the spume torn from the backs of the maelstrom waves was red. Even as Tsirtos, frozen in the doorway, watched, bow waves like the runoff in a giant's slaughterhouse exploded hundreds of feet into the air. The long hull faltered in her motion once again. A cascade of detritus flew onto the floor and slid forward. A tidal wave seethed back along the deck and exploded at the foot of the superstructure with such force that a wall of it rose to block the clear view in front of the helmsman's narrow eyes. The sound was incredible.

Tsirtos had seen all he wanted to see within seconds. "I'll be in the shack," he bellowed at Ben Strong's back. Ben raised a hand to show that he had heard, but he was occupied with his own preoccupations. "Still at 983," he yelled to the captain, who was sitting comfortably in his big black chair on the port side of the bridge. "I think it's slowing."

The captain raised a hand: he had heard.

There was something indefinably calm about him. No danger could approach too near while he took his confident ease in that chair. Tsirtos took comfort from this and went back below.

Half an hour after that, Ho brought the soup.

"Hey," said Tsirtos happily to the chief steward. "Thick vegetable soup. Now I know we're in winter waters." He toasted the rock-steady Chinese. "First of the voyage," he said.

Half an hour after he drained the last drop of it, he started to vomit helplessly.

It was one of the worst storms Richard had seen, but there was really nothing in it to cause him more than a moment's worry. He was in a well-found, well-prepared ship. Only if the cargo had been incorrectly loaded; only if the tanks had been so inexpertly balanced as to put an unacceptable strain on *Prometheus*'s long hull, was there anything to fear. And if that had been the case, she would have broken up long ago. And he knew his godson well enough to have no doubts at all on that score. The wind could howl until it blew the world awry, therefore; the seas could become more mountainous than the Himalayas: they would not overwhelm his command. Nothing outside could seriously threaten the supertanker.

Ho appeared at his shoulder bearing a large tray well-stocked with brimming mugs of soup. He took one of them, amused to note that not a drop had been spilled on the long trip up from the galley.

Ho crossed next to Robin, then to Ben and John. "Some of this going below?'' asked Richard, knowing the answer would be in the affirmative: the engineers were just as much under the chief steward's wing as were the deck officers. '' 'Pity poor sailors on a night like tonight.' '' He raised his mug, saying the old toast to John, who grinned and toasted back. John was close, by the Collision Alarm Radar, the only one close enough to hear him above the cacophony of wind and sea.

This was still John's watch, though he would technically be relieved by Robin soon. But they were all on the bridge, of course, each doing a vital job, working as a well-trained team under the eagle eye of their captain, the only one of them apparently idle. And in the Engine Room it would be the same. Each engineering officer with his set task and particular responsibility, and Martyr overseeing, making sure each vital task was done well. Ready and able to do any task himself if necessary, and yet at the moment probably doing nothing.

He finished his soup and stood up. Angling himself carefully so as not to be thrown by the motion of the ship, he crossed to the chart table where Ben was carefully plotting their course, matching it to the course and reported size of the storm. "We'll be in the eye in ninety minutes, maybe two hours," Ben yelled, though they were close together. "We should be about here by then." He pointed to a spot farther south and west than Richard would have expected. Ben saw his frown. "Yes," he yelled. "It's pushing us over pretty fast. Lucky you gave us the extra sea room earlier. Be a bit embarrassing if we bumped into Africa!"

"Damn right! We'd better come to port a few more degrees." He went across to Robin by the helm to check on their exact heading. The compass read almost due south. They were at slow ahead, making about five knots, if the instruments could be trusted in this. Their heading and speed were only notional anyway. The storm, pushing on their port quarter, was moving them west almost as fast as they were heading south. The Agulhas current under their keel was in motion too, the whole mass of water moving like a river toward the Cape. And the hurricane wind above, of course, was using their massive superstructure like a sail.

He turned to his third mate. "Come to . . ."

He never finished what he was saying. Even as he spoke to her, in a ghastly sort of slow motion Robin sank to her knees. "What..." He went over to her and went down on one knee beside her. Her arms were crossed on her belly, her fingers buried in the taut flesh under her ribs, knuckles white. As he reached her, she rocked forward, obviously in acute pain. She was white as chalk, her eyes huge and wide with shock. "ROBIN..."

She vomited as he said her name, folding forward with the wrenching effort, smashing her forehead on the deck. He reached for her, but she could not straighten, her stomach obviously locked in a cramp. As he tried to lift her she vomited again.

He looked desperately over his shoulder. John was still by the Collision Alarm Radar, his own face looking pretty ghastly in the green glow from the dish. "JOHN!" he yelled.

The Manxman had taken two steps when the cramps hit him too. His face twisted, muscles writhing terribly. The angles of his jaw stood out in stark relief. His pipe fell to the floor, its stem bitten right through. Automatically, he tried to catch it and he lost his footing.

During the next minute they all went down, as though this were some kind of virulent plague spreading among them. One moment the bridge was functioning normally, the next they were all in fetal positions, puking helplessly on the floor. Even the helmsman slid down, the tiny wheel slipping from his numb fingers. And the agony hit Richard too, a massive shock that warned of severe damage to the system. From solar plexus to pubis, the muscles of his belly spasmed. Vomit flooded out of his throat, washing into the sensitive passages behind his nose, burning there and blinding him with tears. When he blinked them away, he found himself on the floor beside Robin, just behind the helmsman.

His whole body spasmed again, raising the hurt to the realms of agony, muscles tearing themselves as they wrenched beyond control. And yet they could not be beyond control. His mind, alert even under these circumstances, knew he must overcome this mutiny in his body and force it to his will or they were lost. And yet even to stand seemed an impossibility. He forced himself half erect, only to throw up and fall down again. Once more—

like some simian ancestor in Darwinian theory—he straightened his back and stood erect.

Three steps toward the helm console. Another spasm. He slipped in the mess and crashed forward, landing with his elbows on the icy metal of the console top. There was a microphone here. When the dry heaving had stopped, he bent the metal stalk until the wire mouthpiece touched his lips.

He pressed the button. "Engine Room," he whispered. He flipped to RECEIVE.

The noise of the answer confirmed his worst fears. But at least it was Martyr's voice. "Captain? It's bad down here."

"Here too. Keep going as best you can."

He pressed the button again. "Sparks ... Tsirtos ..."

The sound of helpless puking answered him. It caused his gorge to rise again. He controlled himself, feeling the effort draining him. God! He was weak!

"TSIRTOS!"

"Cap ... Captain ..."

"Can you radio for help?"

"... Try ..."

A hand came onto his shoulder and he actually jumped with the shock. He turned so quickly that his grip on the console slipped and he crashed to the floor again.

It was Robin. She had pulled herself up, obviously with as much grim effort as himself, and she stood now, filthy, agonized, sick unto death. Simply refusing to give in.

Richard rose, inch by inch until they were in a position to collapse against each other. Breathlessly, speaking almost in shorthand, sentences—often words—broken by bouts of heaving, they discussed what they should do.

She must take the helm and try to keep *Prometheus*'s head around into the storm, away from the dangers of the African coast. He must go below and check on the others. Tsirtos must be made to call for help. Anyone with any strength at all must be made ready to act when that help arrived.

In many ways, the most difficult bit was simply making it to the door. The atmosphere on the bridge was so foul now that he had to stop every few steps, find something to cling to, and puke weakly. Once or twice the cramps hit him again and he fell down. It was impossible to bend and check his other officers. He looked down on them with a rigid back as they lay curled on the floor, beyond help at the moment. At the door he looked back, just in time to see Robin fold forward, start to go down, and pull herself erect again, using the helm to support her. He could not express how proud that made him feel.

In the corridor, things were marginally better. Certainly, he could at least breathe without being overcome with nausea. Right from the start, he blessed whoever had retained the old-fashioned strong wooden railings along the corridor walls. Without these to cling to, his progress would have been slow indeed. As it was, he simply leaned upon them and collapsed forward into a staggering half run. This way, as long as his arms could bear him he made progress and, although he was weaker than a sickly child, he hardly fell down at all. The retching got worse, of course, now that his stomach was empty and dry.

The atmosphere in the radio shack set him off again. He found it hard to breathe, such was the twisting and heaving of his stomach and he stood crucified in the doorway, choking and sobbing for breath. Tsirtos was lying on his chest, backside just out of his filthy chair, chin just above his filthy desk, speaking into his radio like a ghost. Every once in a while—Richard stood there long enough to perceive a pattern in it—Sparks's left hand would depress the RECEIVE button, and Richard would hear a whisper of conversation from the headphones Tsirtos was wearing. Miraculously, the sick man was in communication with somebody. Hope and relief gave Richard added strength, though the simple good luck of the circumstances almost beggared belief. North and west of them, altering course even as they spoke, a mere three hours distant at the top of the green, were two South African oceangoing salvage tugs. If they could get their lines aboard in the relative calm of the storm's eye, they would take *Prometheus* back to the safety of Durban.

But there would need to be someone in the forecastle head to take the lines aboard.

Three hours. Automatically, Richard looked at his watch. As soon as his hand came away from the door frame, his legs gave out again and he crashed to his knees on the threshold, but he had made the calculation. They would be here at 22.30.

He crawled over to the nearest wall. He pulled himself erect and leaned on the railing once more, gasping as though he had just run a marathon. He was going to have to find himself some help.

The crew's quarters were as bad as the bridge—was there no one aboard who hadn't eaten that accursed soup?—but, just as on the bridge, the strongest were up and about. Salah Malik and Kerem Khalil met him at the door. In the event, although three hours seemed like a long time, they only just made it.

First, the three of them—they didn't feel like splitting up again—went down to the engine room to try to drum up another recruit or two. They were luckier here. McTavish had been in his bunk when the soup came and had only taken a sip or two before the others became ill. Martyr had used the relatively strong young Scot as a sort of workhorse to help and support the rest so that the Engine Room, though it reeked disgustingly like everywhere else, was comparatively orderly. The gaunt American, like the captain, had simply refused to give in, so he was still in charge.

Rice was beginning to come out of it, so Martyr agreed to keep the piratical Welshman and release the one strong man aboard to join the deck party. McTavish himself was less than enthusiastic about going on deck—and who could blame him?—but it had to be done and these were not the circumstances to ask for volunteers. The four of them went off like intrepid paraplegics to get their wet-weather gear.

Their strength did not return miraculously. They did not stop feeling sick; the stomach cramps did not abate. Nothing got easier. But they did what had to be done, inch by inch, little by little; knowing there was no alternative and therefore never pausing to count the cost.

By the time they had got themselves ready it was nearly ten o'clock. There was no real question of checking further on the others; it was enough to ride up a couple more decks than necessary, check with Tsirtos that the tugs were on schedule, then ride back down again in the blessed lift.

They took it for granted that the helm was—at the very least—still in the hands of the indomitable Robin. With luck, they reckoned, some others up there would have pulled themselves together by now as well. And, indeed, it seemed so: for as they exited the port A deck bulkhead doorway into the terrible night, all the deck lights came on.

In out of the massive howling blackness, there still tumbled gigantic seas, rearing out of the shadows, foam-webbed but slick like the backs of incredible monsters. The cloud cover was gone, however, save for a high, light scud; and the moon and stars were out.

Once in a while, at random points all around the compass card, great bolts of lightning would plunge down, defining the inner edges of the storm. On a level that was almost subliminal, below the occasional noises close by, they could hear the insane cacophony of it—like Armageddon all around them; in the distance and coming closer.

From side to side, the storm covered more than a thousand miles. A thousand miles of towering clouds reaching from wave-top to troposphere in unbroken columns of swirling air thirty thousand feet high; a thousand miles of banshee winds gusting to 150 miles per hour, a thousand miles of waves whipped up house-high from abyssal trough to mountainous crest.

But at the middle of the circle, at the hub of this madly whirling wheel, there was a disk of calm over one hundred miles across: the eye.

Around the outer edges of the eye the black battlements of cloud rose up. Through them the wild winds raved. Down them jumped the lightnings. Out of their foundations ran the tall, tall seas. But within them there was calm.

Down the center of *Prometheus*'s deck, among the pipes, fifteen feet in the unquiet air, three feet wide with railings four feet high, nine hundred feet long, there was a catwalk. There were eight steep steps up to it from the restless, foam-washed deck. Up these they went, in Indian file, Richard first and McTavish last, all hanging on to the railings for dear life. Although the wind had dropped, and the rain and clouds had gone for the time being, the sea was still running murderously high and the combination of movement and slipperiness was fatally dangerous to their weak legs and uncertain feet. Time and again one or another of them would go forward, back, to one side or the other with bone-shaking force. Elbows and knees had the flesh on them bashed away. Ribs were bruised, welted; cracked. Every few yards some-one would turn and retch helplessly down onto the deck.

There was little conversation, however, until they reached the forecastle head. Then Richard said, "If they're not here in twenty minutes or so, we'd better start back. If the storm closes down again and catches us out here in this condition, we're dead."

Nobody had the energy to point out that if they went back without securing the tugs' lines before the storm hit *Prometheus* again, then everyone aboard was as good as dead anyway.

But as it turned out, they had no real wait at all. The tugs came scudding down from the north almost at once, exploding out of the storm wall and igniting huge halogen searchlights visible for miles.

Time, of course, was relative, especially to the men on the forecastle head. One moment it seemed that the tugs were distant; the next they were all but alongside. One moment their great searchlights were mere beams shining up from the horizon like a distant antiaircraft battery; the next they were illuminating every nut and bolt nearby and making their faces like eyeless death masks carved in ice.

Lines came aboard. Light lines caught, eventually, secured to the winches and pulled until the towing cables rose like serpents from the sea. And when the fat, strong hawsers writhed up onto the deck, they had to be secured. And so they were. It was im-possible, but it was necessary. And so it was done.

But how it was done, no one could ever clearly remember.

There came a time when the lines were secure and the tugs, like tiny horses towing a huge barge, began to turn *Prometheus*'s head.

A time when the men stumbled back up the catwalk and into the warm bridge with the outriders of the returning storm threat-ening to overwhelm them at each faltering, exhausted step.

There was a time when McTavish returned to the Engine Room

and Richard via the shack—where he referred laconic tug captains to the owner—to the bridge. When Salah and Kerem joined Ho and his men, beginning to tidy up.

There came a time, now the storm had returned, when Richard and Robin stood side by side at the helm while intrepid shadows moved behind them, clearing the bridge and taking the stricken down to their bunks.

There came a dream time when the storm was gone and men with broad South African accents teemed out of helicopters on the deck and took over the running of the ship, but still the captain and his third mate would not leave the helm; nor would the chief leave the Engine Room.

There came a bright, winter-clear morning, brilliant after rain; and out of the heart of the morning came South Africa, and Durban where they could safely rest at last.

Atlantic

14

Sometimes, when conditions are right, off Cape Agulhas where Africa comes to its southernmost point forming a wedge between the oceans, there is a cliff of water. Ships going west must step down into the Atlantic. It is there because the warm Agulhas current, which sweeps constantly down the east coast, meets at this point the cold Benguela current, spawn of the perpetual West Wind Drift, which flows forever up the west coast to the equator.

At 09.00 Cape time on August 17, ten days later, *Prometheus* crashed forward over the twenty-foot sheer drop, causing even the sure-footed Robin Heritage to stagger.

Richard was seated behind her in the captain's chair and, inevitably, now, he found himself watching her; what was it they said? devouring her with his eyes. She had her back to him, gazing out over Salah Malik's shoulder as the Palestinian held the helm. He could see the merest ghost of her reflection in the window, just enough to guess at its expression: that tiny frown of concentration she habitually wore when wrestling with a problem. Her shoulders were squared, her hands clasped behind her. He watched the unconscious play of her long muscles as she rode the movements of the deck.

How well he knew every inch of that supple back. Dreamily, he watched the shoulders move microscopically, hips readjust, buttocks and thighs tense and relax.

He wondered what she was wearing under the starched, razor-creased, tropical kit. Probably the practical, almost unfeminine combination he had first seen while helping her back up the side after the wreck of the felucca. Certainly not the breathtaking confections she had favored in Durban.

In spite of all he had said about observing the proprieties once they got back aboard, he was still hungry for her.

The South Africans have a strained relationship with the huge ships that pass and repass their shores on the Cape run. Forbidden by OPEC embargo from obtaining the oil in their holds, they tend to see instead only the filth they leave behind. Sludge from illegally or carelessly cleaned tanks. Tar from oil dumped overboard by overladen ships in foul weather; slicks seeping from wrecks. It is oil in the only state they do not want it, for it decimates their fiercely protected coastal wildlife and puts at risk some of the most magnificent beaches in the world.

Richard expected the authorities in Durban to be less than polite, therefore. But this could not have been further from the case. They treated the whole crew, but himself, Robin, and the chief in particular, with something between kindness and awe. It robbed him of any real moral force when he came into conflict with them.

He dealt with—was dealt with by—a big, bluff, cheerful man called Jan van der Groot. Such men exist in any organization and are universally successful. Certainly Richard tried every tactic he could think of to enforce his will over the South African's and got nowhere. But he was playing from a position of absolute weakness. And van der Groot—"call me Jan, man!"—concealed beneath his bearlike bonhomie a steely resolve which, given the circumstances, could not be overcome. And the area of their disagreement was so small, Richard was soon made to feel positively petty.

Though when he talked it over with Robin he found she had run into the same wall for much the same reason, and van der Groot's charm had impressed her not at all.

As soon as they arrived in Durban, *Prometheus* was put into a specially prepared quarantine dock and everyone aboard was removed to the Addington Hospital overlooking the harbor for observation. Tests soon established virulent but relatively simple food poisoning; the suspect foodstuffs were destroyed and replaced. A thorough search of the ship at last revealed the final resting place of Hajji Hassan's bloated corpse. It was removed, and a postmortem held as soon as the relevant officers and crew were well enough to attend. A verdict of accidental death was returned.

As a gesture of respect for the strength of the officers above deck and below, especially that of the chief, the third mate, and the legendary captain, all of whom had remained at their posts, and technically in charge in spite of the distress signal, salvage claims were waived. A local harbor watch was put aboard, awaiting the return of the crew.

In the Addington—and afterward—things were not quite so simple. The deckhands and stewards had a ward each; the officers had rooms. Everything possible was done for their comfort. The doctors and nurses were kindness itself. Patients responded, for the most part rapidly. Put in his room at dawn on the 7th, Richard was well enough to receive van der Groot on the evening of the 9th and to check himself out on the 10th.

As soon as he was well enough to walk, he went around the others. First he checked on Robin, and he found her in better shape than he was himself, fuming from her first interview with van der Groot. Martyr, too, was on the mend, but some of the others were still in a bad way. Ben was in a coma—not dangerous, apparently, but not too healthy—being fed by a glucose drip. No one was allowed to disturb him. Rice, Napier, and John Higgins were almost as bad. A visit to the crew's quarters, accompanied this time by the restless Robin, revealed almost the same story. Some were nearly well again; some were still quite ill.

"About half our complement are well enough to go back aboard, Mr. van der Groot," said Richard firmly on the 9th.

"Call me Jan, man," boomed van der Groot in answer, with a broad grin.

"Quite. I'd like to get them back aboard as soon as possible, ah . . . Jan."

"Impossible, I'm afraid." The South African lost none of his charm. "We had to put together a slightly unusual package under the circumstances. Immigration were not too happy about letting you all in, my people not too happy about leaving your kaffirs out in the harbor to die. We came to an agreement, therefore. They agreed to let you all in together: we agreed to see you all out together."

"And that means, precisely?"

"What it says. Like any good crew, it'll be 'one for all and all for one.'" He saw Richard's growing impatience and leaned forward to explain in detail. "As the crew get better, we take them out of hospital and put them in the Seaman's Mission down by the docks. As the officers get better, they check out of the Addington and into the Edward Hotel. We have rooms reserved. When the last man is one-hundred-percent fit, we bundle up the whole lot of you and put you back aboard. All at once. Together. Not one at a time. Not in dribs and drabs. All at once. It's what we agreed. It's the way it has to be."

"And in the meantime?"

"You get better. You check into the Edward. You have a couple of days' holiday."

And that was that, bar the arguing. Except for the distant formalities of Hajji's inquest, which seemed to be looking into the death of someone utterly unattached to their current, fairy-tale existence. The practicalities were taken care of without Richard being involved—for all that he tried to be, in every stage of everything that affected the welfare of his crew. The owner, without contacting his captain except via telex, arranged such payment as was necessary; provided funds at the Standard Bank of South Africa for all officers and crew; even for the third mate, though she had independent funding of her own.

So, as each officer improved, he moved in Robin's footsteps down the road to the Edward Hotel on Marine Drive, and into a suite in one of the great hotels. There were no complaints, of course, but Robin, Martyr, and Richard all looked at their surroundings with a great deal of suspicion. During the day, the three of them were together quite a lot; visiting the sick and convalescent, attending the inquest, doing a little sightseeing, wandering, apparently aimlessly, round the docks.

In the evening, however, they split up. Martyr was a lonely

man who preferred his own company, spending most of his eve-
nings writing long letters that never seemed to be answered—as,
indeed, he did aboard ship. As the younger officers came out of
hospital so they entered into the swing of Durban nightlife, visiting
the nightclubs, especially those with the most daring cabarets.
Richard and Robin would have been thrown together by circumstances in any case, even had the chemistry not been so potently
at work.

Richard arrived at the Edward on the evening of the 10th, a
mere twelve hours after Robin had done so. They moved, with
the rest of the crew, back aboard *Prometheus* at 18.00 local time
on the 14th. The hours in between were like a honeymoon for
the two of them.

There was no hesitation, no courtship. These were people who
had known each other too long, knowing that in the other lay
almost everything they had always wanted. Robin had loved Richard to the exclusion of almost all others for ten years. Richard
saw in Robin everything that had attracted him so fiercely to
Rowena, plus a certain indefinable extra. An extra made up of a
heady combination: Robin's own strong, open character; the fact
that she shared all of his interests and preoccupations; the fact
that, subconsciously, subliminally, like a child with a beloved
parent, she mimicked him in so many ways. The combination
would have been irresistible, even had he felt the slightest inclination to resist.

It was a shock to him to see her at dinner on the 10th, dressed
as a woman. The sheer magnificence of her left him breathless,
choking like some callow boy on his first date. He had seen her
under a bewildering breadth of circumstances during the last
weeks; seen her fighting him for the position of third mate with
vivid passion, seen her turn humiliation into victory over Neptune, seen her throw away her life to help what she thought
might be a child in danger. Seen her refuse to give in to the
greatest extremes of physical discomfort when all around were
helpless. But he had never, until she swept like a princess into
the restaurant where he and Martyr awaited her, never seen her
as a woman.

They were dining in the hotel on that first night, the three of them together for the first and last time. They had put aside their vexation with the cheerfully intransigent van der Groot, put aside their worries about the others—and some of their suspicions about what was really going on here—and were simply dizzy with the joy of being alive; as would be any group of people who had survived what they had survived.

They were waiting for her in the cocktail lounge outside the Mandarin Room, with their table booked for 8.30. Both of them were in Number One whites, having had no chance to arrange civilian clothing, and individually were quite distinguished enough to be turning a few heads themselves as they sat at their ease at a table near the door.

The first they knew of her arrival was a sort of communal intake of breath. A rustle of movement as every head in the place turned. Richard glanced up with the rest and was suddenly unable to inhale.

She stood in the doorway, framed to perfection, accepting the reaction she was causing as of right—as Rowena had—but waiting there not for effect but because she could not see the others in the gloom. She had had twelve hours longer out of hospital than they, and had used some of that time to the greatest possible effect.

The golden curls had been cropped close to her head giving the effect of a glistening Juliet cap. Around the long neck, the theme of gold was taken up by a modest chain. Tanned gold too were the naked shoulders and back, the sheer slopes of the breast. And there it stopped, contained in black silk. The dress was by Chanel. It was tulip topped and backless, flowing out from a tight waist in a controlled cascade to the gathers midcalf. It was, like the necklace, simple as only the greatest art can be.

A perfect dress perfectly filled. The raw silk and the gold flesh complemented each other perfectly. Seemed to have been created for each other and probably had been. Richard stood, fighting the most ridiculous desire to applaud, and she saw him. Had she been breathtaking before, now she became incandescent, seeming to light the room as she crossed to him. He stood tall and awaited her, feeling for the first time in many years the cynosure of all eyes. Knowing from experience without a trace of vanity—that couples all around the room were looking at each other and almost nodding. Of course the golden girl was with the dashing, distinguished officer. Such creatures belonged together.

It was a feeling more powerful than the strongest drug.

"Hooks and eyes. At the back. Oh! Quickly!"

He fumbled, clumsy with desire.

They were in each others arms at last, in her room simply because it was the nearest, too impatient even to switch on the light. He slid his thumbs between the hot tight silk and the smooth skin, closing the sides of the dress together, twisting them back apart. And her hands were busy too, on his simpler, more accessible buttons.

The slick silk and the crisp cotton slid away miraculously at the same time and each partner paused, reveling in the sensation of skin on skin; of softness crushed against firmness; of heat building upon heat. They kissed again, crushing each other, terrified to slacken their grip in case the beloved slipped away. Yet slacken their grip they did at last, dominated by more than childish fears.

And later, when they lay in a tangle of bedsheets, she curled against him, his hands lazily exploring her back, learning her by feel in the dark like a blind man, he asked at long last, "Robin, what is all this about? Really?"

"I want you. I want you back. That's why I came out to *Prometheus*."

"Only your idea?"

She should have been shocked at the question, he knew: enraged at the implication. But he asked, somehow safe in the knowledge of her.

And she answered. "He's too proud. And anyway..."

They paused. There was no suspicion between them, no bitterness left. During the last few hours they had also laid Rowena, in the way she would have appreciated most, to rest. It was time for the simple truth, and they both knew it.

And the truth did not seem so very dreadful, after all.

"Oh, Richard! I'm so very worried about him. He won't tell

me—and I can't find out for sure—but I think there's something dreadfully wrong. He hasn't been the same since Rowena died. He seems weaker, somehow; hesitant. But it's more than that now. He's been seeing his doctor, usually when I'm at sea and he thinks I won't find out. He's had a whole battery of tests and I think he was afraid that he had a brain tumor."

"And has he?"

"No! Not as far as I can find out. But there is something. And he still does the strangest things..."

"Like buying the oil?"

"Like waiting until I took the first holiday in years and *then* buying the oil. I was halfway to the Seychelles when I found out. It was quite by accident. I'd forgotten to tell my secretary I wanted complete rest and he telexed me the news. He had my itinerary— he'd booked all my flights—and the message caught up with me on Bahrain. I came south instead of heading on east. Came onto *Prometheus* instead of onto the beach."

"Some holiday!"

"Some lifeguard."

There was a silence, then she continued. "If he was his old self, I might have suspected it all as a convoluted plot to bring us together..."

"With what object?"

"To bring you back," she conceded. But there was no reluctance about the concession.

"Explain."

"Well, as I see it, it really takes two to run the company. One in London and one at sea. I can take care of either end. But if he feels he can't handle the other end, for whatever reason..."

"All this, just because he wants me back as son and heir? Gambling much more than he can afford to loose, if the papers are correct?"

"No. It's not just that. It's me, too. It's what I've always wanted. He knows that. He would never have risked it all for himself. But for me..."

Silence.

"I'm all he has left..."

Silence.

"And there's so much there, Richard! So much to be done."

A lesser man might have used Crewfinders as an excuse. Someone not so deeply in love, less involved than he. Someone wishing to keep his distance, to retain a sense of proportion; to hold on to a little sanity. But Richard had been too sane for too long. There would be a way to guard his own beloved company and still to help the Heritages.

And she was right. There was so much to be had. It was breathtakingly exciting.

As was she . . .

So, at 09.20. Cape time, August 17, with Robin still on watch, seemingly unaware of his hot gaze on her back, Richard pulled himself up out of his big captain's chair and crossed to the chart table. For a few moments he stood studying the chart lying under the clear plastic sheet: the chart of the Southwest Atlantic.

It was time to turn north for home.

15

During the first ten days of sailing north they covered four thousand miles. As the long, glass-green Atlantic swells passed with monotonous regularity under her giant keel, *Prometheus* returned also to routine—except in one area: during that time she was redecorated from stem to stern, from keel to truck, wherever storm had damaged or sickness soiled her.

Only the Pump Room remained untouched.

The routine, of course, centered around the captain and his day. The routine had come into being early in the voyage. It had varied according to circumstance but it was honed to peak efficiency now. Even though he was surrounded by properly qualified officers, the quiet Englishman seemed to be involved with everything, available at all hours.

Richard's day began at 06.30 when the chief steward brought him his teak-dark morning tea. At 07.00 he would appear on the bridge and relieve John Higgins of the last hour of his watch. At 08.00, when Robin came on watch, the captain went down to breakfast. He ate and chatted for half an hour then retired to his dayroom to put the finishing touches to the agenda for his daily conference, which began at nine on the dot and was attended by all officers except those on watch. It was a rigid ninety minutes long and concerned every aspect of the day-to-day running of the ship. It was here that the exhaustive—exhausting—work schedules for the ship's redecoration originated; and everything else that affected the lives of all aboard.

At 10.30 coffee was served, and, in the more relaxed atmosphere, any other problems could be brought to the captain's notice. At 11.00, Richard returned to his dayroom to centralize and generate the paperwork arising from these meetings—notices read quietly but clearly over the ship's PA system; notices punctiliously typed and individually signed to be displayed on the various notice boards.

At noon precisely, the PA would sound and the gentle but compelling tones would say, "Your attention. Your attention, please. This is the captain speaking..." and everything would come to a halt while officers and crew alike would listen to the daily notices; any items of news that Tsirtos passed up from the World Service of the BBC; the official figures of miles sailed since yesterday, exact position now, time left before destination was reached; the exact bearing of Mecca for the Moslems among the seamen; and—most importantly (at least, so suspected C. J. Martyr watching these eccentric English officers)—the latest score in the current test match.

He lunched lightly from a tray in his dayroom but always appeared on the bridge at one o'clock, when the first officer went to lunch. He would hold the bridge watch until three, pacing up and down, his eyes everywhere, restless fingers setting everything just as he liked it. Restless hands clearing the chart table of everything except the current chart (only on the rarest occasions was there anything else there: his officers respected his neatness in a way that many captains would envy to the foundations of their souls) setting out the pencils in regimented rows like Guards on parade. At first even Ben Strong thought this endless adjusting and readjusting petty and irritating. Then it occurred to him that in an emergency, the captain would know where everything was, right down to the smallest item that he might need.

At three, Strong returned to the bridge to complete the last hour of his watch and Richard was released to prowl the ship on an unofficial captain's inspection. Between three and four, everyone aboard who was involved in anything of importance could expect a visit from the captain and a few quiet words of encouragement. On the rare occasions when something was not up to standard, corrections would be suggested mildly: only if corrections had not been instituted by the next visit was censure actually employed. Richard didn't want them to think he was trying to catch them out. Actually, they thought nothing of the sort, vying like students with a popular professor, each trying to outdo the others and impress him most.

At four he returned to his dayroom to complete the day's paperwork, sometimes visiting the bridge to check the logs, but never interfering at that time; "Not actually there at all," as he put it.

At six, 18.00 hours, he and Martyr, newly showered and shaved, in clean uniforms, proceeded like some theatrical double act down to the Officers' Lounge for Pour Out. Like the noon announcements, this was an unvarying ritual of the day. They drank and chatted for three-quarters of an hour. Dinner was served at 6.45. At 7.30, they would return to the Officers' Lounge. Richard had not been absolutely idle—or utterly lovestruck— when in Durban. His negotiations with the owner had resulted in a laden relief ship coming out, as was routine, from Cape Town bearing all sorts of goodies, most welcome among them a library of two hundred books and a selection of watchable videos. Having arranged for them, however, Richard did not avail himself of them. He would chat for a further half hour, then go up to the bridge. From 20.00 to 22.00, while she had dinner and watched the film if she wanted, he kept the third officer's watch. But Robin never actually watched a film either. Instead, she would eat as quickly as possible and return to the bridge.

Nobody made any comment about this. You would have thought it was the rule rather than the exception for captains and junior navigation officers to share two quiet hours of each others' company around sunset each evening. Between 10.00 and 10.30—the only timing that was not particularly precise in the routine—the captain would silently leave the bridge.

In his dayroom, he would do paperwork or read until 11.55; then he would rise again and return to the bridge one last time. At the end of her watch, at midnight, Robin would accompany him below. Silently, almost like children about some secret adventure, they would creep down to the Officers' Galley and make themselves a cup of cocoa.

Then if the third officer came back to his cabin with her captain, there was never any evidence of it next morning when the routine began all over again.

In the bustle of redecoration, Tsirtos found it easy enough to wander round the ship at odd hours without arousing too much suspicion. But he was always wary. A willing part of the late Captain Levkas's plans, with responsibility for some action, he felt increasingly isolated from the rest of the crew as the time to take that action came inexorably nearer. As he had said to Martyr on the night the old officers died, Nicoli had found him this berth, got him involved in this lucrative business. But Nicoli had also been his only contact with what had been planned and now that he and the others had been replaced, nobody at all seemed to know what was going on. Tsirtos became nervous, then genuinely scared. He began to wander around the ship trying to discover—without asking too directly—who else was involved. Nobody at all rose to his bait. In the grip of an increasing sense of unreality, he began a systematic search of the ship, for he knew that, in secret places, there were things like life rafts hidden, left by those dead men who had wanted to make assurance double sure. It seemed to Tsirtos that if he were going to act alone and abandon ship alone, a life raft would serve him better than one of the lifeboats in any case.

He first became convinced that there were ghosts following him at 03.27 on the morning of the 19th, just as he found the life raft hidden on the forecastle head. He had risen sometime earlier, determined to make a thorough examination of the deck, starting with the forecastle head. It was dangerous, he knew, to go wandering around out there in the dark with too large a torch—he would be seen by the officer of the watch. He took the smallest of lights, therefore, secure in the knowledge that there was no watch in the forecastle head tonight and that the light he was carrying was unlikely to cast its beam ten feet, let alone a thousand, when he switched it on.

There was no question of his creeping down the catwalk. That was far too risky. Instead he slipped out of the starboard side door of A deck and tiptoed stealthily forward, guided between the various obstacles by the light of the stars and a nail-paring moon. It was a sultry night. They were north of Walvis Bay at that time, though well out, and heading back into the heat. There was a faint, salt-smelling wind, just enough to whisper over any obstacle or irregularity. The Benguela current pushed them over the Walvis Ridge and the great long Cape swells rose higher, became busier against the hull. There was an air of stealthy activity about the ship that only became apparent when one left the antiseptic confines of the bridge. Though from the bridge, carried magically to him by the whispering wind, came the haunting music one of the stewards played nightly on some strange Oriental flute.

The infinitely distant music, the ghostly bustle, insinuated themselves into his subconscious as he crept along the deck; of such things, perhaps, are hauntings made—if of nothing more. Certainly by the time he reached the faint moon shadow of the Sampson post halfway down the deck, Tsirtos was beginning to suspect that he was not alone. Under the uncertain starlight, the deck stretched vastly away. The safety of the bridge was already distant; the lights already dim. The night gathered itself around him.

Of course, he had been used from childhood to the vagaries of the dark, raised in a Peloponnesian village south of Neapolis, overlooking Kíthera and Crete, which, even when he left to go to sea had still to be connected to any electricity supply. But this night was different from the sage-scented, cicada-singing nights of his childhood. This night smelled of salt and oil and cooling iron. There was nothing in it but the whispering of the wind, the chuckling of the sea, that lone flute like a lost soul crying. There were no familiar hillsides, bush-clothed and precipitous; only the geometric, unnatural planes of the pipe-divided deck. The farther out he went, the more the steel claimed him, having a sort of spirit of its own: cold, inhuman, overpowering.

Conscious of none of this, he crept forward, his way illuminated only by the heavens, and that light shadowed now and then by the faintest trace of high scud.

The forecastle head was more lonely than he could ever have imagined, a great metal blade coming to its blunt point far from the rest of the ship, seemingly; far, far from the rest of humanity. Under only the sibilant wind and the faint, shrouded sky, like the last man at the most distant end of the world, a sort of rapture overcame him; like the rapture of the deep, of high places and great spaces. The sort of rapture that kills.

It crept up on him, however, for he was at first preoccupied with his search. On the forecastle head itself there was a maze of heavy equipment. The massive winches, one each side, which raised and lowered the anchors. The great posts, in pairs, to which the tow ropes had been connected on the way in to Durban, all sorts of equipment which, as radio officer, Tsirtos was rarely if ever called to deal with. But someone else was, regularly. That was the problem. Who would be stupid enough to hide something in or near a regularly used piece of equipment? If anything had been hidden in the winches, for instance, would it not have been discovered or destroyed when the South African tugs' hawsers were being winched aboard? Where else was there out here in this terrible place? Increasingly nervously, he switched on his torch and flashed it around. And its weak beam fell upon the spare anchor.

Prometheus had two anchors ready to be deployed, hanging from the massive hawse holes athwart the bow. Like most great ships, she had a third, for emergencies, in case one of the others was lost. And it was kept out here, fastened securely to the deck. Tsirtos crossed to it at once, certainty flooding through him. Certainty well placed. Wedged under the anchor, well out of sight of all but the most prying eyes, was a large black canvas bag. Tsirtos pulled it out and opened it. Inside was a deflated rubber life raft, packed tight. On top of this was a box the size of a small hamper. It was locked, but the lock was weak. Inside the box was a radio, a neatly packed bundle of emergency rations, survival equipment, fresh-water distillation equipment, and a handgun. Tsirtos was tempted to take the gun, but thought better of it in the end. He would only have to find another hiding place for it, and he was not confident of finding one as good as this. Well, if the person who had hidden this were still aboard, he would have to move very fast indeed to beat Tsirtos down here when the crunch came. And if it belonged to one of the dead men, Tsirtos was sure he would not begrudge it.

He began to pack it away, still thinking about those dead men, unconsciously soaking up the atmosphere of the vast night around him. He could not begin to understand the forces within and without that held him as helplessly as Robin had been held by the bow wave against the side of the ship. Unable to comprehend the dark wonder of what was really happening to him, he translated what he was feeling into a superstition he could more readily accept.

On the vastness of the forecastle head he suddenly turned, breathless. "Nicoli?" he whispered.

But Nicoli did not answer, preferring to tease him with the almost-silence.

"NICOLI!" he screamed.

Nicoli, ghostly, chuckled in the darkness with a voice like water on steel. And mad Gallaher was there in the shadows as he rose.

Tsirtos flashed the torch around increasingly wildly, not caring who might see it from the bridge. But they hid from him, Nicoli, Gallaher, Kanwar, and the others, lurking at the edges of shadows, always in the corners of his eyes. Their dead voices murmured just behind him; their dead fingers touched his neck. He suddenly realized just how far he was away from the light: how absolutely alone he was way out here in the dark.

Covered with sweat, fighting the shakes, using his torch to light every inch of the way and lucky to be overlooked by Ben Strong on watch, he stumbled all the agonizing, terrifying distance back into the brightness of the empty bridge where the accusatory murmurs lay just beneath the grumble of the generators.

In his cabin, he began to recover; and as he did so, he began to make his plan. No matter what the cost, he had to get to that life raft first, as soon as *Prometheus* began to sink.

16

It was a hot night. There was no moon. A high overcast obscured most of the stars. *Prometheus* was just coming east of north. She was at 14 north and 18 east, less than two hundred miles off the coast of Senegal.

Some of the general restlessness might have been attributable to these facts. Even in the air-conditioned confines of the accommodation areas something of the night's heat lingered. And these latitudes traditionally proved dangerous to ships. Even ships the size of *Prometheus*. For these were pirate waters. Not those sailed by Edward Teach or Henry Morgan, but waters where from time immemorial right up to the present day, it has been a flourishing village industry for men to crowd into the largest boats available and sail out on dark nights to surprise ships that pass too near.

VLCCs have long proved favorite targets—if hard ones to reach, for they sail far out. They have small crews. They sail unarmed. Even those few who do carry officers with guns do so more for show than effect, for who is going to risk a spark from a ricochet setting the cargo alight?

But *Prometheus* had nothing to fear from African pirates that night. It was the last-but-one night of August, thirteen days since they turned north. The Cape Rollers that had followed them almost to the equator had moderated and they had left the Flying Dutchman's haunted waters without the expected crisis overtak-

135

ing them. This good luck in spite of the report by Nihil the flute player of a distant, pale three-master heaving up over the horizon at midnight exactly four days ago, then turning away and running south, glowing eerily as she went. There had been a stir among the superstitious at the news: it meant there was bad luck coming.

The signal came in at midnight. Tsirtos was in the shack, not because he was really expecting the signal anymore, but because he had been put aboard to be in that place at that time and so he was. And the signal came in at midnight. Absolutely. Unmistakably. When and as expected—in spite of the fact that everything had changed.

He made no acknowledgment: there was none to make. He simply sat, unbelieving, looking at the equipment in front of him as though it had changed, become monstrous, nightmarish.

He knew the routine. He was to destroy the radio and then take the message to Nicoli. Nicoli would take the message to Captain Levkas. The captain would sound "abandon ship." They would all pack their suitcases and stock up with everything they needed or wanted before reporting to the lifeboats. They would abandon leisurely but would explain to their rescuers in a day or so's time that there had been too much urgent confusion for any logs or records to be saved.

There would be no distress calls broadcast except from the lifeboats later.

The last man off would be Nicoli and he would have opened the sea-cocks so *Prometheus* would sink swiftly, silently, and deep.

But Nicoli and all the rest were dead. Who to tell, therefore; what to do? He sat for a moment in an agony of indecision. But he hadn't been put here to hesitate. There was only one course of action that he could see: the one he had been preparing for since he discovered the life raft. He would do his bit and then get off *Prometheus* just as fast as he could. He leaned forward and hit the button he had watched Gallaher add to the equipment nearly two months ago. There was a fierce hiss from behind the radio equipment and a cloud of acrid smoke filled the shack as it all destroyed itself. He slammed the Radio Room door on the first billow and ran down toward the main deck. The sense of being alone in all this was compounded by the normality of the scenes he stealthily sped past. Past the Officers' Galley, its door ajar, where the captain and his third officer were drinking their cocoa looking back over the ship's pool and her fluorescent wake in the dark sea astern; past the crews' quarters where the hum of quiet, sleepy conversation was punctuated by the plaintive wailing of Nihil's flute; past the Cargo Control Room, empty now, where the computers stood in rank upon rank, their lights shining like multicolored stars, overseeing the safe disposition of every drop of cargo aboard. And out through the A deck bulkhead door onto the main deck itself.

Into the arms of "Slugger" Napier taking a breather at the end of his watch before he turned in for the night.

"Here!" said the big Mancunian, catching hold of him. "What's your game?"

In a frenzy of impatience, Tsirtos tore away and ran for the forecastle head. He had gone only half a dozen steps before Napier tackled him. Wrapped around each other like all-in wrestlers, they rolled toward the Pump Room hatchway in the center of the deck immediately in front of the bridge. Desperately, knowing he would be no match for the huge English bully in anything even approaching a fair fight, Tsirtos drove his head up into Napier's face. His forehead connected shrewdly with Napier's nose, flattening it even more. The huge engineer pulled back and Tsirtos thought he had won. He wriggled out of Napier's embrace and gathered himself to get up. He never even saw the left hook that caught the point of his jaw with professional perfection. His head slammed back against the deck and that was that.

Like Gallaher, he was unconscious when he died.

Gallaher's bomb had two timers. The first, the clock, had been reading 00.00 for uncounted hours; it should have detonated days ago. It had failed to do so because Nicoli had knocked loose a wire when he touched it. The second was a much more simple device, designed to trigger five minutes after Tsirtos destroyed the radio. It was a little fail-safe the Irishman had included in this bomb to make certain it did its job. Gallaher had reckoned on being safe and sound back in Durban when it went up in any case.

It triggered now.

The second part of the bomb was plastique, carefully molded to spread its force sideways among the pipes like a scythe through corn. Because Nicoli had moved it, however, its force cut up and down instead of side to side. It destroyed not many pipes but one, filling the air with microscopic droplets of oil from the bunkerage—the oil used to drive *Prometheus's* engine.

The third part of the bomb, designed to detonate a millisecond after the plastique, was a magnesium-based incendiary. Working with the air-suspended droplets released by the first explosion, it created a fireball that blew open the decking beneath Tsirtos and vaporized both him and Napier at once. It blew away the great steel door below and filled the corridor with flame. It would have incinerated anyone nearby, but the engineering decks were empty at that time.

It is doubtful whether the lethal firefighting equipment could have stopped the process even had the canisters been as full as their faulty gauges boasted. But they were mostly empty, so the fire burned unabated.

The deck split open. The Pump Room hatch flew away like a champagne cork but that was nowhere near enough to alleviate the forces unleashed by the exploding oil. The deck split open from the foot of the bridge to the front of the coffer-dam space separating the engineering area from the first cargo tank. The edges of the wound folded back, white-hot in an instant, into a gap more than ten feet wide, nearly twenty feet long.

Up out of the steel volcano came a column of force too great to be called mere fire. As it rose it pushed the air above it to either side with incredible power.

All the windows on the front of the bridge exploded inward.

As it passed, it sucked air back with hurricane strength into the vacuum left behind it.

Everything loose on the bridge was sucked out except for those things closest to the floor.

The helmsman and the watchkeepers never stood a chance. They were mowed down by the shrapnel glass from the windows coming in. And what was left of them, before it had time to fall, before it had time to do anything other than mark the scorched back wall, was sucked back out a second later as though it had never been.

So that John Higgins, at the rear of the port bridge wing trying to get a decent midnight shot of the stars, was aware only of a terrible screaming roar that robbed him of sense and breath, which was there and was too much to bear—and which was gone in an instant.

John pulled himself to his feet—though he would never remember falling down—and staggered over to the bridge door. The handle was hot and the door stiff, but he tore it open and ran onto the bridge. He was utterly alone. Stunned, he looked out of the holes that had been the windows down into the volcano on the deck. The first blast may have passed but there were still combustibles out of control down there. The decking below him was curved up into a blistered, dully glowing hillock sloping most strongly to port and starboard. Through the ragged lips of the opening at its summit, white-hot flames still roared, their breath enough to singe his eyebrows, fifty feet above.

One look was enough. He hit the emergency button.

Then, thankfully, Richard was there by his shoulder. John had never been so glad to see anyone in his life. "You all right?" asked the captain. John could only nod.

"Pray the PA is still working," said Richard, coolly in control even under these unimaginable circumstances. "You'd better get below, John. Find Robin. I left her in the Officers' Galley." Then he spoke crisply into the microphone. "Attention. Your attention, please. This is the captain speaking. There is a fire in the Pump Room and we are in danger of exploding. Abandon ship. Abandon ship."

In the confusion after Richard gave the order to abandon, the man who had poisoned the soup had no real difficulty in sneaking away alone. The tanker might explode; it might not: there was still work to be done.

The saboteur's course was fraught with danger. The possibility of an imminent explosion he took for granted, quelling his fear with thoughts of the immensity of his reward if this continued according to plan.

Where in hell's name had that bomb come from? Acutely, for he was a greedy man, not a stupid one, he suspected that the bomb had been part of the original plan, the one that had died with the bulk of Levkas's crew. What incredible luck that it should have gone off just at the right moment. Ah, but was it good luck or bad? Only time would tell. In the meantime, there was no use crying over spilled milk. It had certainly panned out suspiciously well for the owner. No one was likely to question the loss of a ship that blew up and sank with most of the crew still aboard.

These dark musings served to take him down to deck level where he almost met some of the crew. A line of wounded men—he could not see how badly they were hurt from the shadows where he hid himself—being led to safety by Kerem Khalil. He avoided them with ease and, pausing only to check in the burned-out wreck of the Radio Shack, he headed for his first destination.

The Cargo Control Room was a mess too. He should have foreseen that, but it came as a surprise to him. One glance through the splintered door was enough to tell him it would be useless to enter. All the machines were dead. The shattered windows were so full of searing flames from the Pump Room that he turned away at once, drenched in sweat. So plan number one—insurance number one—was ruined. All that time setting it up in Durban had gone to waste after all. Now he had to go on down below. It was the heat, he told himself, not fear, that made him sweat. And, indeed, the heat was building fiercely as he went down. As though he were nearing the center of the earth, he told himself. Or hell. Yes, all in all hell was much more likely. But down he plunged regardless, into the bowels of the ship.

The noise increased disproportionately as soon as he got beneath deck level. It became a deafening roar, echoing through the corridors as though the ship were bellowing like a beast in agony. He was used to the incessant grumble of engine or generators, which caused a perpetual trembling in everything aboard, but this was infinitely louder and dangerously overpowering. A deafening, disorienting din that made the floor vibrate so hard the soles of his feet itched unbearably and his teeth chattered painfully. Were the walls shaking, or was it just that his eyeballs were trembling in their sockets? Tears sprang onto his cheeks, born of the acrid smoke and the juddering of his eyes. He leaned against a rail to catch his breath, but the vibration only shot up his arm and caused his very heart to palpitate. He thought only of the half a million pounds he had been promised; it bolstered up his courage. And after a moment more he went on with his secret mission to ensure the death of the ship. Unable now to log in his secret program on the cargo control computers to move the cargo and break her in two, he was going to open the sea-cocks and let the Atlantic into her. Even ablaze as she was, he could not rely on her cargo blowing up. And her destruction had to be ensured.

The Engine Control Room was empty. He glanced around it quickly and did not linger. His mission must take him farther down still.

His procedure for opening the sea-cocks and flooding the ship was designed to be relatively simple. Down here, out of the way, in a place where it would not be too hard for the engineers to overlook it, was a switch. As soon as it was turned, the sea-cocks would begin to open. Not too complicated, even under these circumstances, which were so much worse than anything ever envisioned. And so discreet! And it was very nearly foolproof, granted only two things: granted that he could get to the switch, and granted that the generators maintained enough electrical flow to make the system work. But if the ship's power died, the switch would be useless. And in the final analysis, after all he had been through, after all his bravery, all his intrepid greed, it was the generators that let him down. He was deep in the ship, in the same place—though on the opposite side—as the one in which Hajji had died, with his fingers actually fastened on the switch itself, illumined by the beam of his torch, when the distant lights went out and that all-important element of the background noise fell silent. He flicked the switch up and down, thwarted at last: absolutely nothing happened.

The saboteur was overcome at once by dread. At first he imagined that the Engine Room must have flooded and he waited for several dreadful seconds anticipating that first cold lick against his legs that would tell him he was dead. It did not come. Thankfully, he began to move—the switch now useless and his presence here pointless. He turned and began to pick his way back along the path that had brought him here. His first priority now was to obey his captain's last order and abandon.

But his steps, which had been quick enough in bringing him here through the fully illuminated ship, were slower now. The dark was an oppressive force. It had weight. It wrapped itself around him like a blanket. The sensation became so vivid that he found it hard to breathe. He pulled a shaking hand down over his running face, gathering enough cold sweat to flick an enormous shower of it away into the massive darkness.

In the Engine Control Room there was a glimmer of light. It did not come from any of the consoles—they were all dark. As were all the hi-tech aids on the bridge now: *Prometheus* without her generators was blind, deaf, dumb: dead. The light came, a reflection of a reflection, glancing off bright surfaces, round corners, up and down, from the sun-bright furnace of the Pump Room.

And still there had been no further explosion.

But that was nearly a miracle now. Even knowing what he knew of that, he could no longer subdue the fear under promises of massive wealth. He had to escape. Now.

He swung the broad, bright beam of his torch over to the door and lit up the startled face of the chief engineer.

"What..." said Martyr, blinded.

The saboteur hurled himself forward, silently offering a prayer of thanks that the brightness of the beam masked him, but at the same time cursing the chief for being here now. Why was he here? Had he come to try to fix the generators so that the others could abandon in greater safety? Or was it he who had switched them off, trying even now to save the ship? The terrible suspicion flashed into the saboteur's mind just as their bodies met.

They met with a shock of force, two big men charging for each other full-tilt. The torch spun out of the saboteur's hand and rolled away across the floor. Then, but for that vague light from the furnace at the ship's heart, they fought in darkness. And, but for their guttural grunts of effort or pain, in silence.

As each was aware of the other only as a darker presence in the surrounding shadows, as the slightest of sounds amid the jarring rumble of the fire, they did not stand back and fight each other scientifically. They closed with each other and half wrestled, throwing in great invisible punches where and when they could; sometimes connecting with each other, sometimes with the steel-hard objects around them. They crashed back against the doorframe, the saboteur driving his head into Martyr's face so that the back of his head smashed stunningly against the wood. The tactic was repeated, equally successfully, before the saboteur drove his knee up into his opponent's groin. This was not so successful. His knee hit the same edge as Martyr's head, turning what should have been the coup de grace into a painful retreat. Martyr shambled forward, punching out by instinct, connecting once by luck. The saboteur hurled forward once more, ducking under the blows to drive his shoulder into the chief's lean belly. The American folded forward and his opponent straightened at once, bringing the bludgeon of his skull back into play.

This time Martyr fell to his knees, badly stunned. The saboteur stepped back and unleashed a massive kick, knocking Martyr onto all fours. Another, from the side, rolled him right over, and he kept rolling, trying to avoid the merciless feet; but he collapsed motionless in the torch's beam as one last kick relentlessly tore into the side of his head.

The saboteur stood, choking for breath, more shocked than exhausted, wondering feverishly what he could use as a weapon. In the final analysis he used the torch because no other club was to hand and his fists were simply too sore.

The first blow, to the back of Martyr's head, broke the bulb so the rest was done in darkness.

Oddly enough, after the first three or four blows—the saboteur was striking wildly and taking no account of numbers—Martyr stirred feebly and started fighting back. He clawed at the saboteur's face and they wrestled briefly for a moment or two. It was an uneven struggle and the American soon collapsed back against the foot of the nearest console. He did not move again. But the victim was now lying face-up, and this made a terrible difference to the would-be murderer. Blind in the darkness, he translated every variation of impact communicated to his sweating palm by the rubberized handle of the torch into a vivid mental image. With his eyes tight closed, he nevertheless saw all too clearly what he was doing as Martyr's long face disintegrated under the wild onslaught.

He saw teeth come bloodily through lips and splinter. He saw the chin shatter and the jawbone break open. He saw the nose crushed and the temples collapsed. He saw the whole face ruined to a gargoyle horror of a death mask before he hurled the torch aside and ran like a lunatic from the place.

He came out onto the starboard side of the stricken ship, having run wildly through the furnace of the A deck corridor, leaving footprints of molten rubber behind him from the soles of his desert boots. The emptiness of the port side had alerted him to the probability that the main escape had been made from the opposite side while he had been on his abortive mission below.

And sure enough, although the forward, smaller lifeboat hung in splinters from its davits, the other two big boats, each capable of carrying forty at a pinch, were gone. It came to him then, with a force that brought a cry of alarm to his lips, that he was utterly alone on the doomed ship. Alone except for the man whose face he had just beaten in.

He tensed himself to dash down the length of the deck, past that horrific column of fire, to his life raft, hidden under the spare anchor on the forecastle head.

But then, above the dreadful roaring of the fire, he heard a voice. "Here's one!" it yelled to someone far away. Close by, between him and his distant goal. No way past but to kill again.

The murderer turned. "Here!" he called.

A figure appeared beside him, its features masked in shadow. The only light on the stricken ship coming from the column of fire before the bridge. "Glad to've found you," said the figure. "Seen any of the others?"

"Who's still missing?" asked the murderer, as though he, too, had been looking.

"Nobody's seen the chief since the generators went."

"No," said the murderer. "I went down to the Engine Room to see if I could help, but there's nobody there at all."

"You sure? We'd hate to lose the chief."

"Absolutely certain," said the murderer decisively. "If there was anyone alive down there I'd definitely have seen him."

"That's it, then," said the other. "Let's go."

17

Richard fought to keep the big lifeboat snug against the side of his blazing ship as the last of Salah Malik's search party climbed down the rope ladder into her. Even down here the sound and the heat were incredible. He licked the sweat off his upper lip and squinted upward trying to see how many more were to come.

The smaller lifeboats, the port one of which he and Martyr had used to rescue Slope, had been reduced to kindling by the blast. They had taken the two large ones from the starboard side, though all of them could have fitted into one in a pinch, in case they needed extra of anything, or in case the equipment in one proved faulty. Robin was in charge of the other one. If he looked over his shoulder he would be able to see her lights seemingly on the horizon, but actually only a couple of hundred yards distant. She had McTavish and Rice with her, together with Kerem Khalil, "Twelve Toes" Ho, and some of the wounded.

He had the rest with him and was waiting now only for Tsirtos, Ben, John Higgins, Martyr, Napier, an unknown number of GP seamen—say five. That meant ten in all still missing.

While he waited, his mind was occupied, his stinging eyes were busy, watching the silhouetted figures coming over the high side, then changing magically from black to white against the black cliff of *Prometheus*'s hull. After Malik only two more figures appeared, and he began to fear the worst even before John, the first

146

aboard, came up the length of the boat and reported. "Tsirtos is gone, Richard. The shack is a mess. It looks sabotaged to me. I doubt he even had time to send a mayday. Napier and the chief are still missing. Salah says two of his men are also unaccounted for. There must be seven more seamen and stewards dead. We've searched everywhere. No sign of life at all. And, with the generators down now too, I'm afraid there's no real chance of finding anyone else, even if they're still alive."

He had hardly finished speaking when Ben was at his side, and his terse report confirmed everything the second mate had said. "That's it, then," said Richard crisply. "Let's go before she blows. There'll be time to mourn them later, when all the rest are safe."

He gunned the engine and pulled the tiller toward him. The big lifeboat gathered way, heading out into the cool dark to join her sister in a great arc to starboard.

Nobody was sitting idle. By the light of the big battery-and-oil-powered lamps, they were tending the wounded, most of whom had suffered bad cuts from flying glass; a few of whom had been deafened and blinded and scorched by the blast. Luckily nobody was too badly hurt. The simple fact was that the explosion had been so fierce that anyone who had been close enough to get themselves seriously injured was dead. Only those well clear or well protected had survived, though everybody, it seemed, was covered in scratches, cuts, and bruises.

While the wounded were being seen to by Ben and Malik, John was checking through the stores, starting, in the light of what they now suspected about Tsirtos, with the radio. Nobody had much to say, or any real occasion to speak. There was the odd murmured instruction to a wounded man, a stifled groan or two; but generally, as they came out of the rumble of the fire into the silence of the night, there was only the growl of the lifeboat's engine and the soft slap of the waves.

So the concern in John's voice as he said to Ben, "Would you mind shining that lamp over here a moment?" was evident to everyone at once.

"What is it?" asked Richard.

"Dunno. This radio . . . Thanks, Ben . . ."

The silence returned for a few more minutes, then, "Nope. That's the damnedest thing. Ben, was it okay when you tested it?"

"Fine," replied the first mate. Then, with gathering concern, "Why..."

John interrupted him. "Could anyone have put them out of action since?"

"Wouldn't have thought so....Captain?"

"You're right, Ben. It's not very likely. And the cover was still on when we swung her down."

"There you are, then," said Ben morosely.

"But has it been sabotaged?" asked Richard, thinking grimly of what he had been told of the mess in the Radio Shack.

"Hard to tell." John was still fiddling with it, trying to find out what was wrong. "Probably find that out when I find out why it's not working."

Silence returned until they came within hailing distance of Robin's boat. Then she called across, "Our radio's been sabotaged. Whole panel of transistors gone. How about yours?"

"The same," yelled back John.

Ben left the man he was nursing. "Maybe we'd better check in case anything else has been mucked about with since my last full inspection," he whispered. He needn't have bothered lowering his voice. His words carried clearly to everyone on both boats.

They looked as carefully as they could under the light of the lamps, and everything else seemed fine until Richard, almost out of sight now of the blazing *Prometheus*, checked the compass. No matter where it was pointed, the needle remained glued to N on the card. Robin's was the same. Even when N was pointed due south by the faint, cloud-masked stars, and the overcast gathered rapidly so that the stars soon were obscured. In the end, the captain and his third mate simply put their backs to the distant column of light that marked their wounded ship, and hoped that they were sailing east into an African dawn.

They were still so far from land that the sun rose through the sea ahead. It was a sudden thing, almost like an explosion. One moment the horizon was a steady line above which the cloudless sky was like a duck's egg gilded with almost transparent foil. Then the sea lit up, first at a point, then from north to south, a dazzling emerald as the sun shone through it. And this was only the beginning. As soon as the rim of the sun peeped over the edge of the world, it sent great beams speeding almost visibly toward them, through the cobweb tendrils rising with silent majesty off the slick backs of the waves. All around them, the huge sea, heaving rhythmically in the dead calm with the great green rollers that would pound Africa in time, was smoking with greater and greater intensity. The nascent fog, rising out of the heart of a warm current into the crisp chill of the clear morning, gave the beams of the rising sun form and substance, seeming to flatten them first into great blades; eventually obscuring them altogether.

By midmorning visibility was down to a matter of yards. Richard had a rope secured between the two boats in case they lost each other. The sun became a pale copper disk. At noon, instead of making his usual announcements, the captain said a service for the dead. Nobody felt like eating. The afternoon began to pass. They remained lost, but safely wrapped in a cocoon of coolness. Richard did not look forward to the moment when a blazing tropic sun burned that protective layer away and revealed to them all the immensity of the ocean on which their frail little boats bobbed so helplessly. *Prometheus* had been so vast that she had kept them utterly apart from the seas they were sailing. The contrast, when it came, was likely to be a shock.

For another day and two more nights they drifted in the fog. The boats, held almost magically in still water at the confluence of three great currents drifting south, nevertheless were pushed by what fitful wind there was so that their heads kept turning north. Indeed, at dawn on the third day, Ben Strong, who had the tiller of the lead boat, looked unbelievingly as the sun lit up the emerald sea behind his right shoulder instead of dead ahead. So surprised was he, for he had been certain that they were heading due east, that it took him a moment or two to realize that the fog had gone. The boats were still tied together and he glanced back into Robin's boat where Rice was dozing at the

149

helm. Nobody seemed to have noticed how badly off course they were. Good. He put her over and took them in a gentle arc toward the bright new dawn. Richard felt the change at once and looked up from under lowered lids, noting what was happening before he apparently went back to sleep.

Two days in the fog had been frustrating, occasionally almost frightening, but in the end simply a sort of waste of time. With little or no idea where they were heading, they kept only rudimentary logs, though sometime during each watch, the watch officer made some kind of observation on the state of sea, weather, anything else of interest; and added a guess as to where they were and which way they were pointing. There was a surprising lack of tension, even though it was plain to all that they were in the middle of something mysterious, murderous. Richard made sure that they talked the situation through—though he kept his own suspicions quiet—and they concluded with the rueful cheerfulness of people who have been the victims of a practical joke that the saboteur must only have wanted them out of communication for a while: not out of the way permanently. They had plenty of food and water—all untouched. They were in busy sea lanes and not too far from land. They were cocooned by the fog—it was like being wrapped in cotton wool. Apart from the boredom, it might almost have been taken for a holiday. A lark. There was no real sense of danger at all.

The third day changed all that. The sun slid up out of the water into a strange hazy shadow line that in the tropics appears at the foot of the sky on clear dawns and sunsets. Moments later it was filling the sky with a disproportionate amount of glare and both Ben and Rice found themselves steering toward it with their eyes shut, so fierce was the brightness ahead.

The simple change in the weather was enough to alter the tenor of life in the boats, just as Richard had feared it would. As the sun went higher, so the horizons withdrew all around. The wider the horizons became, the smaller the boats seemed. Their total fragility, riding on the back of the Atlantic as though it were some fierce but sleepy monster, was brought home to everybody in an overwhelming rush as they woke. They had grown used to seeing the ocean from a great distance, tamed by the size of the tanker. Now they were face to face with it. All too aware of its unimaginable force; its overwhelming capacity for violence. Even its simple depth became a source of fearful wonder. They sat in silence looking over the side. The ocean floor lay some three thousand fathoms, eighteen thousand feet, two-thirds of the height of Everest beneath them.

With visibility so good, there was no need for the boats to remain tied together, so the line was slipped and Robin's boat came up alongside Richard's. They both took the next watch and sat, side by side, separated by as little water as possible, watching their crew with increasing concern. John was in his element, of course. Ben was fine. Rice and McTavish weren't too happy. Malik and Ho were hard at work trying to keep some spirit in their men. While covered with the fog, they had tried all the singing, storytelling, jokes, and games they knew, and now everyone was being required to recall anything new, or to recount the favorites. Under other circumstances it might have been an interesting cross-cultural exercise, but not now. Now everyone watched listlessly as the great swells came out of the west behind them, seesawing them rhythmically, but seeming to push them no nearer to land. Even the stewards had given up betting on which of each series would be biggest.

The fishing contest seemed a stroke of genius. It galvanized them as soon as Richard suggested it. As the lines were being prepared, a babble of excitement spread between the boats. The stewards arranged a dazzling array of wagers. The more staid Palestinians joined in of course, many of them the offspring of generations of fishermen. McTavish glowed, having fished the Clyde estuary from Largs to Ardrossan as a boy. Ben looked down his nose at them like a schoolmaster with an unruly form, but he took a line. Then, thinking that no one was looking, he took another and tied them both together, doubling the length and the number of hooks. John became adjudicator, even though he was taking part himself. Watch officers, it was decided, should remain aloof. Such tinned meat as they had would have to do for bait. The lines were readied, and on John's signal, dropped.

A concentrated silence descended. The boats moved apart slightly. They had to. With more than twenty lines out, the risk of a massive tangle was high. The contest began.

The day was hot and bright. The sun might have been overpowering, but the steady south wind that had blown away the fog remained surprisingly cool. The boats rose and fell easily on the shoulders of the great waves. The water was limpidly clear, though once in a while the telltale rainbow effect would blemish the glassy surface, showing where oil had been spilled. Every now and then they would see small black globules of tar. The first man to pull in his line, certain that his bait must have fallen off, found his hands covered in sticky black marks.

One of the stewards caught the first, a small tuna. He made much of the effort required to pull it in, drawing out the performance skillfully, convincing the others that he had caught something big. Taking it off the hook for him, John said to them all, "Remember. If you hook into anything really big, just let your line go." He said it without thinking, and it was a wise thing to say; but it reawoke that very element that Richard had been most hard put to quiet: the nervousness they all felt at the simple size of the ocean.

As the morning wore on, the sea moderated and the waves became smaller, though they continued to roll silently by, like the backs of huge fish. With their attention on their lines, they all became intensely aware that they had entered one of the great currents of the deep, at the point when the Canary current swings west to become the North Equatorial current. It jerked and pulled at the lines like a live thing. One moment they would all stretch away to port then for no reason they would be pulled to starboard, kicking and twisting as the strength of the water grasped them. The lines plunged down out of sight, though the water remained so clear you would have thought the seabed should have been easily visible, and there was no way of telling what was at the bait. Even John became depressed, unconsciously suffering from agoraphobia and an overwhelming sense of his own frailty. Suddenly a particularly vicious cross-current tore at the lines and there was pandemonium in the bow of Robin's boat. One of the stewards, convinced the current was the jaws of some monster clamped around his line, had let go of his tackle with a cry of fear. "He say it just pull an' pull," yelled Ho to the adjudicator. "He say he couldn't hold on no more."

"It was just the current," John called back bracingly.

"Maybe yes. Maybe no. You look out all same."

Ben gazed dreamily into the limpid water. The effort of holding the long line had proved too arduous for him some time ago and so he had just tied it to the boat's side and was sitting with one finger on the bright, braided nylon line, daydreaming contentedly.

Noon came and went. There was no change of watch. Some of Ho's stewards desultorily set about preparing lunch. It would be baked beans. The meat content of this particular meal was being offered to the fish.

"Hey," called Ben in the middle of this, "I've got a bite!" He knelt up on his seat, leaning over the side like an excited boy, pulling in his catch hand over hand. Lunch forgotten, the men in Richard's boat strained round to see.

The line stretched straight down in the still water, jerking and jumping as the still invisible fish fought every inch of the way. After a few minutes he came to the knot that joined the two lines and he wrapped the heavy-duty nylon round his hand for a breather.

"There it is," shouted someone excitedly. Vague at first, but becoming clearer as it swam up, trailing the line behind it, came a large tuna, its blue-and-silver flanks flashing. "Twenty, twenty-five pounds," said John knowledgeably. "We'll have a job getting that one aboard."

"What's that?" Robin's voice came sharply over the water. She had pulled closer so that her lot also could see Ben's tuna come aboard. She was leaning over the side, looking down. "There . . . No . . . But there was something." She looked across at Richard. "Something big."

"It's bleeding a bit," said Ben cheerfully. "You probably just saw the blood."

"Better get it up quickly, then," snapped Richard. But he was too late.

"There!" called Robin urgently. She said more, but her words were drowned out in the pandemonium.

Ben, the line still wrapped around his hand, was slammed against the thwart. His arm stretched out, a taut extension of the humming spitting line. He looked down unbelievingly. The tuna was gone. In its place, a mere sixty feet away, firmly attached by the tangle of line to his right hand, was a hammerhead shark. Not a monster by any means. A powerful, deadly fifteen-footer. The line angled out of the corner of its mouth, stretching up behind the protuberance housing its left eye. It didn't seem to know that it had been caught. Yet. One more beat of its majestic tail was enough, though. The flat, alien head turned. Even as Richard leaned forward to cut the line, the hammerhead turned back and began to circle inquisitively around the two frail boats.

After a few minutes it was joined by another, a twelve-foot tiger this time.

Then another . . .

18

The danger of the element they were now so close to could not have been brought home to the dejected crew more clearly. Above the surface, everyday normality. Below it, scant inches of wood and Fiberglas away, was horror and death. And, as if to emphasize the lesson, the dangerous predators followed them, cruising in menacing circles around them, every now and then brushing against side or keel with a sound like distant thunder.

And so the rest of the day passed, with Richard and Robin sitting together with the thinnest possible strip of water between them, the only contented people there. At sunset, the watches changed. Ben, recovered from his shock, came back to relieve Richard; McTavish came back to relieve Robin, and Richard stood up so that he could move down his boat with her, the need to be near her almost unbearably strong in him.

And, because he was standing up, the only one doing so at that moment, and because he was looking away from the sunset into the crystal calm of the gathering night, he saw her first, surprisingly close at hand, her upper works painted blood-red by the rays of the setting sun. He knew her at once, although he could not see her name. There could not be two like her. No other would present all those black windows, lacking the glass to reflect the sun. No other would have that great scar up the middle of her bridge. And he knew her as a parent knows its child, by something deeper than sight.

She had crept up to catch them unawares, because the watch had been watching the sharks or each other and not the horizons, and because she was moving in silence like a ghost, like the Flying Dutchman sailing north. Drifting without her engines. Safe, with the fire out.

Robin rose and followed his gaze the second she realized he had frozen where he stood. So it was she who had whispered, horror-struck, "Look!"

One by one, it seemed, they turned, and an awed murmur went through them like a breeze through dried grass. They watched in scarce-believing silence, each a prey to myriad conflicting emotions, as *Prometheus*, back from the dead, drifted down on them.

All of a sudden, Richard, for all his misgivings, was possessed of a fierce joy; an immense feeling of the goodness of life filled every fiber of his lean, hard body. It was one of those moments that come to men and women when they know without a shadow of a doubt that what faces them, no matter how daunting, is the task that they above all others were put upon earth to overcome.

Still standing, he began to speak, his ringing tones dragging their eyes back from the silent ship to their shining captain, outlined in fire by the setting sun. "At least one person here doesn't want us to go back aboard: the person who sees *Prometheus* as what she was always meant to be: a coffin ship. A worthless hulk brought cheaply up to scratch so that she can be lost at sea as part of an insurance fraud. There is someone among us, perhaps more than one person, who knows she cannot be allowed to come safe to port in Rotterdam. And I believe that behind this person, behind the whole sickening mess, stands the owner, Kostas Demetrios, involved in an act of fraud. Nothing else makes sense.

"But *Prometheus* is my command and I will bring her home, to expose the fraud. I will bring her home for my father-in-law whose oil fills her holds and who stands to lose everything if I do not. I will bring her home for us, who have been cheated, tricked, lied to, and killed to make a rich man richer. And I will bring her home for herself, because she is not a worthless hulk but a great lady: perhaps the greatest I have ever sailed aboard, and I will not let her die.

"So I'm giving any secret enemies in our midst fair warning.

I'm taking my *Prometheus* home come hell or high water. And the only way you'll stop me is to kill me."

Robin, still on her feet in her boat beside him, added dryly, "And me." Her narrowed eyes raked the boat and a shark's back rumbled against the keel. Then Ben was up, and John and all the rest of them, crazily, carried away, cheering once more until the boats began to rock dangerously and they had to sit down.

When the cheering died, Richard sat at his helm once more and led them past the lazily cruising sharks, back toward *Prometheus*.

As they drew closer, however, their buoyant confidence began to diminish under her icy air of desolation. It was all too easy to see the ghosts of their dead friends and enemies in the shadows gathered behind her shattered windows. It was hard not to hear them whisper in the lapping wavelets against the black precipices of her leeward side or in the thunder of surf as the occasional roller broke against the iron cliff of her windward side. The rapidly gathering dark brought with it a chill after the clear, hot day; a chill that seemed to emanate from her, making her strange to them and eerily forbidding.

Quietly, a little nervously, they came down her leeward side, under the accommodation ladder folded level with the deck almost fifty feet sheer above their heads. They snugged the heads of their boats at the exact point where Richard had held his more than three days ago, waiting for the last search party to come off, down the rope ladder.

But the ladder was gone.

They continued around, to the windward side of the silent, forbidding hulk. But that, too, was empty—there was no other way to scale her sheer sides.

Richard watched the pale afterglow of sunset, deep in thought. This was going to be even more difficult than he had anticipated. He had assumed the ladder would still be in place and had planned to send the engineering officers up it to restart the generators so the accommodation ladder could be lowered for the rest of them. They had to use the accommodation ladder somewhere in the scheme because they would never get the wounded up otherwise. It had been all very well helping them down rope ladders in the emergency of the fire when there had been no alternative—and when several had fallen into the water anyway; but expecting them to climb one now—even had there been one—with the hungry sharks waiting for one wrong move, was simply out of the question.

But now it looked as though he was going to have to come up with some alternative. And fast.

More to keep them occupied than because he thought they had missed anything on the first circuit, he moved the lifeboat forward and began another circuit of the forbidding ship.

The air of desolation had been depressing when they first approached her. Now it was overpowering. The last light of the brief tropical evening gleamed on her upper bridge works. All the rest was fast-thickening gloom. In almost shuddering silence they rounded her stem, innocent now of bow wave as she drifted without headway on the gray-black sea. They went wide enough to look up the full length of her just as the last light left her, leaving the scarred bridge gray as a corpse's face.

The crystal beauty of the night, star-bright in the east already, only served to make her look worse by comparison, and the lightest breeze, blowing over them toward Africa, suddenly brought the charnel stench of her, an overpowering amalgam of burned steel and blown flesh.

One of the stewards leaned shakily over the side and began to vomit. The others were muttering nervously, overcome by her unexpected hostility. The air of tension became almost palpable.

So that several of them actually cried out with shock when, just at the very moment they were passing underneath it, the accommodation ladder jumped noisily into motion and, apparently under its own sinister volition, hissed out and down to meet them.

19

Martyr woke up in hell. A New Englander, born and raised in Salem, Massachusetts, he had a clear idea what hell would be like—it would be a hot place, full of pain. It would be filled with the roaring of those eternal fires whose stench would make breathing another agony. Shafts of firelight would gleam through billows of acrid smoke like the livid glow of a distant furnace. Hell would be full of caverns—perhaps as many as there were mansions in heaven—and in each cavern would be a soul like his own, condemned to roast forever on the hot metal floor.

He sat up and his head swam, pulling him back to a nauseous reality. He rested for a few moments, gathering his strength. Then he tried to stand. His first attempt wasn't too successful. He staggered like a terminal drunkard until his feet crunched on something unexpectedly and the surprise made him lose his footing again.

Sitting on the floor, he explored in the darkness with his fingers, trying to find what had caused him to fall. It was the broken torch. More than broken, by the feel of it: smashed to pieces. The memory flashed into his head of a figure cloaked in darkness behind a blaze of light, throwing itself at him, wrestling him down, bludgeoning him about the head in the shadows with a torch.

Rage came. Sheer, overwhelming, bone-deep, blood-hot red rage.

It was a feeling he knew well. It was part of him more than

159

any other feeling in the world. "I'll get you, you son of a bitch," he said. And the rage gave him the strength to stand.

He felt his way to the door and opened it. He was just about to step outside when his dazed mind warned him that he did not know which door this was. There were several doors opening from the Engine Control Room. One led to the corridor. The others led to balconies overlooking the engine. If he walked off one of those in the dark, he would simply fall to his death. He laboriously knelt, feeling sick and slightly foolish, and checked with his fingertips. The linoleum of the corridor: not the patterned metal of a balcony. He was safe so far.

His mind had been suggesting subliminally for a time that the battering about his head might have affected his ears. Now he consciously took on the problem and found the logical answer: he was not going deaf, the fire was dying down. He stood again and walked purposefully out into the corridor. Apart from the fitful roar, the ship was absolutely silent. He felt his way along the corridors and up the eerie stairways.

There was dawn light enough to see the charnel house of the crew's quarters. By the time he made it up onto the deserted bridge, the sun was coming up, bringing the first ghostly tendrils of fog. Martyr sat in the captain's chair and wondered what he should do first. Wondered what he should do, period. He was the only man left alive on a drifting, half-derelict hulk. It seemed unlikely that she would blow up now, but in becoming less of an immediate danger to Martyr, she at once became a terrible hazard to other shipping. She was drifting, without lights or horn to give warning of her presence, through busy sea lanes in a thickening fog. If the watch officers of passing ships weren't very wide awake indeed, there could be a major catastrophe here. Which would be all the better for that murderous little bastard Demetrios.

He sat for a long time, thinking dark thoughts about his relationship with Kostas Demetrios, such as it was, and the Greek's fail-safe scheme. While to Richard the owner seemed American, to Martyr he seemed Greek. Still, the Greek had paid the American's share up front, quite a lot of money, simply to turn a blind eye to the one extra circuit that would automatically open the sea-cocks—and make sure nobody else got too suspicious about it if they found it—and the money was performing its designated function now; so that even this way the sea was giving back a little of what it had stolen from him.

Obviously, the first thing to do would be to get the generators working again. Without them, *Prometheus* was worse than helpless. And there was clearing up to be done. He would need light for that. And after. Plenty of light. He needed those generators.

But they were down in the Engine Room where the sun never shone. So, step one was to find another torch. Simple.

Why the diesel-powered alternators should have chosen to switch themselves off when they did was something that Martyr was never able to fathom. There seemed nothing wrong with them when he looked at them closely under the bright beam of a battery-operated lantern some twenty minutes later, and they started with ease. After the first kick and bellow of sound, light flooded the Engine Room and he felt comforted somehow. He patted the bellowing machine and turned away. He had taken four steps precisely when the realization of what he might actually have done swept over him.

When it came right down to it, his involvement, expensively bought, consisted only of one thing: turning a blind eye to the one circuit down here that could not be explained. The one circuit that the real accomplice would close in order to open the sea-cocks, if the generators were still running.

He stood there, frozen with the certainty that this was what his mysterious assailant had been doing down here the better part of twelve hours ago. The sea-cocks had obviously remained closed then, but what if that were only because the generators had failed? What if they were opening now?

Impulsively he turned back and killed the power, plunging the Engine Room into echoing silence and darkness again. He strained his ears. Could he hear the sound of water gushing into her? He could hear little. Not enough to distinguish between imagination and actuality. Cursing quietly to himself, he reached down and lit the lantern again. Was it enough just to cut the wires? He wondered. Possibly. But even in these circumstances his natural professionalism overcame him. He laboriously followed the wire to the hidden switch and checked that it was in fact turned off before he would allow himself to feel satisfied or safe.

He was a man well acquainted with death and it seemed to him fitting that, above all the others, he should have been chosen by fate as an undertaker. He moved the bodies and pieces of bodies—mostly Palestinian—into the ship's cold room. His inclination was to throw them overboard, but some glimmer of rational behavior stayed alive during those hours, hazed as they were by shock and concussion. Some certainty that at last *Prometheus* would be found and taken in tow, as she had been to Durban, and then there would be full reckoning for Demetrios, and the devil to pay.

He lost a day altogether, working like an automaton at instantly forgotten tasks. He slept, without knowing it, wherever his legs gave out, and woke to take up where he had left off, apparently mere seconds later. Night drove him belowdecks because one of the more eccentric side effects of the blast was that, while much of the equipment seemed untouched, every light bulb in the front of the bridge was smashed. He woke at noon on the third day and found himself, much to his surprise, in the captain's chair on the bridge. His overalls were stiff with filth. His long, aching body stank foully. He was nursing an empty pint bottle of bourbon and the mother and father of all hangovers. His mind, for the first time since the murderer clubbed him with the torch, was absolutely clear.

During the next three hours he toured the ship from stem to stern, giving her a thorough inspection; surprised to find how clean and tidy she was. Surprised to find just how much he had done while concussion blanked almost everything out. The tour, unsurprisingly, ended at the engine, and, as far as he could tell, this, like the generator, was undamaged and would start again, if asked. As long as there was enough oil in the bunkerage. But it would be pointless to get under way. He could not hope to control *Prometheus* on his own. Far better to let her drift and hope she kept out of trouble. But the idleness, once his elementary engine checks were complete, drove him up to the bridge once more, to keep an eye out for any passing ships.

And so it was that he, standing high and armed with powerful binoculars, though looking almost directly into the setting sun, saw the forlorn specks of the lifeboats long before anyone aboard had any idea that the stricken giant was drifting down on them. His first impulse was to let them know he was here, but it was dismissed instantly. Instead, he veiled his eyes calculatingly and returned to the captain's chair. Here he sat, lost in thought as the sun set and the three craft closed together. By the time Richard saw *Prometheus* the chief was in the forecastle head watching through carefully shaded binoculars, taking careful note of who was there.

He had just pulled up the rope ladder when the lifeboats came buzzing in and paused, like strange water beetles, puzzled at the point where it should have been. He gave a lean smile. Good. Now they would have to wait for him to welcome them aboard in his own way. As far as he was concerned, after all, one of them had tried to kill him and the rest had simply left him to die. He found he was deeply disappointed in Richard Mariner, though. He would have reckoned on the tall Englishman for at least one search party. It never occurred to him that the search party might have been fooled by the murderer's lies. So he busied himself as they explored the other side, and was in position when they came back, with his next few moves at least worked out.

As they passed beneath the accommodation ladder, he hit the button on its electric motor and, silently on desert-booted feet, he ran for the shadows of the black-windowed bridge.

The accommodation ladder clanged down to its fullest extent and stopped. They sat and looked at it in an awed, superstitious silence. Then Ben stood up in the first boat's bow. "Someone alive up there after all," he called cheerily. "Hope it's the chief. Still feel bad that we didn't manage to find him." Then he sprang nimbly out and up. John automatically took his place, leaning out and holding the boat still, looking up after the first officer with the ghost of a frown.

Ben vanished up onto the deck, hallooing cheerfully, but there was no reply, and after a moment, his tousled head was shoved out over the side. "Nobody here. No hide nor hair. Damnedest thing."

Richard sat for a moment longer, face like a mask, mind racing. More mystery. He, too, hoped it was the chief, but this behavior was too eccentric for the American—unless Martyr was motivated by something as yet unknown to him. But there was certainly someone left alive on board. He would find out soon enough who it was. In the meantime it was nearly full night and he had to get the wounded aboard. He rose stiffly, raising a hand to Robin to warn her that he wanted her to stay where she was for a moment; then he stepped carefully down the boat past John and climbed swiftly up the ladder.

Stinking, strange-atmosphered, inhabited by mysteries or not, it seemed to him as he came onto the deck that *Prometheus* was glad to see him. But that was perhaps mainly because he was so pleased to be back.

Ben was busily examining the top of the ladder. "Might have tripped as we passed under it . . ."

They both listened in the silence above the muttering from the boats below. The ladder was powered by electricity. That meant the generators had to be on, but it was hard to tell down here. And the bridge was in darkness. They looked at each other, already almost lost in the gloom.

Then, unexpectedly, with a sort of silent explosion, all the navigating lights and most of the forward deck lights came on.

"It has to be Martyr," said Richard decisively. "You oversee the unloading of the boat. I'm going up to the bridge at once."

Ben hesitated. "He's acting pretty strangely, Dick. Maybe I'd better come up with you."

"No. I'd say he tripped the ladder then ran back to get the lights on before it got absolutely dark. Nothing strange in that."

"If you say so. You're the boss. All the same, I'll get a couple of Malik's heftiest up here first in case anyone needs restraining."

Richard walked briskly down the deck, his mind switching from speculation to planning; his eyes wringing the last drop of information out of the gathering shadows as the deck lighting, also smashed by the explosion, sought to hide the wounded deck and bridge-house in darkness. But a simple sense of equilibrium told him of some of the damage, for the deck canted up increasingly steeply on his right, as he came past the last of the three tank caps nearest the bridge. Unable to resist, he walked to the edge of the gaping pit where the Pump Room hatch had once been and looked down into the black void. There was nothing to see. The stench was overpowering. He did not tarry long.

The lights in the A deck corridor were on and the brightness nearly dazzled him. There was no doubt here: he could hear the generators clearly and even feel the hum of them through his feet. Even so, he did not trust the lift, preferring to pound up the stairs two at a time.

The instrument panels, most of them miraculously still working, lit the bridge with an eerie green glow, in which he could just make out the figure of Martyr sitting in the captain's chair. At once he thought about Ben's concern. What if he had cracked during the last three days? But his voice sounded calm enough. "Hello, Captain. Welcome back aboard."

"Evening, Chief. You the only one here?"

"Only one alive." Martyr turned and Richard gasped. The chief's face was a total wreck. Brows thrust out above swollen eyes. The nose was out of line. The lips, simian in their thickness, were split in several places. The high forehead was welted and raised in mountainous lumps. There was dried blood at the corners of nostrils and eyes, and in the ears.

Without thinking, Richard was in action. As first officer, he had acted as medic on enough ships to know the basics. His hands gently took the ruined face and probed with infinite care, checking for telltale tenderness that would tell of fractures. There seemed to be none. Martyr's bright eyes watched him quizzically. "Teeth?" Richard asked.

"Still in place," answered Martyr. "You should have asked about my heart. The shock I got when I first looked in a mirror damn near killed me."

20

Nobody except the sedated got much sleep that night. Martyr's job of cleaning had been rudimentary. There was still much that needed immediate attention even before the bridge could be properly manned or the great engine restarted.

Of course, Richard's dream of bringing the great ship to port in better condition than when she sailed had necessarily gone by the board, but there was some tidying and painting that had to be done. All the windows needed boarding or replacing. Electrical light was needed at any price, and it returned to the bridge-house little by little. Only the places that needed to be used regularly were illuminated, as and when necessary, for light bulbs were now few, because, as Martyr had observed, all those in the blast area had been broken. The radio shack was sealed and left in darkness, finally, because there was no way of fixing the ruin in there.

Martyr and his team, shaken to a man by the sight of his face, but warily silent and apparently incurious, had the engine started before first light next day, so the new dawn found *Prometheus* under her own power, sailing determinedly north, back onto her old course.

All the navigating equipment had survived except the suspect Sat Nav, so John brought up his beloved sextant to replace it, and, because the chronometers also seemed undamaged, this was quite good enough.

* * *

166

Richard sprang awake and automatically looked at his watch. 07.30. Last half hour of John's watch. Half an hour until Robin took over. He looked down at the golden crown of her sleeping head lying lightly on his chest. The emotion that swept over him as he looked at her was so poignant it made him feel like a boy again, stunned by the beauty of a world that could contain so much happiness; so much excitement. For the last few days he had lived on a plateau of contentment above any he had ever known, knowing that she shared it with him.

They lay, fully clothed, on the bunk they had collapsed on the night before. Her arms and legs wound round him, clutching him to her. He smiled and returned her gentle embrace for a few moments, luxuriating in the feel of her, then he softly disentangled himself and rose. As he put his feet on the floor, something chimed quietly: a tray with cups and saucers, sugar and reconstituted milk. And a thermos of teak-dark tea. Richard smiled. Ho's one concession to the emergency was the thermos—he would not wake his captain at 06.30 anymore; nor would he let his captain's tea go cold while he slept. He opened it and poured himself a cup, then left it uncorked by the head of the bunk, knowing the warm fragrance of the hot tea would waken Robin more effectively than anything except the emergency siren.

With his cup in his hand, he crossed to the vacant windowframe to look down across the scarred deck, through the balmy morning toward his distant goal. If they had maintained course and speed through the night—and if they had not, he would have been informed—they should be north of Cancer by now. The Canaries and the Azores beckoned temptingly: they still had not sighted another ship. They were still in enforced radio silence. There was, creeping over the men, a sort of fantastic suspicion that something unimaginable had happened to the rest of humanity, some unannounced holocaust that had left them alone in all the world. Like the Flying Dutchman, whose waters they had so recently crossed. But Richard was not going to stop at any of the islands unless he absolutely had to. He was going to take her home. If they limped into some safe harbor on the way, they would simply be taken off and flown home, leaving the massive, impersonal machinery of the investigation to work itself out distantly from them while they were occupied with other things. Like getting on with the rest of their lives. There was a temptation, but Richard could not entertain it. He could not allow the resolution of all this to come about through the workings of others: men and women who had not earned the right, as his crew had, to lay bare the whole truth of the matter.

No. The only thing that could have made him turn aside now was if their rudimentary medical facilities began to fail, putting the lives of the wounded at risk. But, as he had observed in the lifeboat more than three days ago, the men were either dead or only lightly wounded. There was no one who needed hospitalization. The worst hurt was Nihil, among Ho's men, who had lost part of a finger. And that only served to make his endless playing of that strange flute even more weird and haunting. The others only needed burial, and they would wait.

He frowned, still gazing out into the still, clear morning, his thoughts taking a darker turn.

"Penny for them..." she whispered at his shoulder, so close she made him jump. She took another silent step forward and wrapped her arms around his waist, crushing herself to him.

"You're due on watch in fifteen minutes, Number Three," he said.

She screwed up her nose. "Just time for a shower, then."

They showered together, not having time to turn it into a game; Richard, in any case, too preoccupied to answer her playful advances. They came out together also and quickly changed into clean, white uniforms. Twelve Toes and his team had performed little short of miracles getting the ship's laundry back in service. And, since Durban, there had always been a complete change of clothes for each of them left, apparently by accident, in the other's quarters. The bomb and the abandonment had not changed that.

There had been enough glass in the ship's stores to replace the bridge windows. Everyone else had to put up with ply or board unless, like Richard, they were willing to risk inclement weather and leave their windows uncovered for the moment. So, with windows in and blast-damage covered if not corrected, the bridge seemed normal as they stepped into it side by side ten minutes later, as though the explosion had never happened. Until, that is, they walked forward far enough to see the crater on the deck.

John Higgins was sitting, worn out, in the captain's chair. His pipe had fallen into his lap. When the rest of them had collapsed, exhausted, at four this morning, it had only been time for him to take over his watch. He was certainly due for some sleep now, and, emergencies aside, he would sleep until Pour Out.

Richard had reinstated the ship's routine at once, as though nothing untoward was going on. He would make his noon report as usual later, having calculated their position himself with John's sextant, and without the international news that Tsirtos used to supply, but still religiously including the bearing of Mecca for the Moslems. They might be working all the hours that God—or Allah—might send, trying to repair the damage caused by their strange, invisible enemy, but the daily routines punctuated their efforts with the calm accuracy of a Swiss watch. The façade of normality was enormously important. It gave them an added strength. So the watches changed like clockwork, with Martyr replacing Napier below, and all the meals were served as normal. They were only an hour behind GMT now, and would not come back onto it until they were entering the Channel Approaches in a little less than five days' time. With luck, they would sight the Lizard at dawn on September 9.

Richard walked forward and put his hand on John's shoulder. The second officer jumped into full wakefulness and looked up. "We've got her now, John. Robin's watch. You get to bed."

"I think we came pretty close to another vessel last night. Strong echo on the radar. Couldn't raise her with the signal lamp, though I thought I could see her lights. Watch must have been asleep."

Richard looked down at the tired man with infinite respect. In spite of everything, the watch on *Prometheus* had been anything but sleepy. He glanced at Robin. She was just signing onto the log. "Logged at 04.45," she confirmed. "Echo's course due south. Closest three miles. Should have seen a signal lamp: conditions clear enough."

Richard nodded. They might find it difficult to raise a passing ship with the lamp. So many ships relied solely on their radios now. But then, *Prometheus* would strike passersby as unusually silent; worthy of closer attention. It should be possible to attract someone's attention to that flashing point of light. And most ships' officers still understood Morse code.

Richard called them into his dayroom and they stood like guilty schoolboys at the headmaster's desk: "Twelve Toes" Ho, Salah Malik, C. J. Martyr. It was the middle of Robin's watch, the first opportunity Richard had had since returning aboard to reconstruct the sabotage and voice his opinions.

The other three knew why they were here. They were wary but, surprisingly, thought Richard, there was no real hostility in the air. And this fact seemed significant to him.

"The bomb wasn't part of the original plan, was it?" he said. "Or if it was, then none of you knew about it."

They watched him in guarded silence. He went on, calmly. "That's the only way I can see to make sense of this. You all agreed, with the others, to abandon and scuttle *Prometheus* off the coast of Senegal so that Demetrios could put in a huge insurance claim. It was supposed to be easy and safe: nobody hurt. But Demetrios decided to do things his way and he put a bomb on board."

"He's put more aboard than that," grated Martyr, his voice slurred by his swollen lips. "There's someone else aboard, a Crewfinders man, whose job is to do what the bomb failed to do." He gestured at his face. "No matter who gets in the way."

Richard nodded silently. Then his ice-cold gaze switched to Salah and Ho. "You both agreed to abandon, like the original officers. I'll give you the benefit of the doubt and suppose you both must have reckoned you would get all your men off safely. But Demetrios and his sidekick have taken this simple fraud and made it murder."

Salah's square shoulders slumped. "It is as you say, Captain. It is as you said in the lifeboat. We were going to abandon. Levkas or one of his officers was going to scuttle her and lead us in the lifeboats to Dakar. It was all agreed. But these men have changed all that. We must find them now and kill them for what they have done!"

"Twelve Toes" made a sound deep in his throat to signify agreement.

Richard's hand slammed down onto his desktop. "Not on my ship, you don't! You tell your men I want watches kept in case the owner's friend tries anything more, but that is all. I want no searching, no detecting, no revenge. I want to take this ship and her crew back home exactly as they are. *Is that clear?*"

All three men nodded.

"Right. Malik. Ho. Back to your duties." The two of them left. "Mr. Martyr," Richard continued, "sit down please."

Martyr sat.

Richard leaned forward, elbows on the desk, steepling his forearms up to interlaced fingers. "I propose to spend the next few hours interviewing everyone aboard to try to reconstruct what happened that night for the Accident Report Book," he said. "But that presents me with something of a problem because two crimes—at the least—happened. There was an attempt to sabotage my command and there was an attempt to murder you. I think the same person is involved in both of these crimes."

"A Crewfinders man," repeated the chief.

"Not a seaman or a steward?"

"Stewards are all too small. Could have been a seaman—but I'd say only Malik and Khalil are big enough."

Richard nodded. "But both of them were with teams of men right throughout the night. They couldn't have slipped away. So it has to be one of my men."

Martyr shrugged.

Richard continued, "I need to know how you fit into this, Chief, if I'm going to make sense of it, make sure that justice gets done."

And Martyr leaned forward and told him. "I'm a long-service man. Twenty years in the American merchant marine. Good years. Happy. Had a wife. A daughter—Christine. Beautiful girl. The apple of my eye. But then it all went sour. Sailor's nightmare. While I was away at sea, my wife found someone new. We divorced. She got custody of my girl. I got visiting rights whenever I had shore leave. I came home one time and Christine was gone. Just plain gone. Vanished. My wife and her new husband put up a reward but they heard nothing. I jumped ship—a chief engineer jumping ship like a cadet—and I went to look. I found her in New York. On drugs. Working as a prostitute. Making videos—like that one

171

Tsirtos put on—to support her habit. I took her back. The little pusher who was pimping for her tried to stop me. I killed him.

"She's in detox now. Getting better. But it costs. You know, Mariner, it *costs!* Every cent I earn goes to help my girl. But I don't earn that much now, on the beach with a federal warrant out on me. Or I didn't till I met Demetrios..."

He paused. Richard watched him silently.

"All I had to do was get the ship around the Cape. Nurse that clapped-out old motor along then look the other way while they scuttled her. There's a circuit—I'll show you—opens all the sea-cocks at once. One flick of the switch and she's gone."

"You willing to say all this at a court of inquiry?"

"No way. No way at all. I'll help you get home, but that is all I'll do. I've got scores to settle and I'll do that my own way. But I won't stand up in court: if I go to jail, who'll watch over my Christine?"

After Martyr had gone, Mariner lapsed into a brown study. What was due to happen to *Prometheus*'s hull was only part of the problem: what was due to happen to her cargo was important too. And the extension of that problem led to very murky waters indeed.

If the oil had been taken off at Durban without his knowledge then Bill Heritage might be in the clear. But if the oil was still aboard, still part of the fraud, then it looked as if the owner of the oil had to be a party to the fraud as well. If only he felt able to run the risk of looking in the tanks. The loading programs on the computers probably held a clue, but they were unavailable until the computers themselves were fixed—if they ever could be. And even the most cursory examination had already revealed that all the tank tops down as far as the Sampson posts were damaged by the blast. Should he get a team of seamen and a huge dipstick and run the risk of opening the forward tank to see what it contained? It was tempting. But in the end he decided to wait because to do so, to run the very great risk of opening the tank at sea on a damaged ship whose safety systems seemed to be working but were—to put it mildly—unreliable, would solve little and might force him to take action he would rather avoid.

For that oil was owned by a desperate, bitter old man. And by

his daughter, who had arrived so conveniently, remained so in-
sistently, fallen in love so precipitately and so convincingly, and
who perhaps—just perhaps—had deceived them all so completely.

Until now.

It was not until that evening, part way through John's second
watch, that the fifth ship they had passed during the last twelve
hours made the cheerful, unexpected reply:

HELLO PROMETHEUS STOP SOMEONE OVER THERE PRACTICING FOR
THEIR ELEMENTARY SEAMANSHI EXAM QUERY

"Cocky bugger's missed his *P* off, " growled John.

Richard chuckled, still half winded by his dash to get up here.
"Make: RADIO OUT STOP SOME CREW WOUNDED IN ONBOARD EXPLOSION
STOP . . . What else?"

They were outside on the port bridge wing. John was using
the lamp himself, and Robin was taking down the messages as
the second officer growled them out.

"Contact my father," she said without thinking, and then
stopped, confused. For the first time in a long time, she had spoken
as Robin Heritage: a different person from the lean, hard Third
Officer, *Prometheus*, she had become. The difference between what
she had been and what she was now came as a shock. So little
time had passed: so much had happened.

The other two continued speaking without pause. If they had
noticed her momentary confusion, they gave no sign.

"Better Heritage than Demetrios at this stage, surely," agreed
John. Robin's confusion lasted long enough to miss the linking
of the two names. And the cold glance that passed between the
two men: so John was thinking along those lines too, thought
Richard.

"Yes . . ." Richard temporized. No matter who they contacted,
Demetrios would know soon enough. But what would the wily
owner do next? He couldn't relay orders to his henchman—or
men—aboard until they got a radio in, and even then it would
be dangerous; perhaps impossible.

But, from Demetrios's point of view, *Prometheus* still had to sink. His man—or woman—aboard knew that. Their only real hope was that he—or she—would find it harder now.

If only he could trust Martyr...

"Richard!" John jerked him out of his reverie. "They're signaling again: PROMETHEUS STOP RELIEVED TO SEE YOU STOP INFORM YOU YOU ARE OFFICIALLY LOST WITH ALL HANDS STOP LUTINE BELL RUNG FOR YOU AT LLOYDS TODAY STOP"

The three of them looked at each other. A chill seemed to settle on them all at once. Robin actually shivered. They had just read their own obituary.

"Well, sod him," swore Richard, suddenly enraged. "He's just a little too sure of himself. Let's spoil the bastard's day. Make: PLEASE INFORM OWNER STOP KOSTAS DEMETRIOS STOP NEW YORK STOP AND HERITAGE SHIPPING STOP LONDON STOP PROMETHEUS COMING HOME STOP ALSO PLEASE INFORM SIR WILLIAM HERITAGE STOP HERITAGE SHIPPING STOP ROBIN ALIVE AND WELL STOP CAPTAIN STOP PROMETHEUS STOP MESSAGE ENDS."

Back on the bridge, Robin asked, frowning, "Are you sure we should be warning Demetrios?"

"He'll get to know soon enough in any case. At least this way he might be fooled into supposing we don't suspect him yet."

"What good will that do?"

"I don't know. But every little bit might help." He was going to say more, but John came in from the bridge wing and interrupted him.

"They'll inform everyone. I gave them an ETA for the Channel Approaches. There'll be some Coastguards waiting, I expect."

"At the very least."

"But what exactly do you propose to do?" asked Robin. It was a subject they had skirted but never really discussed. The Manxman looked speculatively at him, but he probably knew the answer as well as did the anxious woman.

"I'm going to park her in Lyme Bay and invite a full inquiry," he said. "Like it says in the Bible, 'All hearts will be open and all secrets known.'"

Robin looked at him and shivered. "Judgment Day," she said.

Channel

21

"There!" called Robin in from the port bridge wing. She took the glasses from her eyes and pointed to the shadow line between the brightening sky and the sea. Richard came out and joined her at once, leaving John beside the helmsman. He took the binoculars she was thrusting excitedly into his hand and looked through them in the direction of her gesture.

At first he thought she was mistaken. Then he thought it was only a shadow. But soon his vision cleared and his heart came close to bursting. It was the Lizard. No doubt of it. They were in home waters at last. He put his left arm around her shoulders and hugged her to him with all his strength. "Number Two," he called through the open door to John Higgins on the bridge, "you may reset the chronometers now."

It was dawn on September 9. He had brought them back exactly as he had said he would, and surprisingly easily. The weather in the Bay of Biscay had been rough enough to ensure that Richard would have been unable to open the forward tank tops even had he changed his mind, but it posed no real danger. There had been no further action by the secret saboteur. Nothing had changed. They had signaled passing ships but requested no further help— Richard wanting to keep Demetrios guessing as long as possible. So now they were entering the Channel Separation Zone still without the ability to contact other ships with anything other than the signal lamp. Still with only John's trusty sextant to pinpoint their position. But, to be fair, that sextant together with Richard's legendary powers as a theoretical navigator, had brought them exactly where they wanted to be, precisely when they were due to be there.

Richard suddenly remembered first reading as a boy, rereading on his journey to *Prometheus*, of Horatio Hornblower's great feat of navigation, guiding his Brittanic Majesty's ship *Lydia* to a perfect landfall off the Gulf of Fonseca after seven months out of sight of land. Five days across Biscay hardly compared, but the feeling of achievement was the same. He knew now why the normally imperturbable Hornblower, hero of his youth, had rushed onto the deck to see the twin volcanoes that marked this miracle of dead reckoning.

John appeared by his side and punched him lightly on the shoulder in unspoken congratulation.

"Ha-h'm!" said Richard.

The first rays of the rising sun struck across the long gray seas and glistened on something tiny and silver lifting busily from the distant land: a helicopter. Richard watched the silver speck growing larger, his mind racing. So much was going to have to be faced now. He had planned it all with infinite care. But now he would just have to see if the plans were going to work. Or whether his suspicions were going to tear the team apart.

Every single off-duty person aboard was standing by the helipad as the copter landed. They looked at it with strange intensity, as though it were something from another planet. Although they had been out of touch for only a short time, they had become so fiercely insular, so closely welded by the power of their experiences, that this came as a shocking intrusion. So the cheerful ball of a man in a blue Coastguard uniform who stepped first onto the deck might just as well have come from a distant galaxy.

If he felt their intense strangeness, he gave no sign, but bustled over to Richard at once. "Captain Mariner? McLean, Coastguard. Heard of you of course: pleasure!" This said, pumping Richard's hand enthusiastically. "Pleasure and a privilege. Shall we?"

He tried to turn Richard away toward the bridge, but the big man refused to move and McLean had no choice but to turn back, still talking, and perform some sort of introduction for the other passengers climbing down onto the deck. "Brought you all the usual offices and then some. Radio and radio officer, of course. Quine, his name is. Senior Trinity House channel pilot: excellent man called Moriarty. Chap from Lloyd's called Watson and..."

"DADDY!" Robin's voice broke off the monologue.

Sir William Heritage paused at the top of the steps. When his eyes met Richard's they narrowed and the two men might have been separated by inches rather than feet, face to face like duelists.

The moment lasted a long second, and held everyone in its power. Richard was taken off balance by the strength of his emotion. It was almost as strong as it had been in that moment when Robin appeared on his bridge like a ghost. He saw through the tear-bright haze of the dawn, the tall, broad-shouldered, soldier-straight frame of the man he most respected in the world. The clear blue eyes; the straight-clipped salt-and-pepper mustache. The steel-gray hair. And, at his side now, arm entwined through his, reed-straight until her golden head easily topped his shoulder, his daughter whom Richard loved.

How could he ever have suspected these two of anything dishonorable? How could he ever have considered standing against them, no matter what they had done? He strode forward decisively, moving for the first time since the helicopter landed.

The older man saw in his eyes something of what was in his heart. They met at the foot of the steps and what started as a handshake somehow turned into an embrace, with Robin's strong arms around them both. Richard was home again, in more ways than one.

He found he had to clear his throat when formality returned. "Welcome aboard, Sir William."

"Thanks m'boy, but it's been Bill to thee this many a long year. Let's not change that now."

Only Sir William would dream of calling Richard "m'boy"; only Richard had ever actually called Sir William "Bill."

Richard turned away from his old friend and looked up at the two men in the helicopter's doorway. A stocky man in uniform:

the radio officer. A tall angular man beside him: Watson from Lloyd's. "Gentlemen," he said, and they sprang to attention like naval cadets.

Behind them, descending in stately consequence, came the portly, spade-bearded figure, again in uniform, which could only be the channel pilot, Moriarty.

When the group was all together, Richard led them up toward the bridge. The silent crew parted, like the Red Sea parting for Moses, and closed silently behind them as they passed. They lost Watson before they reached the A deck door. The Lloyd's man lingered behind them gazing with awed wonder down into the gaping wound in the deck that the others hurried by.

On the bridge, there was an almost embarrassed pause. It was past 08.00, so Robin went about relieving John. Richard hardly knew where to start. But the others did. The radio officer opened the black case he was carrying and began to set up his portable radio on the shelf between the port windows and the captain's chair, having almost apologetically placed the captain's binoculars, cast there in the excitement, back into their holster on the chair itself.

McLean turned toward Richard and started talking again. "Should we have brought medical help? The message we received wasn't too clear on that point, and space on the helicopter was limited. We can radio..."

He said more, but Richard hardly heard him. In many ways he was the least important visitor. As soon as the radio was working, Richard would offer the con to the Channel pilot and let him get on with his job. Then he could talk to Watson, in private. He had also to talk to Bill Heritage—did the man have any idea of what he was really caught up in? He ought to talk to Watson at once, show him the logs and Accident Report Books; to do anything else would look suspicious. But he had to know what Bill was up to first. He would not run the risk of damaging him or the Heritage Corporation through an unwise word.

There was only one course open, no matter how suspicious it looked. He hesitated no longer. "Bill," he said quietly, gesturing with his head toward the bridge wing.

Sir William paused, holding the heavy door wide for his son-in-law, but before Richard could step through it, Robin was out into the bright, clear morning. This looked damned suspicious. Richard could feel their eyes on his back. Well, a captain answered to no one on his own bridge. Let them think what they liked. He stepped out, and Sir William followed, closing the door tight.

"Right. What is it you want to know so desperately, Richard?" The slightly flat vowels of Sir William's northern childhood colored his speech, showing that he was not quite as relaxed as he seemed.

"How much do you know about what's going on here, Bill?"

"Nowt. Nothing at all. Smells fishy to me, though . . ."

"You know it has to be fraud, Daddy. You know the oil must have been . . ." Richard watched her narrowly. Of course, with her lively intelligence she would have worked it out too, even if she hadn't been implicated.

The bridge wing door opened. Moriarty pushed his massive frame through. "They've given us the all clear on the wireless, Captain. I'll be taking her down to a safe anchorage in Lyme Bay now, with your permission." There was a chilly note in his precise Edinburgh accent.

"Yes, Captain Moriarty, you have her," snapped Richard. "I shall be back on the bridge in a moment."

He turned away as the door closed with a decided slam and took up Robin's surprising accusation. "You know the oil has to have been taken off at Durban. That this is all a fraud."

"That seems quite obvious, now, yes."

"That the idea has always been to break the embargo by selling the oil to South Africa, then to sink the ship and claim full insurance on both cargo and hull."

"Seems logical."

Richard took a step forward, forced near the edge of his self-control by Sir William's calm agreement.

"But it's your oil!" The agonized accusation rang out in Robin's voice.

Suddenly Richard understood her involvement completely and clearly. Her arrival at Dubai, her presence aboard, all the things that had seemed so suspicious because they couldn't be as pat as they appeared in spite of what she said. She had been lying; lying all along. But not because she had come as part of the plot. She had come because she, too, suspected her father and was trying to stop whatever was going on before it dragged the old man down. But of course she had found herself working with the one man she could not bring herself to trust in this one matter alone. As far as she knew, Rowena still lay between her father and her lover, making them the bitterest of enemies.

God! She had been strong to hold together through this tangle.

Horror showed on Sir William's face as he recognized the accusation in their eyes. "No!" he cried. "No. It's not true. I knew nothing. Nothing at all. I bought and sold that oil in good faith. I've done nothing. How could you . . . Either of you . . ."

He turned away, overcome by sorrow and rage.

They looked at each other, shocked. That one word *sold* raising the terrible weight of suspicion from their minds. Robin went forward to lay her hand on one bowed shoulder. Richard went back onto the bridge. He felt a new man. He met each suspicious gaze and held it till it fell.

Now he could deal with Watson, though he suspected the tall young man was only the vanguard of a full Lloyd's team that would descend upon them once they were safe in Lyme Bay. That would be in a little less than twelve hours' time. Sunset. Then they could all relax—all except those guilty of complicity.

It would all be over with the day.

It seemed hardly possible.

Watson's clouded blue eyes were set deep in a face composed principally of chin and cheekbone, framed with unfashionably long hair. He carried a small Dictaphone tape recorder. They went out onto the starboard bridge wing; Robin and Sir William were still out on the port one. Watson started talking into the little machine at once, giving day, date, exact time; but Richard's mind was elsewhere. On this side of the ship he was looking toward the south rather than the north, and, as is sometimes the case, the different side meant different weather. It was only the slightest imaginable difference, but it made him narrow his eyes looking away over France nevertheless. Yes. There it was. The narrowest possible band of mackerel cloud, preceded by some high, feathery whisps of mares' tails. He remembered John's doggerel said in the blue waters north of Durban where he had last seen such a cloud formation:

Mackerel skies and mares' tails
Make tall ships wear short sails.

He suddenly realized he hadn't heard a weather forecast in well over a week.

At that moment, the helicopter lifted off again and Richard followed it with his eyes, forgetting about the weather for the moment. It was gone out of his sight in a few moments and his eyes turned south again, remembering the storm.

But Watson had started his inquisition and he readily turned his mind back to the present. Then, over the next half hour, each contributing knowledge and speculation beyond the other's ken, they began to reconstruct the bare bones of the fraud.

They discussed Lloyd's history of Kostas Demetrios, a former lieutenant in the U.S. Navy, lucky to be in Naples instead of Vietnam, leaving the service at the end of his tour of duty apparently clean—though medical supplies kept vanishing from the Italian port—returning to civilian life rich, but not lazy. He worked his way through business school and moved into shipping, rapaciously ambitious; infinitely greedy. The purchase of *Prometheus* was his first really big venture in the most lucrative market of all. Running it legally, he would have been well in profit, and able to build his fleet slowly and safely. If the fraud paid off, his profits were likely to be colossal.

The crew selected for *Prometheus* might just have stood up to scrutiny, even had she sunk. There was nothing concrete against Levkas the registered master. Only Gallaher, the ship's electrician, had a serious criminal record as an IRA terrorist, still wanted for bombing an Army patrol.

Had Demetrios's plan gone unhindered, it would have been foolproof. *Prometheus*, under an assumed name, would have sold her oil in Durban. She would have blown up and sunk off Senegal. Insurance would have been collected. Kostas Demetrios would have been very, very rich.

Everything that had happened to Richard and his crew had been an increasingly desperate variation on that simple plan. Desperate, but not wildly so: there was still no absolute proof.

Until the tanks were opened.

"But if you couldn't open the tanks?" asked Richard. "If we hadn't brought her home?"

"We'd have paid up. Simple as that. Still might have to, if anything goes wrong."

"But the suspicion..."

"A story. Nothing more. The sort of thing you find in novels. I doubt it would ever stand up in court. Unsubstantiated hearsay, most of it. No damn good at all, without proof."

There seemed little more to say at the moment. Both men knew there were still a lot of loose ends to be tied up, but for the time being they had sketched out the broad outlines of the plot. Watson went below to check through the records, now he had a clearer idea of what he was looking for.

Richard made a mental note to get the police aboard the moment they dropped anchor in Lyme Bay, then stood looking south, lost in thought. After a few moments, the door opened and closed. He turned to find Sir William beside him, his back ramrod straight and his shoulders square again.

They stood in companionable silence, then Richard, unable to say how happy he was to be beside his father-in-law again, said instead, solicitously, "Robin said you'd not been well."

"Told you that, did she?"

"Yup."

"Ah, well. Happen she thought she had reason." A hint of displeasure, like distant thunder in his voice.

"But there was no cause for alarm?"

"No!" The northern accent drew the vowel out derisively. As though there could be anything wrong with Bill Heritage! The very idea invited scorn.

Richard was lifted by the negative—and the old, familiar confidence beneath it. This was the man he remembered. Obviously he had found some way to strengthen the weak, broken man Robin had described so long ago...

"How's the oil market?" Richard asked, as though the suspicions, as though the last five years, had never existed.

"Very buoyant. Rumors of another cut in Middle Eastern production. Prices going through the roof."

"You were lucky to buy in at the start."

"I was owed some favors by someone in the Foreign Office."

"And you sold it on ... When?"

"Ten days ago."

"That fits. Who to?"

"Some outfit I'd never heard of. Good profit."

"Too good?"

"Good enough to make me feel dirty? That what you mean?"

"No, Bill. We're over that. Good enough to look suspicious?"

"Not with the market jumping like that..."

Richard nodded. Then something further occurred to him. "Why'd you come out, Bill?" he asked. "It was more than just seeing Robin. She's been her own woman for years now. You knew she was safe, like the rest of us. You've never fussed before."

"This was different!"

"Right about that!" His tone was mild, robbing the words of offense.

"And anyway ..."

"I knew there was more. What?"

"It hardly seems important now. We're headed for safe anchorage. Only a matter of hours to go."

"Right. So?"

"I heard yesterday morning, and it frightened the life out of me, I admit."

"Out with it, Bill. What?"

"*Prometheus*'s sister. Doesn't have a name anymore. Last registered as *Tethys*. Tied up in the next anchorage to *Prometheus* in Valparaiso all these years..."

"Yes?"

"Broke in half. Sank in minutes. Complete harbor watch gone. Riding in ballast. Clear day. No warning, nothing. They reckoned it was the long seas did it, bending her like a piece of wire, never varying. Bending her like a piece of wire till she snapped."

Richard felt his body chill.

"No warning at all?"

"One of the watch aboard was talking to his daughter on the ship-to-shore phone line. Cut off in midword. That's how they found out so quickly. She looked out of the window and it was gone. Bloody great supertanker gone. No ship: no father. Nothing." He snapped his fingers. "Quick as that."

22

The helicopter was back again in minutes, ferrying in a doctor and a nurse, another Coastguard, a customs officer who looked like the sailor on the front of the old cigarette packet, and the first policeman, a self-effacing detective sergeant from Falmouth.

They might just as well have called in at any of the islands after all, thought Richard grimly. The only difference would have been the nationality of the officialdom that overwhelmed them.

But all these new—and not particularly welcome—faces had the unexpected effect of bringing the crew even more closely together. If they looked upon the first influx as aliens, they looked upon the rest as little short of vermin. On the one hand, Richard found himself rapidly running out of patience as all sorts of bureaucratic pygmies made importunate demands on his time he could not begin to fulfill; on the other, the rest of the crew, from the first lieutenant to the lowliest of Ho's stewards, flatly refused to do or say a thing without referring either directly or through the chain of command, to their captain. He had, after all, brought them this far against unimaginable odds; he would stand by them now.

And he did. Although he would far rather have been leading a team to check for possible weaknesses in the hull that might trip them, fatally, at the last fence from home.

The awe in which they seemed to hold him, therefore, became

187

a source at once of great strength and of great irritation. And of increasing isolation.

He felt alone, but he was not. They all, to varying degrees, felt isolated too. Robin, even though she was with her father, to whom she had given a lifetime of filial devotion, looked almost with pity on the grand old man because he had not shared what the rest of them had. No matter what he had seen or known, it could be nothing like this. There was a part of her that he would never be able to reach again. Which any other one of the crew, no matter how little known or how faintly remembered, had direct access to. And each of the others, looking at the interlopers, felt the same. Events, and Richard's titanic abilities as a leader, had welded them together into a combat unit. Had strung between them those bonds almost of blood, which would see the passing of years as nothing compared to the enduring of this experience.

As midday approached, the captain firmly extricated himself from the clutches of the insistent customs man, swept past the policeman, and entered the bridge. His impatience was instantly obvious to his crew. It was pleasant to have the radio aboard, but the current news concerned only pop stars and drugs. They had missed the final test match, of course. There was nothing of real interest. He listened for a few minutes, then swung round.

"Bearing to Mecca?"

Ben was just relieving Robin, and it was she who rattled it off. She hadn't seen Richard in this mood for many years, but she remembered it vividly and stood in awe of it. When he turned and exited the bridge, the mate and the third lieutenant exchanged a long look.

A moment or two later, the ship's address system came on. "Attention. Your attention, please. This is the captain speaking..." Absolute silence fell. Even the engine seemed to quiet.

Surprised by this simple demonstration of this captain's power, Moriarty turned, and his eyes met the awed glance of Quine, the new radio officer. They stood in respectful silence until the bearing of Mecca completed the messages.

Then, "What sort of a man is he, your captain?" Moriarty asked Ben.

"The only man alive who could have brought us through like

this." Ben might have been going to say more, but the subject of their discussion came back onto the bridge just then.

"You can go down to lunch, Number Three. Tell them to send the rest of us up some sandwiches."

Robin was happy enough to leave, but he stopped her at the door. "Oh. And find that policeman. I don't want him being sick all over my ship."

She turned away. Too soon.

"And if you see Sir William, tell him he is welcome either to join us here or to eat with the officers below."

"Aye, sir." She hadn't called him "sir" since Durban, and not very often before Durban, either.

The afternoon passed in that air of dangerous calm. Richard stayed on the bridge, unable to do anything else without tripping over importunate officialdom. Anyone who wanted to see him— fewer and fewer as the day progressed—came and were growled at there. Off their port beam the coast of England loomed and receded as they swept past bays and headlands most had never thought to see again. They had passed the Lizard, Black Head, and Manacle Point while Moriarty was getting used to her. They had passed distant Dodman Point and Chapel Point. They had passed the Eddystone Rocks soon after Richard's curt broadcast; and now, looming large across Bigbury Bay, lay Prawle Point, and beyond it, Lyme Bay.

What had started as a bright day was gathering itself into a dull evening. The mares' tails that Richard had seen this morning were replaced by a flat, gray overcast. The sea, gray-green at the best of times, now seemed almost black, rolling in on the starboard quarter from Biscay and the southwest.

The detective sergeant's name was Bodmin, like the moor; and he wasn't either as self-effacing or as seasick as he seemed. He had been born and raised in Falmouth, able to sail a boat before he could ride a bike. Only education in London, at Hendon, and his detective's course in Manchester had taken him far away from the sea. And as soon as he had passed out of police training college, he had transferred back to the Cornish force and his childhood sweetheart, content to make his way slowly and happily down here.

Nor was he a fool, for all that he played up his accent and acted before the ignorant a little of the country bumpkin.

So when he told the chief engineer to consider himself under arrest, Harry Bodmin knew well enough what he was up to. The American took it surprisingly calmly, and at first the detective thought he couldn't have heard above the grumble of the engines in the Engine Control Room. But Martyr had heard all right, as had Rice and McTavish. Their reaction was more marked than the chief's, for, as it was with Captain Mariner and the deck officers, so obviously it was with Martyr and his engineers. For a moment, Bodmin wondered if he had miscalculated after all and was about to meet a sticky end.

But Martyr swung round slowly, wearily. "Can't prove nothing, son," he said. "But you're welcome to try like the others back home."

"Thank you, sir. At least I can assume you are not going anywhere for the moment, and I know you are necessary to the running of the ship, so it's a notional arrest. Unless you try to escape before this inquiry is over, of course." He saw the skeptical look in the chief's eye and added dryly, "Scotland Yard is of course aware of the warrant for homicide outstanding against you in New York, though I believe that to be a federal offense; and, together with the investigator from Lloyd's, I cannot see how this alleged fraud could possibly have been perpetrated without your active or passive connivance. You are the last of the original officers left alive. This ship was always bound, illegally, for Durban. You and your dead colleagues must have known that from the start. When we have proved what is actually in those tanks, we might well be adding our own charges to the federal warrant against you."

Rather pleased with that as an exit speech, he swung wide the door into the strangely misshapen, blast-damaged corridor past the Pump Room and went to pursue the rest of his inquiries.

He spent the rest of the afternoon in the first mate's office, interviewing everyone aboard. But it really got him nowhere. No one actually admitted to knowing anything, and he began to realize that unless he and Watson could prove that the ship had visited Durban on purpose—and the food poisoning was going to make that difficult—then there was precious little proof that anything illegal had been done since Mariner had assumed command.

And yet it was quite obvious that here was a massive fraud, attempted mass murder by the use of explosives, perhaps the same thing by the use of poison off Durban, and heaven only knew what else. Grievous Bodily Harm at the very least, if the American's face was anything to go by. He had better get ashore, he thought, and turn this lot over to his superiors.

He found Martyr and the captain on the bridge, both looking morosely across the choppy expanse of Lyme Bay to where the lights of Exmouth twinkled in the distance. As soon as Mariner saw him, he went straight into the attack. "I hear you've put my chief under some kind of arrest."

It was only to be expected, thought Bodmin, without a trace of resentment at the hostility. It hadn't taken him long to see how close-knit this crew had become, like some station-houses he had known on the force. He hoped if he ever got into trouble there would be people like these to stand beside him. He calculated that this was the time for a softly-softly approach, if he wanted to get ashore.

"Only notionally, sir. I'm not quite sure of my authority. If Mr. Martyr were considering coming ashore, I might be able to arrange some sort of accommodation until . . ."

"He's not. Now that we're at anchor, we're keeping a harbor watch until the rest of the authorities come aboard in the morning."

"And that watch will include the chief?"

"Yes. It includes all the crew."

"Fine. How do I get ashore?"

"If you hurry, Captain Moriarty may let you have a seat with Mr. Watson in the pilot's cutter. It's just about to pull away."

Bodmin left at a run.

Richard had not been lying to protect his chief. He did fully intend to keep watches above- and belowdeck all night, no matter how exhausted he and his crew were. He had a feeling that their safety was by no means assured now they were at anchor—indeed, he was absolutely certain that this position was not the beginning of safety but the climax of danger.

The real investigation would not start until tomorrow after all. Anyone left active in Demetrios's murderous plot, therefore, would have to act tonight.

So, after Bodmin left, Richard remained on the bridge and Martyr remained in the Engine Room, each one of them at full alert.

And the hours began to pass.

At a quarter past midnight, Robin found herself in the same spot as usual, outside Richard's door in the C deck corridor. She had come down here straight off watch as though driven by some Pavlovian reflex.

The situation and the time were so correct that she paused, though she knew Richard was up on the bridge keeping the first part of Ben's watch while Ben tried to fix the computers in the Cargo Control Room for the morning. She paused for a moment, then, almost ready to turn left toward her lover's empty berth, only to turn right after all and knock quietly on the door opposite.

The owner's suite was occupied again. Oddly—or perhaps not so oddly at that—without a word being said on either side, Sir William Heritage had joined the team. In what capacity it was not quite clear, but when the other interlopers left by helicopter and pilot's launch, he was still aboard. And he had no intention of being anywhere else. Though no great sailor himself for many years past, he fitted into *Prometheus*'s routine as he fitted every-where—quietly and without fuss.

The battered but sizable expanding briefcase he habitually car-ried held as much as he needed—a few office things in one side and a few overnight things in the other; and a small, two-way radio, which could transmit as far as Exeter, perhaps, but which could receive from very much farther afield.

He was speaking quietly into this as Robin entered. He glanced up, grinned, and waved her to a seat. "Please wait," he said into the small microphone and took his thumb off TRANSMIT.

"New toy," he announced, pleased. "It can transmit as far as Exeter, and I arranged a relay there on the way down. Just having a word with the twenty-four-hour secretary at the office." He depressed the button once more and began to speak.

It was from another, half-forgotten world. Robin watched, bemused; amazed anew at her father's grasp of his business. He would have settled everything important before leaving Town and yet here he was, still tying up loose ends with no reports or memoranda—with nothing to help but a few crisp notes from his personal tape recorder.

Abruptly a tidal wave of warmth swept over her. In the weeks she had been aboard *Prometheus* she had forgotten how much she loved this man.

Finishing, he leaned back and massaged his eyes gently, fingers and thumb almost lost beneath his shaggy brows, in a gesture that she remembered with poignant affection from childhood. Unaware of her scrutiny, he leaned forward and flicked a switch on the radio. At once the quiet voice of a BBC newsreader filled the room.

At last he turned, the routine complete. "Well now, lass, you're looking gradely," he rumbled. "Seems I wasn't working you hard enough."

She had come down to see that he was all right. She had no intention of staying for long, but a chat and maybe a drink wouldn't go amiss. Smiling wryly, therefore, she crossed to his small bar-fridge. "You're looking better yourself, Dad," she said.

"Mebbe I am at that."

"Whisky?"

"Grand."

As she poured them a whisky each and turned back toward him, so the news bulletin on his radio finished.

"You want water with this?"

"Has it been that long, lass?"

"No; it's ice-cold."

"Ah well. No help for it."

She turned back and opened the fridge. There were some small bottles of Perrier in the door. "And it's fizzy . . ."

"Gah! The privations of ship-board life, eh?"

"Pity poor sailors..." she said.

"And here is the shipping forecast issued by the Meteorological Office at midnight tonight..."

She crossed to her father and handed him his glass. Then she sat comfortably on his bunk. He sipped the amber liquid. "So," he said, "what exactly have you been up to then?"

"German Bight, Humber: six to seven, southwesterly, strengthening. Showers. Moderate to poor..."

"Well, it's a long story..." She was suddenly a little defensive; unsure how much she wanted to share.

"We've got time now, lass..." He spread his hands wide, holding the whisky firmly in the left.

"Thames, Dover: seven to gale eight, south-southwesterly, strengthening. Intermittent rain. Poor..."

"Not too long. I'm going back up onto the bridge in a minute or two." Already she sounded distracted. She sipped her whisky.

"Nay, Robin. What good can you do? And you're worn out. Look at you."

"I'm third officer here, damn it, Dad. I can do my duty..."

"Wight, Portland, Plymouth: gale eight to severe gale nine. Strengthening. Heavy rain. Poor..."

"Don't you swear at me, my girl! You're mixed up in something pretty dirty here. Dirty, and, by the look of it, dangerous. I'm your dad. I want you safe out. It's only natural..."

Erect now, she put her glass on his bedside table and turned. "Don't you patronize me, Father. As I have already said, I am third officer here and I..."

It hit her then: the weather forecast.

"Biscay: severe gale force nine gusting to storm ten, southerly, strengthening. Heavy rain. Visibility poor and worsening..."

"My God! Did you hear that?"

"What..."

"South Finisterre..."

"*That!* There's a southerly storm coming and we're anchored on a lee shore. Jesus!"

She crossed to the door.

"Robin," he called.

She turned in the doorway. A vibrant, controlled, competent person he had never seen before. "Make it quick, Dad," she snapped, "or we'll all be sitting hard aground on Exmouth promenade long before the dawn."

The VDU screen flickered. A column of figures appeared then vanished in the twinkling of an eye. "Nearly there," exulted Ben. "McTavish, is that circuit going to hold up?"

"Aye. There's nothing uncou' complex about it, Mr. Strong. It's just been blown tae hell and gone. That's all."

"Well, if we pull this one off my bonny boy, we'll be able to hand in our papers here and get a job with IBM."

"And gie up the sea, Number One?"

"And give up the sea indeed."

They worked for a while in silence; then McTavish ventured, "But what'd there be tae catch the lassies af I'd no ma uniform tae wear?"

They were working in the Cargo Control Room as they had been since the anchor went down. The two of them, with occasional help from Quine, had been at it for nearly eight hours solidly and were quite prepared for eight more. But there would be no need: if this last circuit held up without shorting out, the end was in sight at last.

Fortunately, the computer's memory banks did not seem to have been damaged by the explosion. Richard had sealed the room against wind and weather once it had been cleared of debris, and now Ben and McTavish were hoping to get it ready for the inspection later this morning.

"That's it!" called McTavish from under the console.

"Right. I'll try it again. Come out..."

McTavish needed no second warning. His face was a rash of burn-spots from their last such experiment, which had shorted like a Roman candle an inch above his nose. But Ben didn't even see him move. Even as he spoke, he pressed ENTER and now the whole screen lit up again. And stayed alight.

"Good..."

Ben's nimble fingers moved across the keys, rattling off the entry codes that would bring up the memory index. He would check that, then the file headings. And if they were all still there, the files themselves.

But the machine was already answering perfectly:

FILE ONE: LADING: LADING SCHEDULES 1–10...

By 02.30 he knew for certain that the bulk of the memory was intact. He sat back and cracked his knuckles, satisfied for the moment. "I'm finished with the first part of this, McTavish. You all tidied?"

"Just about, Number One. Screwing down the last panel now."

"I know someone I'd like to *screw down*: the S.O.B. who did all this in the first place."

"Aye." McTavish picked himself up and dusted off his knees punctiliously. "It's nothing short of criminal ruining all this expensive equipment."

"Still, it's working now."

"That it is, Mr. Strong. I'll tell the chief so too. Do you want tae tell the captain?"

"I'll clean up first. You run along."

"Aye. It's been a dirty job." The young Scot paused at Ben's shoulder, looking across the room. "But it's done now. And well done."

Then he was gone.

Ben's hands hovered over the keyboard an instant longer. Then he, too, left.

He did not go to the bridge, however, but to his own quarters. He wanted to check that everything was ready. He was still busy there when Robin arrived.

Bang Bang Bang! The hammering at his door was so unexpected that he nearly fainted. He answered as quickly as he could, still pale from the shock.

"Lord!" said Robin. "You look terrible!"

"I'm okay. What is it?"

"Where've you been for the last few hours, Number One?" she demanded, taking a leaf out of his own book. "It's a bloody great storm is what it is. Got us trapped against a lee shore. It's either hard aground on Exmouth Prom. or safely afloat in the Seine Bay—so we're off to France, says our less-than-happy captain. Off to France. Right now!"

"Can't you get anyone on that radio, Mr. Quine?" snapped Richard.

"No, sir. It's not really powerful enough to handle all this atmospheric interference."

"Then our departure will have to remain unannounced. What's our bearing, John?"

"One twenty."

"Steady at that. What are we?"

"Slow ahead. Making five knots."

"Okay. But I want more speed as soon as possible."

It was the earliest part of John's watch, and he stood by Salah Malik's left shoulder while Ben stood at his right, both peering through the fogged glass. Robin was guarding the Collision Alarm Radar, which, though set at its lowest calibration, was mercifully quiet. The first big seas thundered into her, beam-on, black and hard as coal. She lurched a little, not liking this at all. Richard remembered the last time he had put her through anything like this, sitting confidently in his captain's chair. Before bombs; before anyone had mentioned anything about sister ships breaking their backs on the long seas of the Roaring Forties.

Another big sea hit her. She moved only infinitesimally, but Richard knew all her ways now, and that one felt as though it had come more from head-on than beam-on. Richard went forward and pressed himself close to the glass, wishing he had a clearview in front of him. He could hardly see the deck. He couldn't see the sea at all.

"Quine?"

"Yes, sir?"

"It's getting increasingly important..."

Just as Richard spoke, Quine at last got something on the portable radio he had brought aboard. The World Service News.

"...And the hurricane-force winds which have devastated

Southern France today turned north, against all predictions, and are currently blowing over the Channel. Coastguards fear considerable danger to shipping. And now, sport..."

Richard exploded. "Hurricane force! That's no bloody use at all, Mr. Quine! I need facts, not journalistic horror stories. I want reports from weather ships and coastal stations. I want accurate wind velocities. I want exact atmospheric pressure readings. I want state of sea and sky, and I do not need the blasted news and sport."

"N...No, sir!" stuttered Quine, unnerved by the injustice of the attack. But Richard had slammed out onto the port bridge wing where he could vent his frustration on the elements, and not on innocent bystanders.

The wind out here was thunderous, breathtaking. It buffeted him with a cold fury, numbing him almost at once. He strode forward and gripped the handrail. Only that unrelenting grasp kept him upright as the wind tore at him, pushing icy fingers through the apparently impenetrable cold-weather gear he was now wearing. This was the last thing on earth he wanted to be putting *Prometheus* through, but he had no choice. The storm, approaching from this direction, simply turned Lyme Bay into a lee shore and threatened to blow him aground off Exmouth. He had to run for the shelter of the Seine Bay, off the north coast of France opposite.

It was a matter of mere miles—little more than a hundred—before the Cherbourg Peninsula would start giving a measure of protection. In these conditions, perhaps ten hours' sailing time. So little and so short a time after their voyage so far. But there was something that made him more than a little uneasy; and it was not just the thought of the use Demetrios's man might put this weather to. Perhaps he thought the old girl had had enough. Perhaps he felt that this was one test too many.

Certainly, it was the one final test he now most dreaded facing with her. Even as he stood there, lost in thought, the first great column of lightning striking the wavetops far ahead showed him the worst.

As it sometimes does, the Channel, under the storm conditions, had pulled in the great Atlantic rollers from the Western Approaches; it had steepened their sides and lengthened the distance between their crests. It had swung them round and was hurling them head-on at *Prometheus*: a perfect facsimile of the seas of the Roaring Forties. It didn't happen often but it had happened now. To get to the safety of northern France, *Prometheus* must sail through a flawless replica of the seas off Valparaiso. The seas that had broken her sister's back. On a clear day. In a calm.

23

Richard remained outside on the bridge wing for fifteen minutes, expecting to be summoned momentarily as Quine managed to contact the Coastguards. When no such thing happened, his patience ran out quickly. The occasionally glimpsed seas looked too dangerous for him to allow the boy much indulgence.

After the icy rigor of the storm, the bridge was almost suffocating. He paused for an instant to reorient himself, streaming water. Nothing much had changed. Quine was palely wrestling to extract sense from his radio. Without success. Richard bit back further recrimination and turned to Robin.

"Number Three. Go down and ask your father if you can bring his radio up here. It may be open to less atmospheric interference than Mr. Quine's."

"Aye, sir," snapped Robin and exited at once.

Robin was quite pleased at being asked to go to her father. Her bladder was about to burst, courtesy of that unwise whisky at midnight, and the mission at least saved her from having to ask to leave the bridge. Really she should have gone straight to the owner's cabin, but her need was too acute. She ran down to her own cabin first and let herself in with a sigh of relief. It was pitch dark in the little vestibule, for the only light bulb in her quarters lit her cabin, perpetually dark now that the windows had been boarded up.

She knew, as soon as she stepped in, that she was not alone, and she swung the door behind her wide again, to let in light from the corridor.

The layout of the cabin was similar to Richard's except that there was no dayroom or office on her left. Only the curtain before her into the shower and toilet, and the door on her right led out of the little cubicle where she now stood, not even breathing, trying to make her ears overcome the bluster of the wind, the rattling of the window-ply. What was it that had warned her? Some fragrance on the unquiet air? Some sound half hidden in the wind? Some more subtle sense?

It was probably only one of the stewards after all. "Who's there?" she called, as though she hadn't hesitated, being careful to open the door to her sleeping quarters before the door behind her closed.

The cabin was empty. There was no one visible and nowhere to hide: even the doors to her wardrobe had gone to fix the windows. She gave an angry sigh, irritated with herself for acting like a nervous child, frightened of her own shadow.

She went back out to the toilet, vexed.

Sitting in the dark, with the shower curtain eerily caressing her as it moved in the draft, her room suddenly became very clear before some inner eye, and she realized just how many things were not quite in the places she had left them.

Her room had been very thoroughly searched.

And the unease that this shock realization brought started another train of thought. Why had Ben looked so shaken when he had answered his door? She let her mind go back and looked at his face in her clear memory. Something was wrong there. She checked her luminous watch. She might just take a further moment to find out what was going on before she fetched her father.

As soon as Heritage was in her quarters, the door opposite across the corridor opened and C. J. Martyr crept out on silent feet. That English policeman hadn't fooled him with his slow speech and hesitant manner. Heads were going to roll over this, and Martyr's was closest to the block.

Bodmin had brought this home with a vengeance. Martyr had been so wrapped up in what he was doing, and why, it simply hadn't occurred to him how it would look from the outside. But now he saw all too clearly. He was the only survivor of the original crew—which had joined willingly in the fraud. He was a party to a huge insurance swindle, sanction-breaking, something damn near piracy, and murder. Again. They were going to lock him up and throw away the key. The only hope he could see to try to prove his innocence was to try to find Demetrios's man. That at the very least might make them reduce his sentence.

It was amusing, in a grim sort of way. Fate had placed him in the same old position—in the middle and at risk from both sides at once. If only he could be certain about Mariner...

Well, Heritage had nothing incriminating in her cabin.

Who was next on the list? Strong.

No. Higgins would just have taken over the watch. Check Higgins first. Leave Strong till later.

Robin came out of her room and hesitated in the flat brightness of the corridor. It was enough to make one believe in ghosts, even in this bland atmosphere, but she had the feeling again that someone had just been there. And, as if to emphasize her fears, the draft in the corridor suddenly brought the soft, other-worldly song of Nihil's strange flute from the crew's quarters. Perhaps it was just the storm, but little currents of icy air were everywhere, disturbing the normally tranquil ambiance of the accommodation areas, as though the ill-fitting boards were giving access to a lot more than mere storm wind. She shivered, tightened her cold-weather gear around her, and hurried down to Ben's cabin.

Richard would be wondering where the hell she had got to, for she had spent some moments checking through her cabin again, completely mystified as to who would want to search it or why. She began to jog down the corridor, possessed of a sudden urgency, moving silently on her Wellington-ed feet, the only sound the whisper of her waterproof leggings.

When she got to his door she didn't even bother to knock. She knew well enough where he was. He was on the bridge.

Or was he?—The light in his cabin was on!

She hesitated in the dark vestibule of his quarters. They were laid out like the captain's: curtain in front, dayroom office on the left, light-edged cabin door on her right.

If the light was on, the man was in, she reasoned. And he would have heard her come in this far. No help for it, then: she turned the handle and entered the cabin.

"Ben..."

The cabin was empty.

Richard forced himself to sit at ease while every nerve in his body was agonizingly taut. He was used to meeting tension with action; he had forgotten how hard it could be simply to sit and be in command.

He had opened the bright yellow waterproof jacket but had made no other concession to the stifling closeness of the bridge. He might well have to go outside again—perhaps in a hurry—and fighting his way into recalcitrant cold-weather gear would only slow things up. The closeness was not simply a matter of atmosphere, either, he realized suddenly: though the air in here was too warm, too full of unexplained currents of tension, it was really the nature of the storm itself. There was no visual element to it. It was as though the hurricane winds were themselves coal-black. They forced themselves against the windows like the flanks of monstrous animals and it was impossible to see. Off the coast of South Africa, the storm, terrible though it was, had at least been visible—had at least attained some scale and grandeur. This was a much more personal—disturbing—thing; and the fact that it had wrapped the howling shroud of itself around the bridge windows made the normally airy place seem constricted, confining.

Nor was he alone in this thought. Ben stirred at last from his brown study at the helmsman's side. "I'll stand out on the bridge wing. Check the lookout," he yelled. Richard nodded.

Ben slopped through the puddle Richard had made on his last entrance and took the door handle.

Several things happened at once.

Ben opened the door. A large sea gave *Prometheus* a right hook that caused her to jump. The squall responsible for the rogue wave took the door and flung it open, then closed.

Ben was hurled backward over the slippery floor. He lost his footing and crashed down, striking his head against the edge of the chart table. He rolled over and lay still.

"Ben!" Richard was at his side immediately, gentle fingers probing along the scalp line to discover a large gash oozing blood. But Ben's eye flickered open at once, bright and clear. "You okay?" Richard asked.

"Yeah!" Ben's own fingers traced the wound. He sat up. "Fine." But even as he spoke, a bright worm of blood began to crawl down toward his right eye.

"Better get that looked at," said Richard, turning toward John, who was looking anxiously across from the Collision Alarm Radar.

"No," said Ben at once. "You can't spare anyone here. I'll slip down and see to it myself."

Richard hesitated, then nodded. Ben was right. If he could see to it himself it would be better. With Robin still below, he could ill-spare John. And Quine knew nothing of first aid. So he helped Ben to his feet and guided him a step or two until his godson could cross the rest of the bridge unaided.

At the door, Ben turned and looked back, but the others were already preoccupied. He wiped the blood back up into his hairline and allowed himself a grim little smile. Couldn't have arranged it better, he thought. Now no one would suspect a thing.

Robin hesitated in Ben's cabin, thinking fast. Under other circumstances what she was about to do would be absolutely unacceptable—and extremely distasteful—but the memory of that look on his face drove her on. She started to search the cabin, but the search revealed nothing untoward. This was hardly surprising, since she had no idea what she was looking for. Committed to doing this now, she moved into his office quickly. And there she found what she had been looking for—just enough to make her suspicious. By his desk was a small safe. As first officer, he was responsible for any valuables aboard. The safe was open. Empty. And, above it, on the desk itself, stood Ben's only real treasure, a photograph of his dead parents.

Except that it wasn't there. The frame remained, lying dismantled on the desktop, but the photograph was gone. She was standing, holding it, thinking like lightning when the door slammed wide.

Ben hesitated on the stairs, a wave of nausea threatening to overcome him. He held on to the banister and wiped the back of his right hand over his forehead. It came away thick with blood. Impatiently, he pushed the congealing liquid back into his hair. It wasn't as bad as it looked but it was worse than it was meant to be. He hadn't felt as bad as this since the night of the explosion going down to try to sink her for the first time.

But the time and the circumstances were too good to be missed now. The storm would cover the sound of the pumps— he had set them low and quiet anyway, expecting them to be doing their deadly work in a quiet anchorage. The storm would cover the loss of the ship—like the bomb was supposed to. It was a cataclysm so large that it would cover everything, no questions asked. He did not pause to consider the loss of his shipmates—right from the start he had known most of them were doomed.

As soon as his head cleared, he ran on down the stairs. He considered going to his cabin—he had enough medication there to staunch the blood—but he went to the Cargo Control Room first.

There was no need to switch the lights on. His deft fingers found the control-console keys in the dark and tapped in the secret code. The screen flickered and lit up:

LADING SCHEDULE 11. LADING SCHEDULE LOGGED IN.

He typed in: EXPEDITE and pressed RETURN.

At once the screen went blank, also according to the original program.

He paused, listening with every fiber of his being, but he could not hear the pumps begin their deadly work. They were lost in the sound of the storm. But he knew well enough what they would be doing. The extra schedule he had programmed the machine to accept in Durban, called for all the cargo to be transferred to one tank. And as the pumps tried to obey the computer's order, so the forces they obediently unleashed would tear the ship apart.

He went out and paused again. Should he close up the wound in his head?

No. Like the storm, it covered up so much. If he alone survived, it would look so impressive at the court of inquiry. And, after all that had happened, he would need to look impressive there.

Or, if any of the others survived as well, then the wound, deep enough to bring mild concussion, would explain why he wasn't on the bridge—why he was doing the apparently irrational things he needed to do if he were going to survive.

The first of which was to get to the forecastle head, where his own personal life raft was hidden beneath the spare anchor.

24

The door to Ben's office slammed wide and Martyr was standing there. Robin looked at him narrowly. She was not really surprised. "Is this it?" she asked quietly. "Is this what you have been searching for?" She held up the empty picture frame and he understood its meaning as readily as she had done: wherever he was now, whatever he was up to, Ben had no intention of ever coming back here.

"Strong..." he whispered. "Where is he?"

"On the bridge five minutes ago. But it looks as though he's not going to stay there."

"Right." He swung round, heading for the door. Then he stopped. "No. Wait." He turned back. "He's got to make sure we sink. He can't leave it to chance. He's got to be sure, but how?"

"Tell you what I'd do," said Robin thoughtfully, "I'd move the cargo so that she breaks up. Easy enough to do. Hell, we need all those machines and years of training to stop it happening in the first place."

"That's it!" he agreed. "It has to be!"

"Right. Tell you what: I've got to get the radio from my father. It's what I came down for. You take this to the captain. I'll get the radio and come to the bridge with it. And I'll get my father to check the Cargo Control Room."

She caught Martyr's questioning look. "Computers," she

snapped. "He loves them. They're like toys to him. If anyone can find..."

The American nodded.

She was away at once.

Robin made no hesitation outside Richard's cabin this time, but crossed to her father's quarters at a flat run. She thundered on the door until light washed over her feet then burst impulsively in. Sir William was standing, clear-eyed but tousle-haired at the side of his bunk. He had been sleeping in his shirtsleeves and as his daughter entered he turned, running his thumbs up under his braces. "Well?" he snapped, none too pleased with being woken.

Once she might have hesitated, cowed by his obvious displeasure. No longer. "Quine's radio doesn't work properly," she responded coolly. "The captain wants to borrow yours."

"Of course. But I turned it off hours ago because of atmospheric interference."

She crossed to it as he was saying this. She nodded once, tight-mouthed, picked it up, and turned back.

Then she did pause, for the first time, suddenly struck by the thought that she might well be sending him into unacceptable danger. He was shoeless and something about his bright Argyll socks made her feel poignantly protective toward him. But she had a responsibility to all the rest of them as well. And he would do a better job than anybody else aboard. So: "Look..." she began. As quickly and accurately as she could—given that some of it at least was guesswork—she explained what she and Martyr had learned. And what she wanted him to do.

Within moments of her first word he was seated on his bunk, reaching for his shoes. By the time she was finished he was laced up and ready to go.

They parted at the lift. He stepped in, to sink two decks. She ran on to the stairs and bounded up them. Running onto the bridge, she had handed Sir William's little radio to Quine before she noticed something was wrong. John was there alone. There were no other officers in sight.

No sign of Richard or Martyr. Or of Ben.

She went cold.

John was at the helmsman's left shoulder. She strode quickly across to him. "John!" She had to yell to make herself heard. "Where are the others?"

"Captain's on the starboard bridge wing."

"But Martyr? Ben Strong?"

"Martyr's in the engine room if I know him. Ben bashed his head open and went below, what? ten minutes ago?"

"Oh God."

"Robin? Robin, where are you . . . Number Three! Christ!"

But she was gone.

Sir William pushed the door of the Cargo Control Room open and very nearly panicked. He found himself confronted with a solid wall of smoke. He unconsciously echoed John Higgins three decks above. "Christ!" he muttered, hit the lights, and plunged in.

There was no sound of flames, merely a telltale hissing. Nor was there any real sensation of heat; just the smoke: McTavish's wires were shorting out again, though William Heritage did not know this.

Sir William paused in the center of the room. His eyes were watering and, for all that he was holding his breath, the acrid smoke caught at his throat. Forcing himself not to cough, he looked around, all too aware that his time was severely limited. But at the center of the room, the smoke seemed thinner and the light as it flickered on revealed the seat of the fire—a thinning column of smoke oozing oilily from behind a blistered, twisted tin panel. Sir William kicked it twice, ruining some of Lobb and Company's finest work, and it fell back to reveal a black mare's nest of burned wires.

McTavish had left a red can of electrical-safe firefighting foam on the nearest work surface and Bill used this to kill the last pungent clouds.

His breath ran out then but instead of going out toward the open door, he crossed to the rattling sheet of board that was trying to wrench itself out of the blast-twisted windowframe. It came away surprisingly easily and the storm wind burst in, blasting the smoke away.

And bringing William Heritage almost face to face with a tall, yellow-clad figure who turned away before the old man could be certain who it was, to vanish down the deck.

The storm hit Ben with full force the moment he stepped out of the A deck door. The solid ram of the wind blasted him back against the ravaged iron of the upper works. A sheet of water, solid as ice, slid along the deck beneath his feet, almost sweeping them away. He turned and was suddenly blinded by a bright light. He turned again, his back to the brightness, and staggered away from the bridge house, feeling acutely the loss of his chance to summon up some reserves of energy and fortitude. But he had to pause almost at once, fortuitously, in the first shadow; then, leaning forward into the brunt of the wind, placing his feet carefully as though planting them and willing them to grow safe roots into the throbbing deck, he began to walk down the length of the ship.

It never occurred to him that the brightness meant that he had been spotted. It seemed unlikely that anyone from the bridge would see him, though he was dressed in the bright wet-weather gear they had broken out before turning to run for France. The bridge windows, plain glass without the benefit of clearview, would hide most of the deck under a vertical sheet of water. He had no intention, however, of using the raised catwalk above the pipes running down the center of the deck. No. He would sneak down among the shadows of the manifolds and tank caps here at deck level, and hope the hell he wasn't washed overboard. Danger of one sort saving him from the far greater danger of exposure.

That was the one thing he really dreaded. He was one of nature's natural spies. Under the bland surface he presented to the world he could hide anything. Even this. But the surface was important to him. He enjoyed the respect of his peers. He needed to have standing in his community. He lived in an expensive little Surrey village where rich ex-Londoners played at being country-folk. He kept his accounts at local stores. He was a church warden and attended services every Sunday when at home; following prayer with a drink or two at the local pub and an occasional slog with a bat on the village green for the village cricket team. Soon there would be a quiet, patient, biddable, preferably rich wife. A captaincy. Children. He had it all mapped out. But it all required money. And that had been too slow in coming. Until he met Kostas Demetrios in a casino one night.

These were the thoughts that occupied his mind as his body fought its way down the deck. Perforce they occupied only part of it. The rest of his consciousness was trying to deal with the physical sensations of the storm. The effect of it was intensified by the darkness. There was no sense of scale, as there had been off Durban. There was simply an unremitting personal attack, as though the wind hated him and was trying to wrestle him to the deck where the rain and spray could drown him. It had fingers that grasped any loose piece of clothing. It had arms that wrapped around him, trying to lift him and throw him. It had legs that thrust against his legs, trying to trip him—and all too often succeeding. It had fists that pummeled his face armed with knuckle-dusters of hail, until he couldn't feel his cheekbones and his slitted eyes seemed as bruised and swollen as his nose. He fought it as it fought him, unrelentingly. And so he proceeded down the deck.

His preoccupation nearly tricked him. The howl of the wind from the south broke and sobbed. He charged forward without thinking. As soon as he was in the open another squall—a rogue, from the east—hit his shoulder like a heavy tackle and sent him sliding, sprawling across the deck.

The steel beneath his face was slick with inches of running water, the surface of it varnish-bright, like something preserved under glass. But as he slid over a section of it, the smooth water began to behave strangely, forming ripples, like a miniature mill race, for no apparent reason. Ben was too stunned to notice. He pulled himself erect and staggered on down the deck. The glassy water behind his boot heels rippled again along a line running from port to starboard right across the ship. Then the ripple was lost as the south wind returned with the rain.

It was the first sign that *Prometheus* was beginning to come apart.

* * *

211

Robin reached the Cargo Control Room door at a dead run, choking as her gasps for breath let some of the dissipating fumes into her lungs. She hung in the doorway as though crucified watching her father turn from the empty, roaring windowframe.

"There's someone out there!" he yelled.

She nodded, her mind running at frantic speed. Unlike her father she saw all too clearly the meaning of the smoke. The only reason for the wires to short out was if the computer was filling them with electrical impulses, trying to give orders to the pumps.

She endeavored, with every nerve in her body from the soles of her feet to her blood-thundering ears, to sense whether the pumps were obeying. It was hopeless. She could sense nothing beyond the storm.

At once she was in action again. She crossed to the VDU and snapped it on. It lit up. That was very bad.

She tapped in the lading schedules. Worse and worse. Her father was at her shoulder, his face as pale and pinched as her own. The four blue eyes scanned schedule after schedule. Under each neat, safe plan for the disposition of the cargo flashed one red word:

OVERRIDE

They read that same word ten times.

"What next?" she asked herself rather than him, concentrating so fiercely that she had all but forgotten his presence.

"Keep going."

She had no alternative. She knew the machine only had ten preset lading schedules, but she pressed eleven anyway.

And up it came, good as gold. She went cold at the sight. The diagram of their ship with that sinister red box midships: the tank all the cargo should have been destined for.

And under it, the blessed words:

POWER FAILURE: UNABLE TO EXPEDITE.

They were hugging each other, still laughing with relief, when Martyr appeared in the doorway.

"He's gone out onto the deck," the American yelled.

Robin turned toward the chief and saw the desperation in his eyes. Crisply, she answered, "Then let's get him."

And for the first time in their brief acquaintance, she saw C. J. Martyr smile.

The storm took hold of them just as it had taken hold of Ben. It buffeted them together, however, and they gave each other strength. Four legs moved faster than two under these circumstances, and they fell over less often. Like Ben they avoided the catwalk: to catch him they would have to follow in his footsteps. At this intensity, the storm would hide anything but the most massive deck feature from forty feet up: the first mate would be able to move easily unobserved unless they were much closer than that. It would take luck even to find him. But one positive factor was obvious to both of them: he was heading toward the forecastle head.

That being said, locating him on *Prometheus*'s vast deck on a night like tonight was likely to be a lengthy, dangerous process, if it could be done at all. But Ben clearly had a plan or he would not be out here now. If...

If... thought Robin. She could hardly believe that it was Ben. Less than twenty minutes ago she had been thinking of the first officer as fundamentally harmless. Now here she was, bound by the massive power of the wind to the one man she had suspected most of all, looking for this "harmless" man, trying to prove his guilt.

The night closed its fist around them, crushing them together. It was as though the wind had ceased its movement but attained solidity, muffling them. The rest of the storm seemed to recede. Even the ship became distant. All that really existed was the huge, water-filled, choking power all around them. It carried them forward for ten feet before it released them, dazed and disoriented, onto the forward section of the deck.

So they, like Ben scant yards before them, failed to notice the widening cracks in the deck.

* * *

213

Richard could feel it, though. Nothing definite. Nothing he could put his finger on. Nothing even in his conscious mind, yet. He felt the movement of his ship beginning to change beneath his wide-spaced feet and he reacted to it viscerally.

He stood by the helmsman, hands clenched behind his back, glaring out through the semiopaque glass that was all the storm left to him. John stood at the Collision Alarm Radar. There were watches out on the bridge wings and forecastle head armed with night glasses and hand-held radios. He was seriously thinking of sending someone else to the forecastle head. But he was two officers short, and there was something he couldn't quite pin down making him grind his teeth together hard enough to cramp the muscles in his jaw.

Robin saw him first, crouching on the edge of a shadow—head, arms, and legs in darkness; shoulders and back bright—on the port side, just short of the forecastle head. Speech was impossible so she beat upon Martyr's arm and pointed. He followed her gaze and broke into a shambling run. She went with him.

There were no niceties. None of the expertise the chief had shown earlier, when fighting the captain. The big American simply threw himself upon the crouching Englishman. It was all the storm would allow. They rolled together, all arms and legs, upon the slick, slippery deck.

Robin was not one to stand around. She thought about warning the man on the forecastle head. Richard had set the extra watch as soon as they had left Lyme Bay, to keep lookout for Channel traffic as they were cutting across the busy sea lanes. It was Kerem Khalil and she was worried that he might be hurt should anything go wrong here. But that would mean leaving these two alone. And that was not why she had come. She threw herself forward and landed squarely on the wrestling men.

At once she became entangled in the fight. A fist slammed into her ribs. A knee dug into the pit of her stomach. She disregarded the pain and lashed back, pausing only to make sure that she wasn't hitting Martyr by mistake. Then after a few wild but utterly satisfying punches, she concentrated on the safer and much more sensible stratagem of trying to capture and hold Ben Strong's right arm.

Ben twisted more viciously, butting the American in the face, pressing the point of his right elbow into the woman's chest and digging it home with all his strength.

He couldn't last much longer. He could feel his energy slipping away. He would have to break free and destroy them both. There was a gun in his life raft nearby. He slammed his head up into Martyr's face again and bore down with his elbow with rib-cracking force.

And managed to break away.

It was that indefinable feeling of unease, so vague but so over-powering, that called Richard off the bridge at last.

He did not go willingly, too well aware that if the grounds for his almost subconscious suspicions were of any real consequence, then his place was here; but for once John Higgins let him down. John could feel nothing wrong at all, beyond the night and the storm.

"There's more to it than that . . ." growled Richard.

"Only the absence of Robin and Ben."

"They'll be here soon. Sidetracked, probably . . ." In all honesty, Richard was so deeply wrapped up in his internal search for what was wrong that he hadn't noticed the time pass. He was com-pletely unaware just how long it had been since Robin left the bridge.

He prowled up to the helmsman's shoulder, peering out vainly into the whirling, screaming murk. Able occasionally to see the glimmer of a navigation light; once in a while the distant ghost of a Sampson post. And, as he looked down the invisible deck, the feeling in him grew.

Until he could stand it no longer. "Quine, get onto the R/T, if you please. Warn a team of GP seamen to wait for me at the port exit from A deck. Get one seaman up here to take over a watch. John, you have her."

He stepped out onto the port bridge wing. The wind hit him like a sledgehammer, sending him staggering back before he an-gled his solid body and fought his way across the pressure as though he were crossing a river in flood. At the far end of the bridge wing was Salah Malik, night glasses round his neck, solidly on watch. He jumped when Richard crashed into him.

Richard thrust his lips against a cold, wet ear. "There's something wrong," he yelled, gesturing at the deck. "We've got to go and check."

The big Palestinian nodded vigorously. In spite of everything else going on around him out here, he had felt it too, that formless chill of unease.

At the A deck door, a group of half a dozen waited. Tersely, Richard explained that there was nothing he could put his finger on, but they had to check the ship from stem to stern. He split them into teams. They checked their R/Ts. They went out into the night.

Out here, the storm was a little more restrained than it had been on the bridge wing. Here there were all the protuberances of the deck; from tank tops to pipes, catwalk-capped, to break the power of the wind. But on the bridge wing there had been safe rails, each upright closed with a steel plate. Here there was nothing small to hold on to; nothing safe. They felt exposed, as though they were on a mountainside, and they gathered together, like animals afraid.

Slowly, painstakingly, they began to work their way down the deck. Every now and then, when they reached some kind of shelter, Richard and Salah would crouch side by side, one checking with the teams, the other with the bridge. Richard was becoming seriously disturbed by the nonarrival of Ben and Robin. And, while it did occur to him that they, too, might be exploring the ship, subject to the same formless fears as he was himself, never once did he imagine them locked in a life-or-death struggle less than one hundred yards away.

But the moment he stepped past the Sampson posts halfway down the deck, all thought of Ben and even Robin was driven from his mind.

Like everyone else who had crossed this line tonight, he did so in the heart of a vicious squall; blind, deaf, dumb: distanced by a quirk of the storm from what was happening on the deck. And yet he knew at once. Even through the thick-soled yellow Wellingtons, lashed securely to his strong calves, the soles of his feet felt it instantly. The vibration of the deck was different. Up to the Sampson posts, the green steel throbbed to the rhythm of the mighty engine. Here it did not. Scant feet back, the deck was alive. Here it was dead.

Ice-cold inside as well as out, he whirled, falling to his knees. Salah came up beside him, reaching down to help, thinking only that the wind had toppled him. But Richard shrugged off the helping hand. He was peering at the green, fat-welded seam that stretched across the deck here. And as he looked, its thin lips ground together.

Was the movement in his imagination? It had been slight enough! He tore off his heavy gloves, pushing his fingers into the glassy streams of water, feeling for the truth before his hands went numb. Salah crashed to the deck beside him—and his hands were also there, long, dark-skinned fingers lost under the mill race of the water on the deck.

And then, proof positive! Simple and undeniable. The deck opened just wide enough to take the tip of the surprised Palestinian's left ring finger and then closed to nip it off.

Salah lifted his hand, unbelieving. The finger was simply gone from the top knuckle, severed with surgical neatness. It wasn't even bleeding. It simply wasn't there. The two men looked at it, thunderstruck. And then Richard's R/T exploded into life. All along the line, from port to starboard, the horrified seamen had seen the deck open and close at their feet.

Richard sprang upright, overcoming the force of the storm by sheer will. He stood astride the breaking seam, facing out to port. There was no denying it: his left leg felt the engine's throb. His right leg did not. Then, in a motion that translated itself almost into seasickness in his taut belly, he felt the bow on his right ride down the back of a great wave while the stern on his left was still riding up it. This time they all heard the *Clang!* as the two halves closed together again.

There was no training for this situation. He kept up, like any competent professional, with the literature of his profession, but nowhere had he ever seen the article he needed now: "Correct Procedures to Be Followed During the Break-up of Supertankers in Heavy Seas." If he survived, perhaps he should write it.

But it was laughable even to be thinking like this. What they needed now was seamanship and leadership. Or nobody would be going home.

Was there time to secure the two halves of the ship together in some way? Out of the question. Dismissed at once.

Was there time to bring her head round so the seas hit beam-on and stopped working the weak joint? The instant the thought occurred he was on the R/T. "John! John, this is Richard. Bring her head round."

"Aye. What bearing?"

"Fifty-five." But would the torque of the turn widen the crack? Cause it to split apart altogether? God knew. What next? He raised his R/T and opened the general band. "Attention all. Attention all. This is the captain speaking. Anyone forward of the Sampson posts, return to the bridge at once. Report in forecastle head watch."

"*Crackle, hiss*...Khalil here, Captain. Returning to bridge as ordered..."

Richard, too, stepped back a few feet onto the living half of the deck. He turned and looked down toward the bow, his mind already lost in the innumerable practicalities of the situation. Better get Quine to send a general distress signal. Have some Vessel Not Under Command warning lights ready in case the bow stayed afloat. Better get those down there quickly. Two red lights in a vertical line, not less than six feet apart, visible for at least two miles.

Visible for about two hundred yards in this lot...

Suddenly, a prolonged, mournful howl burst out of the throat of the storm. Richard jumped, looking wildly around, before he realized it was the cry of his own ship. John had managed to get the fire-damaged foghorn working. It would sound a prolonged blast every two minutes now until visibility cleared.

He turned and looked back toward the bow. The wind rammed him again, sending him staggering back into Salah, who had put his glove back on as though his hand were still complete. It would be useless to order him to the sick bay until Kerem came safely back from the forecastle head.

And there was a figure now, stumbling out of the screaming murk. Running oddly, but that was surely the effect of the storm...

And, behind, two more figures...

Richard stepped forward onto the dead section of the deck. Immediately it seemed to jump down a couple of feet, throwing him flat, as though his extra weight were too much to bear.

He picked himself up. The running man saw him and froze. Then he turned and was gone sideways into the shadows.

Richard staggered forward again, only to be driven down by another lurch as the whole bow fought to tear itself free. The other two figures fought to pick themselves up as he did, staggering in toward him. He recognized them at once—Robin and Martyr; there could not be two others like them aboard. And the running man... Ben!

What in hell's name was going on here?

Yet another figure appeared, this one much closer. Kerem. He jogged unsteadily up to Richard, gesturing over his captain's shoulder away toward the bridge, his normally impeturbable countenance twisted with concern. Richard turned again. The dead deck beneath his feet had fooled him, giving no warning. Behind him, what had once been a plain was now an escarpment. The stern was riding three, perhaps four, feet higher than the bow. The edge of the decking gleamed dull silver, sharp as though machine-tooled.

He looked back. Martyr and Robin had vanished again. He swore and turned away, running back toward the bridge, aware that in all probability only the horizontal pipes running along the center of the deck toward the forward tanks were keeping the ship together. As he reached the edge, the gap yawned again and he saw, incredibly, sixty feet below, clear water boiling through the heart of his ship.

He hurled himself forward wildly into the waiting arms of Salah and Kerem. "Get me rope!" he yelled.

"On its way," yelled Salah in reply. "I counted three still on the other side."

219

"That's right. We'll set up near the walkway. Those pipes are all that're holding her." They stumbled across the deck, reeling like landsmen as the stern section began to ride the waves with the beginnings of freedom, like a normal ship.

The rope arrived at the same time they did, carried by Bill Heritage himself. Pausing only to clap the grand old man on a yellow-coated shoulder, Richard led them up one of the midship companionways to the walkway amid the flexing hawser of pipes. It was like some terrifying fairground ride, half remembered from his youth: as he and Salah stood side by side while Bill and Kerem secured the ropes around their waists then belayed safely behind them, they watched the narrow path they were to walk twisting and writhing like a live thing. Steel was flexing with more and more freedom; beginning to steam in places where the cold rain hit. Wood bent like a bow, sparking and splintering. The halves of the ship ground together like toothless jaws, moving with wilder and wilder motion.

She had never had a real keel like a lesser vessel, so you could hardly say her back was broken. She had been constructed simply of great U-shaped sections—six in all—welded together. The bow and stern sections had been added later. Within these sections, the tanks had been placed, discrete and solid with huge double walls at their ends. And the join between the third and fourth U-shaped sections, currently breaking open, mercifully coincided with the double wall between the two main midship tanks. Both bow and stern remained, for the meantime, watertight; and there was little or no leakage of oil.

—Or of South African water, thought Richard grimly. Even now, dying like this, *Prometheus* was keeping her secrets safe. Like a battered child protecting its parents with silence.

A blow on his shoulder broke the train of thought. The rope round his waist was secure. He shambled forward onto the snaking, roller-coaster walkway.

At once he was glad of his heavy gloves. He had to keep tight hold of the railings, and the mahogany—not the most flexible of woods—was quilled with splinters already. He was glad, too, of his thick-soled boots, for the metal beneath them was hot—and getting hotter—as he moved through the steam over the yawning, snapping chasm in his ship.

Wildly in the blinding bluster he searched below for the bright wet-weather gear of the officers on the dead deck. At first he could see nothing, but then the storm relented and he began to see glimpses of furtive movement.

There was a bizarre game of hide-and-seek going on down there. What in blazes was happening? Didn't they realize the danger they were in? He could have screamed with frustration. And, at the very thought, one wild figure hurled up a companionway immediately in front of him.

"BEN!" he bellowed.

Ben whirled to confront him and Richard staggered back. The expression on his godson's face was beyond belief. Their eyes locked. Ben stopped and suddenly pulled something from his pocket. It was a gun.

Then Martyr and Robin came up as well, one from either side, erupting out of the shadows to hurl themselves at him. But he was too quick for them, dancing nimbly back toward the bow, still holding the gun.

Richard was jolted out of his momentary inactivity as Salah hurled bodily past him and tackled Martyr round the waist, lifting him clear of the catwalk to drag him back. Instantly he dived forward himself, lying along the wooden handrail, belly down, to grab Robin. The rope jerked him back onto his feet and his shoulders popped, crushing her to his chest. Staggering backward on the wild, hot steel, he lost his footing and sat. She sat in his lap.

The wind stopped.

There was a second of calm. Just long enough for Ben to dance forward again, to tower over them, the gun held firmly, familiarly, in both hands. He froze, his face a mask of confusion, the gun wavering between them.

Ben's mind was a whirl of blood lust, but he had a bewildering choice of targets. He was going to kill Richard because he was responsible for Ben's father's death. He was going to kill Martyr for interfering in his plans. And he was going to kill anyone else who knew what he had done. Starting with the girl.

He pointed it at Robin first, therefore, snarled, "Good-bye!" and pulled the trigger.

The instant Ben said, "Good-bye" and pressed the trigger, the greatest of the storm's rogue waves hit *Prometheus*'s bow exactly from the side.

The concussion, like a right hook to a boxer's jaw, threw the whole bow section to starboard, against the steady pressure of the ship's turn to port, and it sheared the pipes already weakened by the movements of the two sections.

Prometheus broke in two.

Ben suddenly found himself flat on his back, completely ignorant of whether he had killed Robin or not. He felt as though he were attached to the wooden walkway; riveted to it: an invisible force was pressing him down so that he couldn't make the slightest movement. Couldn't even breathe. The breath was crushed out of him in a long, wheezing scream. As he realized the whole earthlike solidity beneath him was spinning, wheeling. *That* was why he couldn't move—he was pressed into place by the unimaginable forces hurling the forward half of *Prometheus* to destruction.

He had time to think, *Noooooooooo* . . .

Richard and Salah, each clasping their human bundle, were thrown up and back as the companionway fell beneath them like an elevator going down. Richard's consciousness snapped shut on the overpowering need to crush Robin to him, the need to wrap his legs as well as his arms around her, as they tumbled vertiginously. Then the rope slammed taut, winding him, while the pull of her falling body came perilously close to breaking his grip. Something slick but solid, whirling madly, crashed into him: Salah, still holding Martyr—just.

Enormous power, mostly liquid, surged over him, bringing his broken attempts at catching his breath right to the edge of drowning. Robin wriggled against him, vivid as an eel, and her arms closed around his neck, then her face was close to his, filthy, icy, running. And she was kissing him, fiercely alive. They clung to each other, held to the great stern section by the terrifyingly thin ropes, tiny bundles of life dangling against that sheer steel wall like mountaineers hanging helpless, high on a storm-lashed precipice.

The force of the storm wave tore the forward section clear, opening it on the broken hinge of the starboard safety rail. It tore loose at once, already sinking, and the great column of spray born of the massive wave joined the first arterial gush from the severed pipes in a thick, freezing Niagara down the naked steel wall that now served the aft section as a blunt bow.

Salah Malik's team, steadied by the massive calm of Kerem Khalil and Sir William Heritage, did not flinch. Even in this most terrifying of nightmares, they hung for dear life onto the bucking, straining ropes.

They saw the air convulse with the concussion of the impact. They saw the whole vista of the deck before them twist and tilt. They saw four figures thrown back and one thrown forward toward the doomed bow. They saw the column of water rise like the hugest of breakers against the forecastle, boiling up, fanning up, exploding up over the side as the forces twisting the very air around them tossed them about in an awesome silence, like toys.

And when at last their vision cleared, all there was to see was the torn pipe ends cascading sludgy filth, the wildly twisting lines plummeting sheer from the splintered end of the catwalk, and wall after wall of black, foam-webbed water charging in toward them, breaking over something that looked for a moment like a slick black reef before it rolled over and under and was gone.

Then, for the first time in her history, slowly to begin with, like a child learning, what was left of *Prometheus* began to pitch, riding over the great storm seas like ships have done over all seas, down from the dawn of time.

Safe Haven

25

They towed her into Europoort after sunset three days later, on September 13. There was a fine drizzle and a high overcast that threatened to bring the night in early, but still, it seemed, half of Rotterdam, Vlaardingen, and Schiedam were there to see her in.

First came the three tugs out of the massive shadows of the gathering dark; the great hawsers, familiar from countless TV and newspaper pictures, stretched up to the crippled giant, which even the smallest television screen had somehow been unable to dwarf. Then, like a bulk of blackness itself, storm-choppy seas thundering against the flat ram of the bow as though against a cliff, she slid into the outwash of the harbor lights. Even cut almost in half as she was, she seemed so big; even broken, she looked so solid. And there was about her still such horrendous potential for disaster.

But *verdammt!* said the onlookers one to another, what a crew must there be aboard to bring her safe to port! And as she detached herself from the rain-misted gloom, and, above the sheer wall of her broken bow the scarred wreck of her upper works appeared, first one or two and then all of them began to cheer and cheer.

As the evening wore on, and the lengthy business of positioning *Prometheus* safely in an anchorage as far from the rest of the shipping as possible, stretched out, so the crowds began to drift away. Only one or two diehards remained, and they were cleared out of the dock complex itself by the courteous but insistent security guards; and they had to content themselves with crossing to the headland opposite and watching from the hillside there.

By midnight, when *Prometheus* was at last in place and the tugs had cast off and sailed away, the rain had cleared and a thin mist was beginning to shroud the anchorage. Even the most intrepid of the boat watchers called it a day once the clammy tendrils began to infest the air; so at last, with his digital watch reading 00.20 local time, on the headland overlooking the anchorage, Kostas Demetrios found himself alone.

All he had to do now was to prime the bomb in his camera carryall and get it aboard the ship.

The original plan had come to him almost fully fledged when he was watching the six o'clock news one evening nearly a year ago. There had been an item on the OPEC embargo of oil to South Africa and he had said to himself, in derision, "But how can they enforce that? Jesus! They can't even *police* it! Anyone can just sail right in..."

And that had been where it started.

All he needed was a tanker, enough money to fit it and run it for a few months. And a cargo of oil—which didn't even have to belong to him, for heaven's sake! And a crew willing to sail into Durban and sell the oil illegally.

But then what? He couldn't bring the ship home. Not with empty tanks. No. The ship would have to sink so that no one would ever know. Which meant there would be insurance to collect on the ship... And on the cargo, because no one must ever suspect she was empty when she went down.

So: *Stage One*, buy, fit, insure, and crew a supertanker. He was a shipping man. He could do that.

Stage Two, contact the South Africans and agree to prices, dates, points of delivery.

Stage Three, deliver the oil and accept payment.

Stage Four, use some of the South African money to buy the now nonexistent cargo on the international spot market. A buoyant market where prices were climbing dizzily.

Stage Five, scuttle the ship.

Stage Six, collect the insurance on his ship and his cargo—worth so much more on the day it was lost than on the day it was purchased.

And that would be that. He would have made the change. No longer would he be just a shipping man. He would be an oil man who owned his own ships.

He was awed by the simple glory of it. Why weren't people doing this all the time? All you needed were some contacts. A little capital. But you could only do it once. And you would have to do it right: there could be no question of illegal practices to stop the insurance payments. No question of people snooping around uninvited—another good reason to buy the "cargo", just before she sank, himself . . .

Well, he could sort all that out later. First, he needed a super-tanker.

Pulling it all back together after the disaster in the Pump Room had been oddly exhilarating. He was by no means addicted to danger but he was the sort of man who enjoyed pressure, and the fact that he managed to save the situation within forty-eight hours finally added to his overall sense of achievement. And it vindicated his decision to put Martyr aboard, knowing he could count on that strange, desperate man in ways he could count on no one else aboard. The only real professional there, doing a professional job, as Demetrios had known he would. The only one not motivated by simple greed. And, Demetrios knew, he had been lucky to have that one strong—very Strong—contact in Crewfinders. But the speed with which he had acted, with his back to the wall, simply added, in the end, to the sense of elation he felt on that afternoon after the Lutine Bell was rung, in that brief time of contentment before it all blew up in his face.

They phoned him at midnight—it must have been the early hours in London—to tell him the good news: *Prometheus* was coming home after all, and he realized that if she did so, he was ruined. Lost, the supertanker was worth millions; afloat, she would cost millions—there would be salvage to pay, docking charges, lawyers' fees. And of course, the authorities would find out what was really in her cargo tanks. If she was lost, he was made. If she survived, he was ruined. Completely. Utterly.

Now here he was in Rotterdam himself, out of alternatives,

with Gallaher's second bomb. The backup he would have delivered in Durban had not things been changed so drastically. Simply blowing a hole in *Prometheus* wasn't going to be any good, he calculated coldly. He had to blow her to hell and gone. He had to manufacture such a holocaust that no one would think to ask what had been in her cargo tanks.

Salah Malik stood by the wheel as the tugs brought them into Europoort. His arms were so stiff and his bandaged finger so sore, that a lengthy turn at the wheel was almost too much to ask. But his usual replacement, Kerem Khalil, was in scarcely better shape. A series of lesser seamen had stood by the rally-size helm throughout the last forty-eight hours, after John Higgins had overseen the bringing aboard of the lines from the Dutch tugs sent out when it became obvious that what was left of the ship was not going to sink. But Salah and Kerem had been there to bring her into port.

Martyr had been unconscious when they brought him up. Salah's shoulders had almost been dislocated by the weight of the big American under the waterfall that had descended on them as they dangled at the end of the rope immediately after *Prometheus* broke in two. After the first full weight of it, Salah's grip had begun to slip, his whole hand suddenly on fire. Some vagary of the massive physical laws that held them in their grasp upended them and twisted them around. Martyr's head had smashed into the unforgiving metal wall behind them with the full weight of two bodies, knocking him out at once.

The dead weight, especially under these circumstances, would have been too much for most men. Indeed, had he been holding any other man, even Salah's strength might have faltered. Above the sickening, choking sensation as he all but drowned in the oily deluge, he could feel the muscles of his arms and torso tearing apart. He held the clumsy, slippery bundle of Martyr's inert body grimly, each second making him more certain that it was all a waste of time, effort, and agony. A few more moments and the chief would slip out of his crippled arms. His right hand gripped his left wrist with bruising force, but the joints in this steely circle at elbow and shoulder were slowly being pulled apart. Salah shook his head to clear his eyes and spat to clear his mouth. Then he ground his teeth together. The wings of his shoulder blades seemed to be tearing away from the muscles of his back. The whole of his torso was burning now, as though he had been severely scalded from neck to waist.

For the last time he kicked away from the black steel wall that swung toward him like an avalanche time and again. The strange forces that had been tossing the two of them around like a feather relaxed for an instant. Salah swung upright. A pause in the torrent allowed him respite to glance upward, and what he saw there gave him the one more ounce of strength he needed.

Kerem Khalil, tied into a makeshift rope sling, was abseiling down the iron precipice toward them.

Kostas Demetrios sat beneath the gentle dew-fall, watching the quiet ship and wondering how best to go about destroying her.

Prometheus had to be totally destroyed—no matter what the risks to her crew, the anchorage, himself. Only an explosion followed by a massive fire would solve his problems. But he was no suicide. Nor any kind of a fool. He had no intention of being caught in the explosion if he could help it.

They had put her in the outermost of the docks, with only the headland Demetrios was crouching on separating her from the restless sea. If he followed the headland back the way he had come all those hours earlier with the Dutch sightseers, he would return to the high dock gates. Security was too tight for him there. Only by revealing himself as the owner would he get through, and even then they would probably search him—especially at this time of night. And even if they did not discover the bomb, they would certainly escort him onto the ship and then he would fall into the same trap he had almost fallen into earlier, on the dock. The slightest gesture on his part would have got him aboard. But that would have landed him with the massive salvage bill. And put him straight into the hands of the crew.

But the simple fact was that he had to go aboard somehow, tonight. There was no alternative. First thing in the morning, the investigators would arrive. Investigators from Rotterdam, Lloyd's, Scotland Yard, the FBI, and God knew where else. And the first thing they would do would be to check in the tanks. And the next thing they would do would be to come looking for him.

And the only way he could think to make good use of the bomb was to get the damn thing aboard. His only real hope was to get it somehow into the ullage where the scum from the unwashed tanks would have oozed enough lethally explosive gas to blow what was left of *Prometheus* apart.

And he had known in his bones for an hour and more that the only way to get across was going to be to swim. And luckily, he had come prepared even for that eventuality. He pulled out the wetsuit from on top of the bomb and started to put it on.

Richard sat in his dayroom, staring at the blank ply over his window, with Robin curled at his feet. Her shoulder rested on the right leg of the chair and her golden head rested on his thigh. She was exhausted, sound asleep. As was her father, gray with fatigue, in the owner's suite. He was on his last legs himself, staring mindlessly at the wood with its swirls of grain like sea ribs on pale sand. He should be writing up the log. The Accident Reports. This was his first chance to do any paperwork since Bill Heritage had pulled the pair of them back aboard nearly forty-eight hours ago with Robin's kisses still burning on his lips. That was the moment he was trying to record in the log. The power of the emotion that memory brought was all that was keeping him awake.

No. Not *all* that was keeping him awake. There was something else. A formless sense of something. Too imprecise even to be called a feeling. Danger. Much less powerful than the sensation that had traveled magically up through the soles of his feet as his command had begun to come apart. It was nothing he could feel, even subconsciously. It was perhaps only the feeling that it was all but over and they were safe, that feeling twisted into a worry by all that had gone before. A thought. A fear. An unprovable certainty.

They were not safe yet. They ought to be but they were not. Not here. Not anywhere above the waves. Not like this. Not as they were, in one piece. Not now. Not until it was too late to stop the inspection. The report. It was almost too much to ask.

After what they had been through already, it might well be too much. But he had to ask it. He had to go round and wake them all up. That was why they were still here, after all.

He had insisted on remaining aboard, on keeping his own watch instead of letting the Dutch harbor watch take over. The port authorities had allowed it, understandingly; and doubled the security on the dock. It was the dock nearest the sea, farthest from the other ships and the refineries. The closest Europoort had to an isolation dock. If they could not have put them, effectively, in quarantine, the careful Dutch would never have allowed them in here.

But were they well enough quarantined? Not from Demetrios. Never from the owner, until his fraud had been exposed.

Facing this, at the end of his long, weary, meandering train of thought, forced him into action. He slammed the log shut loud enough to disturb Robin, though this was not his object. She sat up sleepily and he rose stiffly, feeling ancient and arthritic, and stooped to help her to her feet. He was about to lift her into his arms and carry her through into his cabin and his bunk, but once she was on her feet she stopped him. "What is it with you?" she asked. "It's like being in love with a guard dog."

He smiled wearily at her. "I know." His voice was rusty with fatigue. "I'm a natural-born worrier."

"Okay," she acquiesced. "So let's go guard something."

He nodded. "Not something. Everything."

She sobered down. "You think he's coming?"

"Maybe not him."

"But someone?"

"Sure as death."

"Tonight?"

"Tonight is all they've got."

"Then let's go."

They went out together, side by side, as though going on patrol in the jungle.

Rice was keeping an eye on the generators. McTavish was with Martyr on the bridge, waiting for them. Quine dozed in the captain's chair, beside the quiet radio. They had run a land-line from the shore and a telephone lay in a cradle beside it. John went over toward the sleepy radio officer as soon as he saw Richard, but the captain smiled and shook his head: let the boy sleep. The youngest and the oldest aboard could sleep undisturbed. For the time being. If all went well.

Salah looked up from where he was standing by the wheel and met their eyes in the glass. Kerem, at Salah's shoulder, swung round.

Richard paused in the door with Robin at his side. Just for a second they looked around the bridge and in that time their eyes met every other pair of eyes there.

No word was said, no obvious message exchanged. Yet when Richard turned away, they were all, except John, behind him.

Damn! The water was cold. No—beyond cold: it was freezing. He eased himself into it inch by inch, thanking God he had got the full wetsuit, just in case. Also what he should have got, he thought ruefully, was flippers. And some way of carrying the bomb through the water. It had been heavy enough on land, but as soon as he tried to swim with it slung over his shoulder, he became certain it was going to drag him under to his death. Reluctantly, he turned round and regained the shore.

He sat there, breathless, looking across at the great hulk of his ship. In a fit almost of temper, he hooked his left thumb into the big metal ring on the zipper of his wetsuit and jerked it down to his belly. The metal teeth of the zipper parted and he automatically began to scratch his chest as he looked around. There was no lighting on this side of the anchorage, but the security lighting cast enough light across the water for him to see everything around him here. He didn't have to look for long. Unusually for Holland, but inevitably for any seashore, there was a line of jetsam at the high water mark, and among it was a half-collapsed cardboard box with a picture of a television on the side.

Demetrios felt a sudden flood of energy. He jumped to his feet and crossed to the box. Two kicks burst it. At either end, originally designed to protect the set in transit, where firm trays of polystyrene. He took them out of the cardboard and carried them speculatively to the water. One on top of the other, they made a raft that was so buoyant it hardly seemed to penetrate the surface.

234

Even with the bomb sitting snugly on top of them, they still had enough flotation to give him a little support. He zipped up, leaned forward, pushed it out to arm's length, and kicked off like a kid learning to swim.

John remained on the bridge because he was on watch. Literally, because from his elevated position, he could see the outline of the deck quite clearly under the security lighting from the dock. But all the many protuberances on the deck, from manifolds to tank caps, cast weird, sharp-edged shadows that might well conceal a saboteur, so a watch had to be kept below as well. And a search made and remade, from now until the first inspection team arrived. He crossed to the sleeping Quine and took the captain's R/T from beside the new telephone. He removed the binoculars from their holster on the side of the chair and returned to his position by the wheel.

A moment or two later, he was joined by two of Salah Malik's best men, each armed with a walkie-talkie and a pair of night glasses. They nodded to him as they passed and each went out onto one of the bridge wings. Just the way they moved seemed to knot up his belly. He had never experienced anything like this before. Most of his endeavors had been lonely ones. He lived alone and raced his yacht for the most part alone. He had never before been a part of such a team. And to think, only a scant matter of weeks ago he had secretly wondered if Richard were finished. But not now. He would never doubt the man again. It was like a miracle.

He had been there when the four of them, with Khalil's help, had been pulled back over the brink of their ship. That brush with death, that exploration they had made into another kingdom, seemed to have added the final touch to their extraordinary relationship. The last doubts and suspicions had been destroyed by the destruction of the bow. To see Richard then with Robin or with Martyr was a revelation. If blood was thicker than water, it was as though they had iscovered something thicker than either.

Effectively leaving him and Rice to run the ship, with young McTavish filling in where necessary and Sir William fitting in where he could, the three of them had gone off into some sort of secret conclave. Robin had turned up first, coming onto the bridge to give John some relief while Martyr, his head bandaged, and Richard went down below and examined every inch of the hull from the Engine Room forward—as far forward as they could get.

Richard had been back on the bridge, of course, when John and Salah's best team had been down at the terrifying new bow taking the Dutch lines aboard. Things could hardly have reached that stage without the full involvement of the captain, who was the owner's representative, the one person aboard empowered to agree to Lloyd's Open Form for the salvage.

But once they were safely under way, Richard had vanished again, first with Martyr, to clarify the last of his suspicions; and then with Robin to write his reports.

But it had been inevitable that the pair of them should prowl back, their almost silent footsteps cloaked by the haunting wail of Nihil's distant flute. He had known the moment Martyr appeared on the bridge that the others would not be far behind. And it was as obvious to the Manxman as to any of the others why all this was going on.

The R/T hissed into life: "Any sign, John?"

"Nothing." He answered automatically, never for an instant wondering that Richard should have known he would be standing there, watching, with the set by his side.

"Okay," said Richard quietly. "We're going out onto the deck."

Demetrios paused under the shadow of the blunt bow, tempted almost beyond enduring simply to put his bomb against the relatively thin metal of the tank wall and get the hell away. But such an action would not be guaranteed to bring success. Success was all that could save him now. On this one last throw of the dice rested more millions than he could readily calculate or absolute destruction. He was not the sort of a man who would go almost all the way and then back off, saying he had done his best really; knowing he had not. He went all the way under normal circumstances, no matter what the risk or cost. He was not about to short change himself now. The bomb was going into one of the tanks and *Prometheus* was going to the bottom. In as many million little pieces as he had dollars coming.

Thirty yards in front of the ship, a set of steps led down from the quay to the water level. Even in docks made for these ocean-going giants, some provision had to be made for smaller vessels. Demetrios swam across to these and pulled himself out of the water. Then he scampered silently up them and paused. With the bomb by his side, he crouched in the shadows, trying to catch his breath, waiting for some vigor to return to his chilled and weary body. Willing his dull brain to plan ahead.

The quayside was deserted. It gleamed in the security lighting as though it had just been varnished. It was far too bright for his taste. But at least there was nobody obviously watching out for him. Silently on his numb bare feet, he ran for the next shadow.

The deepest pool of darkness lay beneath a squat crane opposite the blunt end of *Prometheus*. He made it safely, and paused there, narrow-eyed, looking at his ship. A set of steps reached up from the quay to the deck just in front of the bridge house, but almost exactly opposite where he was standing, the automatic accommodation ladder also led down to his level, more because the mechanism was broken than because it had been set, by the look of things. That seemed his best bet. He took it without further hesitation.

As soon as he reached the deck, he ran for the nearest shadow again. This one was at the foot of the Sampson post that had once marked the halfway point of the deck, starboard side. Now it marked the end of the ship. He flattened himself against the white-painted steel upright and looked around. The deck seemed deserted. He could see a figure in the distant bridge windows, and he suspected there would be others invisible in the shadows on the bridge wings; but the deck at least was his alone.

He sucked in a great ecstatic breath. He had overestimated his enemies. He stood an excellent chance of pulling this off.

But then, in the distance, the A deck doors opened and in the brightness he saw them all coming out, the beams of their torches like golden swords cutting the darkness before them.

* * *

Richard led the starboard team, with Kerem, Robin, and a gang of seamen to back him up. Martyr led the port team, with McTavish, Salah Malik, and more seamen. Behind these two teams, in another thin line stretching from port, overlooking the water, to starboard, overlooking the dock, came Ho and the stewards.

They moved forward slowly, inch by inch, disturbing anything that might conceivably hide a man, their eyes busy at their feet. They remained quietly in contact with each other and with the men on the bridge, using the R/Ts that at least two of each team carried. The teams searched the most likely places methodically and thoroughly. The stewards behind them searched everywhere else. It was a system that should have been absolutely foolproof.

And there is no doubt that if Demetrios had stayed on the deck, they would have caught him with that first sweep. But he did not. Desperately, lent a touch of genius by the pressure, he ran forward from shadow to shadow, toward the line. He was lucky. Their eyes were on their feet and they did not see the pale oval of his face or the flash of movement made by his black wetsuit. The watch on the bridge wing missed it, too, and so did John, because the wily owner chose that moment to move when one of Martyr's men called out and all eyes were on the port side for an instant.

There was no scupper at the edge of the deck. The flat green decking curved down to become the side without any runnel or channel to collect and guide the water. Welded to this rounded edge, just inboard of the line where horizontal green became vertical black, were the uprights supporting the deck rail. At the foot of one of these lay a small pile of rope, perhaps thirty feet in all, neatly coiled. It was obviously far too small to hide anything, and its neat, flat, circular shape made it obvious that there was nothing under it. But its edge was exactly at the foot of the upright. Demetrios saw all this and formed his plan, such as it was, in an instant. Then he had slid silently over the side, and was dangling there invisibly, a black shape against the black side, with his pale hands hidden beneath the rough coil of rope.

A slow count of ten brought the footsteps close. Unashamedly, he squeezed his eyes tight and ground his forehead against the icy side. If they found him like this, he was lost. Watching them come nearer would only make the tension unbearable. Then their voices came. Not the captain's, thank God; but the girl talking to one of the Palestinians. "What's that?"

"Where?"

"There! By the deck rail."

"Rope."

"Right."

"Check it out?"

A pause. Demetrios could feel the sweat streaming down between his tanker and his cheek. The tip of his nose itched unbearably.

"No. Leave it. We're falling behind anyway."

Their footsteps moved away. Demetrios took a great shuddering heave of breath . . .

. . . and nearly lost it at once in a scream of fright as the rope moved. It was a Chinese steward. Demetrios had heard nothing. The man had approached on silent feet and conscientiously looked under the rope.

But he had looked under the inboard half only. Demetrios's hands stayed safely hidden by the outboard coils as they lay piled against the white upright.

The movement of the rope stopped. This time he heard a sibilant shuffle of footsteps, like the slither of a snake over tiles, as the steward moved away.

At once, near the end of his strength in any case, he began to pull himself up. He paused with his eyes at deck level and glanced around. Fortunately there was no one nearby so he did not have to wait—he could not have done so in any case, for his muscles were jumping with fatigue. He hurled himself forward under the bottom rail. Luckily the bomb case landed on the rope with the dullest of thuds. The stewards, ten feet away, heard nothing. Sensed nothing. He was in a squat in an instant, bowed like a sprinter on the blocks. Then he was off into the shadow of the central walkway, under the fat, safe pipes.

"Richard!" John's voice hissed over the captain's R/T. Demetrios could just hear it. He froze and listened, running with sweat again. How could someone as cold as he was perspire this much? He slid the heavy metal ring of his wetsuit's zipper down to the middle of his chest absently, listening with all his might.

"Yes?" The captain's crisp reply.

"I thought I..."

"What?"

"No...It's...Starboard bridge wing: did you see it?"

"Starboard bridge watch here: Did I see what?"

"...Nothing. It must have been nothing, then."

"Captain here. Okay John. Keep looking. We'll do another close sweep on the way back. Did you get that, everybody?"

"Robin: affirmative."

"Martyr: affirmative."

All the rest of them.

Demetrios slithered into the shadow of the tank cap. The cap itself stood three feet high, and it was circular with a radius of three feet. It was designed to take the great pipe that would rapidly suck the tank dry. The cap itself was almost like the top on a massive bottle, except that it was held down by a series of clamps, like a hatch cover. In the security lighting from the dock, it cast a hard shadow like the center of a sundial. On a clockface with 12 at the bridge, the shadow would be pointing at five.

As quickly as he could, constrained only by the need for silence, he undid all the clamps concealed by the shadow, then he slowly began moving into the light, crawling to his left, toward the starboard side, fighting to keep the hatch itself between himself and the keen-eyed man on the bridge.

Things were becoming increasingly dangerous, second by second. When he reached the point of realizing he was unlikely to walk away from this, he never knew; but the realization that he would be lucky to survive did not slow him down.

Abruptly, the hatch moved.

His heart lurched within him with enough force to wind him, like a punch in the belly. The rest of the clamps, the ones closest to the volcano-sided hole in the deck, must all have been broken by the explosion in the Pump Room.

He forced his stiff body into a crouch, and he forced his fingers under the edge of the cap.

"*There!*"

The cry seemed to echo over the whole anchorage. A lesser man might have frozen. Demetrios worked even more feverishly, trying to wrestle the top of the tank off. But it was no good. One man simply could not move it. Defeated at last, he left the top to itself and used one last second to tear the bomb and the remote control out of the camera case.

Then, just as the rush of feet gathered itself at his back, he leapt up onto the tank cap. He held the bomb just high enough for them to see it and pressed the ARM button. At once the digital readouts started to flash. They were red and looked every bit as dangerous as they actually were. He needed to do or say nothing further.

They gathered in a circle around him, looking up; and he was almost shocked to feel the depth of their rage, and their hatred toward him. It came up from them in waves. From every shadow-etched, black-eyed face, stained old ivory by the security lighting. He had never counted on this and it frightened him most of all, because it shocked and disoriented him. He had never really thought of them as human beings, with wishes, hopes, emotions, before. He had only ever thought of them as counters. As chess pieces to be moved about, allowed to live or sentenced to die according to the dictates of his plan. Now he saw them as they really were, as people; as human beings who abominated him for what he had done. And he could identify with them completely now, for he had become one of them—though they would never recognize the fact—destined to die with them, according to the dictates of the plan.

Richard Mariner stepped forward to face him. "You realize we are all dead if you detonate that thing?"

"Of course." Demetrios kept his voice calm. Certain. There was no use in letting them see that he thought they had a long chance of survival. It was an incendiary, after all, designed to burn rather than to explode. It was possible that he might detonate the thing and immolate himself without setting fire to anything else.

Or on the other hand, he might set fire to the very air itself and destroy the whole of Europoort.

The second possibility abruptly became the most likely: a pungent stench of petrol fumes suddenly brought tears to his eyes.

He fought for breath, keeping a close watch on them as they all fell back. But then the stench began to fade and he could breathe again.

Mariner was still talking. "Look, why don't you just hand it over to me and we'll talk the whole thing through..."

Demetrios gave a bark of laughter, almost a choke. The fumes had got into his lungs. Luckily the air was clearing of them at last. He was beginning to feel light-headed. "What do you expect? A great confession? The full story? Repentance? Forget it!"

"Now, look..."

"What you don't know now, you'll never know!" he spat. "Now back off or I press the button!" But before he could say or do anything else, he was struck with stunning force behind the knees.

Richard had been concentrating absolutely on keeping the madman's attention while Malik and Martyr crept round behind him, and so he saw all too clearly through the stunning flash of action that their plan was about to backfire. And it was neither of the men who tackled him after all. It was Robin. And as he fell, Demetrios pressed the button.

But Demetrios pressed the wrong button, the button that tripped a part of the bomb he did not even know existed: a small, powerful electromagnet designed to hold the device hard against any metal surface. The bomb slammed into his chest, attracted by the nearest metal—the toggle and zipper of the wetsuit. The blow from in front and the tackle from behind knocked Demetrios back. Flat on his back. His shoulders missed Robin's horizontal body and slammed down onto the metal of the tank cap itself. And the damaged metal sheered. Before even Richard could move—and his reactions had been honed to almost superhuman speed—the ragged disk of metal had tilted and vanished, taking with it Demetrios, Robin, and the bomb down into the gas-filled ullage.

They all hurled themselves forward. Martyr was already at the edge, half hanging over the black hole, for he had thrown himself forward an instant after Robin. To the others as much as to him, Richard called: "Don't breathe! It's deadly!" His voice was raw, as though he had been screaming for many hours. If it was deadly up here, he was thinking, then what was it like down where Robin was?

But none of them—certainly not the canny chief—really needed reminding. They all knew the sequence that Demetrios did not. It was ingrained into every tankerman there. The sequence of hydrocarbon gas poisoning. Twenty seconds—at the most three-quarters of a minute—can render the fittest man unconscious. Four minutes after that, unless oxygen is administered, serious brain-damage starts; one minute more brings death. The first and only sign is a strong smell of hydrocarbon gas, which soon fades—not because the gas has gone, but because it has destroyed the nerves in the nose.

Demetrios had smelled the gas as soon as he stepped onto the leaking tank cap. By the time he started falling, with Robin wrapped around him and the bomb still clinging to him, he was only semiconscious. And, automatically, because he was unable to think clearly, he did the most obvious thing. He took a deep breath to clear his head. His body went into spasm. His lungs automatically emptied themselves. His right hand clasped the bomb to his breast—where the gentlest movement would have freed its grasp on the zipper—and his left closed spasmodically on top of it. This time his thumb hit the DETONATE button, just as his body hit the scum-thick surface of the water, twenty feet down.

As soon as she felt the body she was holding curl into that rigid fetal position, Robin knew Demetrios was dead. There was nothing else she could do now, one way or the other, so she let go and fell free, holding her breath and praying feverishly. It was absolutely dark down here. There was no possibility of seeing anything at all. The water and the distant walls were all tar-covered. They would soak up light. Even a torch beam would vanish down here.

She had perhaps a thousandth of a second to complete these thoughts before the semisolid surface of the cargo exploded against her with unexpected violence. And the thick, icy liquid seemed to suck her down. She began to struggle at once, fighting to regain the surface, though she knew she was unlikely to do so, and even if she did, all that awaited her there was a minute or two's pointless struggle to hold her breath followed by a choking death like the owner's at the hands of the deadly gas.

Her only real hope was the knowledge that somewhere nearby, oil-covered, slippery, and probably useless, a set of steps led up from the bottom of the tank to the tank top itself. Intrepid to the last, she planned to find that flight of steps and climb to safety. She reckoned she had perhaps two minutes before her breath ran out. She had no idea that Demetrios had triggered the bomb.

Martyr straightened at once and, turning toward Richard, swung his leg over the side of the tank top. "No!" barked the captain. "I'll go." The chief stepped back. From twenty feet down came the double splash of two bodies hitting the filthy liquid.

Richard was speaking urgently into his R/T. "John! We need some breathing equipment down here. Now!" Then he gulped the oil-smelling air into his lungs and stepped forward.

Salah Malik rushed up to him, holding the rope that Demetrios had used to hide his hands. He glanced at his captain, who nodded. Richard had been waiting for this, not for the breathing gear. If they waited for that before he went after her, Robin wouldn't stand a chance. Not that she stood much of a chance anyway, he calculated grimly.

Richard found the top step immediately inside the tank top and stood on it impatiently for five more seconds while Salah knotted the rope expertly around his waist, then went back to where Kerem, Ho, and some of the others had tight hold of the far end of it. Richard held his R/T out to Martyr. The big American took it and replaced it in Richard's fist with his torch. Shining this into the pit at his feet, Richard started down. More than thirty seconds now since Robin had fallen in. Richard also started to pray.

Martyr, keeping the channel to John Higgins open, started moving back toward the bridge. Oxygen mask or Drager compressed-air gear, it didn't matter to him: as soon as anything arrived, he was going to put it on and go down into the tank himself. If the tank, if anything, still existed. He was surprised to discover just how fiercely he cared for his captain and the girl.

One of John's men, no longer needed on the bridge wing now, hit the emergency siren. The scream of it boomed out into the night, warning Europoort of the danger.

On the tenth step down, Richard slipped. The rope snapped taut and he swung there, still twelve feet above the surface of the cargo. He had his torch secured to his wrist with the loop at its end, so he did not drop it. Instead he hung there, watching amazedly as the wild beam flashed away into nothingness, showing him the great, flooded black cavern he was descending into. The roof of the tank stretched away above him, darker than any stormy sky. The immense cargo spread below him like a basalt ocean, the surface of it semisolid, cracked into great thick floes, like black ice. And all he had to aid his search was that puny glimmer of light. All he had for support was that treacherous, invisible, thread-thin stair. He swung until it hit him solidly on the shoulder, then he grasped it once more, and carried on down.

Five seconds later, the black sludge of the surface was sucking at his legs and there was nothing to be seen but the measureless, still, tarry crust of it. Robin must be out there somewhere, perhaps nearby. But she would be enveloped in oil sludge like a nymph in a spider's web. He listened with desperate concentration. Was she too weighed down with the thickness of it even to move and make a sound? Heart breaking, he opened his tight-pressed lips and into that immense, tomblike silence, he called her name.

"ROBIN!"

And a bright light spread through the water, shining up through that black crust in a breathtaking array of emeralds, sapphires, and indigos. All the cargo seemed to have lit up by magic, as though, beneath the thick, floating scum of tar, a sunrise was shining through the sea, summoned by the magic of her name. And silhouetted against the brightness, surprisingly close at hand, almost indistinguishable from the black scum around it, was a human shape. Without another thought, Richard hurled himself bodily forward.

Then, incredibly, it all exploded up into a gross black fountain, sweeping him under even as he reached for her.

Sir William Heritage came panting out of the bridge-house carrying a heavy white Drager pack, completely unaware of his daughter's terrible danger. Martyr took it at once and started to strap it on. "Get some oxygen cylinders too," he ordered, gesturing at McTavish and the nearest stewards to go and help. "And more rope." Then he was turning back, tightening the buckles and impatiently ripping the bandage off his battered head so he could slip the face mask on.

As he went past Salah Malik, he gave him one curt nod. That was all. No time for words. Nor any need for them. He was going down: the big Palestinian was in charge up here now.

He had just stepped onto the first rung down when the black geyser thundered up past him and hurled him back out onto the deck.

Demetrios's bomb operated with a built-in sixty-second delay. He had hit the button during his death spasm as he hit the thick surface. The bomb, clutched to him by his dead hand, was heavy. His lungs were empty. During the next minute he sank more than sixty feet. Then the bomb detonated. It generated very little in the way of blast, but an enormous amount in the way of heat. While the seventy thousand tons of ice-cold Cape seawater with which it was surrounded soaked up an awful lot of that heat, there was still enough generated during the next incandescent seconds to set up a violent upward current. A mixture of hot water and rapidly expanding gases.

But the hot water had to travel up the best part of seventy feet to the surface, and through every one of those feet it was mixed with more cold water, so that the geyser it caused in the end, though it rose twenty-five feet at its apex, erupting straight up out of the tank top itself, was never more than tepid.

And the explosion never came.

Martyr was thrown forward over the edge of the tank top and

almost swept away by the force of it, but he held himself doggedly still as the filth from the tank cascaded up and over him and sucked him toward the deck's edge with astonishing force, and only his own iron grip saved him from tumbling overboard, down into the sea. A foul tidal wave of the stuff broke over Salah's team, staining overalls; filling eyes, noses, and mouths; but they remained unmoving, holding on to Richard's kicking, twisting lifeline like grim death.

When it was all relatively calm, a moment or two later, Martyr pulled himself up onto his knees and turned to look down. The tank was absolutely dark again. Only the mess all over his clothes, the Drager gear, and the deck stood as proof that the incredible had happened.

Then, close enough to make him jump and cry out, a perfectly black head thrust up over the rim, and, almost at once a second appeared.

Martyr was on his feet immediately, helping first Robin, then Richard out. And Salah Malik was by his side, frowning slightly, hands busy, still holding his breath, just in case.

Sir William joined them almost at once, stunned speechless, as they pulled his daughter and son-in-law away from the deadly hole, down toward the safety of the bridge. Salah and Sir William pulled one slack figure each, and Martyr walked hunched up between them, feeding compressed air from his own mouthpiece into their filthy mouths.

As soon as they were sure the air was safe, beside a pile of oxygen cylinders from the emergency room, they stopped and began to use artificial respiration properly, adding to their ministrations with more and more pure oxygen, until first one, then the other, coughed and started to breathe normally. By that time even John Higgins had joined them, rushing impulsively down from the bridge.

Only when he was satisfied they were breathing properly, did C. J. Martyr find the leisure to remove his Drager gear and collapse onto the deck, exhausted. Then Richard was sitting up, gulping great lungfuls of air, filling his chest until it hurt wonderfully, officially in charge again. "Better take the pair of us down to the sick bay and check us out properly," he ordered John, first officer and medic since Ben Strong had gone to the deep six with *Prometheus's* bow section.

But Robin had one word more. She sat up at once with a shudder. "Sick bay be damned," said Richard Mariner's new second mate. "Get me to a shower."

She reached up and wiped the filth from her captain's face, then wiped a matching handful from her own. *"Oil!"* she cried. "God, how I hate the filthy stuff!"

I
+9